PARADISE IN RUINS

Levent Şenyürek: Born in Istanbul in 1975, author Levent Şenyürek is an electrical, electronics, and systems engineer who has worked in various fields as automation, sales support, product development and educational simulations. His first book of short stories *Çıldırtan Kitap* (2007, Çitlembik) was published in English in 2009 with the title *Book of Madness* (Nettleberry/Çitlembik). His first novel *Alacagöl Efsanesi* (The Legend of Alacagöl, 2008, Çitlembik) was recognized as one of the most noteworthy books of the year in Turkey. The same year Şenyürek was listed as one of *Turkey's up and coming young writers* in the catalog prepared for the Frankfurt Book Fair, of which Turkey was the guest of honor. Şenyürek's second novel, *Cennetin Kalıntıları* (*Paradise in Ruins*, 2011, Çitlembik) was included in the "Best 100 Turkish Novels of the Year" list published by the Sabitfikir literary magazine.

Both *Cennetin Kalıntıları* and Şenyürek's latest novel *İsa'yı Beklemek* (Waiting for Jesus, 2013, Çitlembik) were named as finalists in the Gio Awards organized by FABİSAD (Fantasy and Science Fiction Arts Association) in 2013 and 2015 respectively.

© Nettleberry/Çitlembik Publications, 2016
© Levent Şenyürek, 2016
The Ruins of Paradise –Cennetin Kalıntıları/Levent Şenyürek;
Original title: Cennetin Kalıntıları
Translated by M. Cem Ülgen.

İstanbul: Çitlembik Film Video Yapım Çeviri, 2016

248 p.; 14x21 cm

ISBN: 978-605-4924-07-3

1.Turkish fiction
2.2. Science fiction, Turkish I. Title.-II. Cennetin Kalıntıları.
-III. Ülgen, M. Cem.

LC: PL248.S476   DC: 894.3536

Layout: Çiğdem Dilbaz

First printing, March 2016

Printed at Ayhan Matbaası
Mahmutbey Mah. Deve Kaldırım Cad.
Gelincik Sokak No: 6 Kat: 3 Bağcılar/İstanbul
Tel: (0212) 445 32 38
Certificate Number: 22749

In Turkey:
Şehbender Sokak 18/4
Asmalımescit - Tünel
34430 Istanbul
www.citlembik.com.tr
Certificate Number: 12369

In the USA:
Nettleberry LLC
44030 123rd St.
Eden, South Dakota 57232
www.nettleberry.com

PARADISE IN RUINS

Levent Şenyürek

Translated by:
M. Cem Ülgen

Nettleberry/Çitlembik Publications 199

PART 1
AFTER YOU

"How much truth can a spirit endure
How much truth can it dare"

W. F. Nietzsche - *"Ecce Homo"*

1

"Yes, sure!" I said, as I rolled up the car window. "The house has a large terrace so we can have a cook-out." I was at pains trying to maintain the artificial joy in my voice. The engine was also having difficulty as the slope of the road was steep. I shifted the phone to change gears and then glued it back to my ear. "Couldn't hear your last words... No, no, of course not!... I know. I'm late in getting back to you. I had already guessed that they might've planned something else. Just wanted to ask anyway. No, no, it's not a problem... Yes, let's definitely get together sometime after New Years... All right, in case I don't see you, Happy New Year, and greetings to all!... All right, thanks."

I hung up and grumbled, "This sucks!" The car windows had begun to fog up, so I cracked the front right window down a bit. I switched on the tape player and turned up the volume. The song continued at the point where I had last left it.

"Did the evil eye touch us, did you forget, why aren't you coming?
My soul is in its dark night. I'm waiting in vain for the morning"

I began to tap the fingers of my free hand on the steering wheel to the rhythm, accompanying the singer. The road ahead stretched like a narrow path through buildings tightly glued together. Most of the windows were still dark, while some glowed orange, reflecting a light from within.

Turning up the volume, I realized that I had the words of the song all wrong. The singer wasn't asking whether "we" had been touched by the evil eye, but rather if "I" had been touched by it. This upset me a bit; my version seemed to make the lyrics prettier and more meaningful. Of course there wasn't much I could do about it any more. I ignored the original and continued to sing my way:

"Rise from the horizon, let me see your bosom if for one day!
My soul is in its dark night; I'm waiting in vain for the morning
Did the evil eye touch us, did you forget, why aren't you coming?"

Startled by the sudden ringing of my phone, I checked the screen before answering. It wasn't "her" calling. I answered anyway: "Hey! Orhan, what's up?" I was simultaneously trying to roll up the window and turn the music down. Why was it that the noisiest vehicles in the city always seemed to pass me as soon as I was talking on the phone? "Of course, I understand, she might get bored not knowing anyone and all... No need to apologize. It was I who planned late. No problem. Thanks for calling. And if we don't see each other in the meantime: Happy New Year! Thanks a lot... See you later..."

I slowed the car, searching for a parking space among the vehicles lining the two sides of the street. Finally I managed to slip into a vacant space I had spotted in front of our neighborhood grocery shop. The car was on the down slope, so I turned the wheels towards the curb before pulling the handbrake and turning off the ignition.

The grocer didn't scold me for using one of his parking spots as I stayed in the car, gazing through the car's window at the shop in front of me, with its packs of chips lying on the dusty shelves outside the shop in front of me, open detergent boxes, and colorful plastic balls hanging by strings from the shelves. I pulled out my phone again and started to scroll down over the names in my contacts. There was a Harun, but for the life of me I couldn't remember who he was. The name Hayat followed Harun. I took a deep breath and dialed the number. The second I heard the phone being picked up, I burst out: "Hello Hayat! Are you free to talk?... Thanks, I'm doing fine, how about you? Long time no see, yes. How long has it been, eight months or nine? ...Whoops, I just remembered that I called you yesterday, didn't I?... Ok, never mind. No, there's no problem. Listen, I wanted to ask you something. I just moved into a new house... Yes, I'm fine, just listen for a second: I've been thinking of giving a house-warming party with a bunch of friends. The flat has a large terrace, so I thought we could barbecue. We'll manage it, even if it snows. And the terrace has a great view too! You can even catch a glimpse of the Bosphorus. I was wondering what your plans are. I'd really like it if you could come... Oh... Ok... No problem. I understand. It's a great time to get out of the city and now that you have the chance you should grab it. We'll do our thing some other time. "

I bit my lower lip in disappointment. Even I could hear the sadness echoing in my voice, so I tried to end the conversation. "Call me when you get back," I added, as if it were my last breath; "No, I'm good, really am. Thanks, I'll catch you later... All right; thanks. See you! Ok, you drop me a message then."

After I caught my breath, I dialed the next number on the list; the number was no longer in service. A female voice was trying to politely explain to me that the number I had dialed could not be reached at the moment. I could have left a voice message but the will had been drained out of me. The silence on the other end of the line gave way to a continuous hum and my vision began to dim.

I opened the door and lunged out of the car as if I were gasping for breath. The cold air would do me good. I hurriedly walked towards home. I felt humiliated. Why had I decided to throw a party? I had only given people a reason to pity me.

At the door of my apartment the silence of the street was jarred by the sound of footsteps approaching from behind me, then a whistle, and someone calling out, "Hey." Although I really didn't like this manner of address, I felt the need to turn around. I got a little anxious when I saw the look of the man who was following me. Even though he was around 30-35 years old and despite the weather, he was wearing shorts held up with suspenders. And his hair, despite being short, was a tangled mess. He was filthy and smelled to high heaven.

Just what I needed, I thought to myself; a loony bin accosting me in this deserted street. Trying to remain calm, I started to plan my next move.

"Stop!" said the man. "Did you see them?"

The man had a huge head, with a rotund face that looked like a crude mask. He seemed to have lost control of his expressions.

Reluctantly, I forced myself to ask: "See who?"

"They're coming to take me away. Did you see them?"

He was terrified. He was mumbling and I could barely make out his words. I didn't know how to respond.

"Did you see them?" he insisted, raising his voice.

I didn't know how I could sustain the lie if I were to respond positively. So –prepared to suffer the consequences– I murmured, "No, I didn't see anybody."

"I told the cops," said the man. "I told them that this thing came and stood in front of me. Then it squatted and watched me from there. I told them, this one here comes into houses too. It's extremely ugly and evil. They stick pins all over my body. I suspect they're demons. What else could they be? I don't want them near me. They scare me shitless!"

Suddenly, he jumped as if he had heard something, jerked his head and looked around in fear. His terror was so palpable that I also found myself gazing around nervously.

"They want to erase my brain!" the man continued to complain. "I'm Suleiman the Magnificent. Look what they're doing to Suleiman the Magnificent! No matter, they'll find me! No, they don't care; we're like bugs, bugs who can be smushed away. What if something were to happen to me? But then again maybe they're trying to tell me something. I believe in happy endings."

I looked into his wild, crazy eyes, trying to search for any meaning in what he was saying. Maybe he was the one trying to communicate something?

"Have you seen my car?" he asked. "Hey! Have you seen my car?"

"Nope, sorry!" I replied.

"Who took my car?"

"I have no idea. I didn't see your car"

"Did you see the girl sitting in the front seat?"

"No."

"That was Aylin. She smoked in my car. It was disgusting. Girls shouldn't smoke!"

He drifted into silence, but continued to stare into my eyes. His stare seemed to continue for never-ending seconds. With a fleeting glimpse of recognition in his eyes, it seemed to register on him that he was disturbing me. With that he turned and ran back in the direction from which he had come. I stood there, watching him go.

* * *

My feelings of dread began to dissipate once I was able to enter the flat and its silence. I thought that perhaps I could write a little before I had another of my anxiety attacks. I walked slowly towards the far corner of my dark living room and switched on the table lamp. The remote control was on the table next to the lamp. I picked it up and turned on the TV, flipping through the channels trying to find anything worth watching. A cable news network was featuring an American military office who was delivering some kind of statement. A line declaring "Breaking News" was scrolling across the bottom of the screen.

"At approximately 17:30 hours today," said the military spokesperson, "U.S. Air Force fighter jets..."

Who knows why but I was suddenly gripped with excitement, ready to believe for a second that the officer was going to announce that they had encountered an unidentified flying object. No such luck...the officer announced instead that they had bombed the southern regions of Lebanon. I turned up the volume of the TV, opened the windows, turned up the heating full force and went to the bathroom where I peed, and then washed my hands. I was bothered by the fact that the sounds of flowing water were preventing me from hearing the news.

Figuring that the room had been aired sufficiently, I re-closed the windows in the living room and then finally removed my overcoat and hung it up on the coat rack. That done, I went into the kitchen and picked up the kettle off the counter and placed it on the stove. The ensuing household sounds of rattles and clinks gave me an indistinct feeling of joy. As I lit the stove and felt its heat on my face, I held my hands a bit above the flames and warmed them for a while. Then I unfolded a napkin and spread it out as a tablecloth on the corner of the table where I was to eat.

I removed some cherry jam, butter, olives, and feta cheese from the fridge and set those on the table as well. I set my pills beside the plate so as to not forget them.

The water in the kettle had come to a boil. Not wanting to waste time steeping my tea, I chose to pour the boiling water over a teabag I had draped into my mug. Back at the table, I spread some butter on a slice of bread and began to eat it along with some olives. It had been a long time since I had eaten a typical Turkish breakfast in the evening as a meal and it felt good. I still tried to rein in on how much I ate, as I knew that a full stomach was unbearable when I was troubled.

Back on the TV the American military officer had now disappeared from the screen, replaced by Turkish politicians who were hurling harsh accusations at each other. Each seemed to be saying something that made sense, but their contradictions left me confused.

I used the last few drops of my tea to wash down my pills and then began clearing the table. I rinsed the few plates and placed them into the dishwasher, after which I wiped the table. When the reporting of the parliamentary session was interrupted by a commercial, I went to the bathroom to wash my hands and brush my teeth. When I returned, I watched the teaser for a new TV comedy drama: "You'll laugh so hard your sides will split," declared the voiceover. It was creepy.

Although I should have begun writing, I really couldn't stir up any enthusiasm for the task. In an attempt to get myself inspired, I switched to a music channel and turned the volume up. I almost dragged myself to my desk and attempted to write for a while.

As I plowed on with my writing, my leg began to twitch nervously; my writing was disrupted by a disturbing thought that seemed to creep and settle into my brain. What if I was unable to

13

finish my book? The mood created by the music was suddenly dispelled by the announcer's sudden interruption. The VJ was trying hard to sound happy, enunciating every syllable and speaking in an overly loud voice. I reached for the remote and switched off the TV, sending the room into heavy silence. I was swept with the realization that nothing had changed, that nothing *could* change.

I saved the document I had been working on and switched off the computer. With that I rose from my desk and wandered into the hall. Overcome with the sudden need to sleep, I decided to go to bed. Going to bed whenever I wanted was one of the perks of living alone. I visited the john, locked the door and put on my pajamas. As I turned back the blanket, the movement created a wind that rustled the curtains of my bedroom, making me uneasy. Then I let my body drop on the wrinkled sheets, enveloped in the beauty of drifting away thoughtlessly into the oblivion of sleep.

2

The phone rang. Despite the tangled cable, I was able to pick up and pull the receiver up to my ear and heard a woman's voice saying, "Good day, Sir."

"Hello," I replied immediately.

"Am I correct in believing that I have reached the offices of TeleTurca?"

"Yes, TeleTurca."

"And am I speaking with Adem Bey?"

"Yes, this is Adem."

"I am sure you're very busy but I will take only a minute of your time. I am calling from Pakbank, Adem Bey, to enquire if you are currently using a credit card."

"No, I am not."

"Would you consider using one?"

"No, I would not. But if I were, I am already working with another bank."

"That is perfectly understandable. But I want to inform you that Pakbank would also be willing to provide you with a credit card. Our credit card provides significant benefits to its users.

Because these benefits are too many to discuss over the telephone, we would like to visit you in your office so that we describe these to you in more detail."

"Please, don't bother," I said, "I really do not want a credit card."

"Anyway," she replied, "I will be in your neighborhood to visit other clients. You won't mind if I drop by to see you as well? It won't take long, just a few minutes."

"Yeah, okay!" I grumbled finally. I replied to the woman's good wishes pertaining to my day and hung up. However I had to pick the phone right back up as it immediately began to ring again. Inhaling deeply, "Yes?" I snarled.

"Adem?"

"Yes, Ibrahim Bey?"

"Come in here for a minute."

"Yes sir, I'll be right over."

After taking a few seconds to straighten my desk, I stood up and scurried over to the director's office. As soon as I entered, Ibrahim Bey began scolding me. "Pull yourself together man! Focus a bit! Aren't you supposed to be finishing up the market share report as soon as possible?"

His already droopy face had become a proper scowl. His lusterless eyes peered into mine, as if he were challenging me. Judging by his face, it wasn't easy to predict what Ibrahim Bey was really thinking any more.

He continued his speech, "I, for instance, got the data about the market share of the PocketCards by calling InterTelekom. You need to use your skills, your talents, to gather market share data from our competitors. I'm trying to show you ways to use your mind..."

"Market research is a new field for me," I replied. "Unfortunately, I have never been trained in this area, and have no experience either. That's why I need your help and will certainly follow your advice, sir. Thank you."

He stood there, speechless. Brushing it off, he said, "Anyway... I called you in for another reason. We've been thinking about letting Osman go."

This time it was my turn to be speechless. I was never easy about handling staff getting fired. Moreover, I had *no* clue why he wanted to share this information with me.

Seeing me remain silent he said, "Even though he has been with us for more than a year now, he hasn't proven to be very efficient. "You agree with me on that, don't you?"

"What can I say, Ibrahim Bey?! Have you spoken to him?"

"Will you continue to cover for him?" he grumbled. I think he thought I was being a spoilsport; he was asking for my validation I suppose. "If you say you will, then..."

"It's up to you," I said. "This is not a decision for me to make."

Suddenly I heard a knock on the door. The General Manager barged in asking, "What happened to the PocketCard business, Ibrahim Bey?" He looked highly-strung. Even though he wasn't speaking directly to me, he still found time to give me a disapproving look from head to toe.

Ibrahim Bey immediately stood up upon seeing him. "Hasan got in an accident Rüstem Bey," he said in a nervous tone. "He's on sick leave and that's why we are a bit late."

"Really now?" he shook his head from side to side angrily. "Why aren't they more careful then? This can't wait until next week! I want those reports on my desk by Friday! Do overtime if necessary. We're running a *business* here!"

Just as Ibrahim Bey was to utter an objection, Rüstem Bey cut him off. He continued to complain: "There are ten engineers in this division. I see people loitering all the time. Give it to one of them to finish it up!"

Then he walked out, slamming the door behind him.

I asked right away, "May I leave now?"

"Wait," said Ibrahim Bey, trying to pull himself back to the state he had been in before the General Manager had descended upon us. "I was going to speak to you about one more thing." He picked up a few thick envelopes full of documents. "We are thinking of going into the monitoring system business," he said. "You must've heard about it. Scada and all... It also concerns this counter of yours too... That's why I thought about you... I don't have much time now. You can read about it in here; the company has standard condition monitoring gadgets. You will undertake the product management side and whatnot."

As I was about to reply, he jumped in: "That is, if you want to continue to work with us." His words carried such a tone, as if he was truly liberating me, as if he was saying *these are the duties I can delegate to you, that's all I can do*, though it was impossible not to hear the implicit threat in his words.

I silently took the documents from his hands and murmured, "All right, I'll get onto it as soon as I wrap up the market research."

"Begin right away," he rebuked. "Work on both together. Get used to working on two things at the same time!"

"All right Ibrahim Bey, may I be excused now?

"Yes, and good luck!"

"Thanks, same to you too."

Clenching my teeth, I went back to my cubicle. I checked my inbox but there was nothing but a few forwarded mails and a funeral notification. Muzaffer Ocak, a marketing engineer at the company had had a heart attack the day before. *He was to be buried after the afternoon prayer at the Söğütlüçeşme mosque.* As I did not know him, the sad news didn't affect me much. I perused the other forwarded messages. In each one, it seemed like either

18

women or men were being reciprocally slandered. In some, peaceful advice was being offered.

I felt my stomach grumble. The clatter of keyboards had died down and it had become silent in the room. I checked my watch; it was lunchtime. I straightened my desk, turned my computer off and began to walk towards the labyrinthine corridors paved with stained rugs that led to the cafeteria.

The department was pretty much empty. Only one of the newly recruited engineers was in his place, still working. I glanced at the wall of his cubicle, reading his name, then asked: "Aren't you going to lunch Soner?"

Without averting his eyes off the computer screen. "I am" he said. "*with friends.*" He seemed to have emphasized the last word.

"All right," I replied, trying to hide my discomfiture. "Bon appetit. I'm off."

Just as I was about to leave the department I saw Osman standing up from his cubicle. I pondered changing my way hurriedly but I took control and remained on my path. As I passed him I called out: "Going to lunch?"

"Yes," he said. "How about you?"

"Yeah. Want to eat together?"

"Sure."

We began to walk side by side. We passed through the mezzanine that was decorated with artificial flowers with the hope that the place would look like a botanical garden. As we couldn't find much to talk about, we walked on in silence. Osman avoided stepping on the lines as he walked, and I was reading the company slogans for the umpteenth time.

Our most important capital is our human resources.

Our vision is to become the leader in communications in Eurasia and to maintain that position.

We are all one big family!

As we queued in the cafeteria, I thought of starting a conversation on politics and the prospects of war in the Middle East. This could be a subject we would both be drawn in.

"America bombed Golan Heights," I said. "Have you heard the news?"

"Yes," he replied, his head bobbing up and down. "I read it in the papers this morning."

"They say Russia and China might also intervene!"

"They'll start World War 3."

He had said this without a hint of excitement, like it was something completely ordinary. Then, as he picked a chocolate dessert from one of the shelves in front of him, he continued: "I dreamed of this the other night. I dreamed of mountains covered in soot and dust."

"Did they look like Golan Heights?" I asked, smiling. In the meantime, tray in hand, I was looking around for free chairs to sit. I did not know if Osman's calm demeanor was due to the fact he could predict the future –which would be quite interesting– or due to his state of permanent depression.

"I guess so," he said as he followed me. "I don't know. I just saw hills being bombed!"

"Strange," I replied. "Did you see things like these before?"

"Nah."

There were some empty seats at the tables in the back, overlooking the windows. We went and sat down.

"You forgot your spoon," I said.

"I eat my yoghurt with a fork anyway," he replied. I saw that he hadn't taken any soup either.

We talked about work for a while. I had no appetite and this worried me and the more I got worried the more my appetite decreased.

As I played with the green beans on my plate with my fork, I said: "I don't take pleasure from eating here. I actually like green beans. The names of the dishes are fine but the taste is so bland it's almost non-existent. Might be the oil they use, who knows?"

When the subject of food began, Osman started to praise the food of the restaurants he had been to over the weekend. He had spent the whole weekend walking around Istanbul by himself. If it were someone else, they might've found his idea of a weekend odd. However, I only felt a sense of profound dismay. It was nice that he could find distractions like this, rather than making life miserable for himself.

"Great!" I said. "How nice! Eating is a pleasant activity, right?"

When it was time for dessert, he told me he liked chocolate a lot. "I...I actually look for it. Especially after meals."

I thought he might be sensing what I was thinking. This could be the reason behind his stutter. In fact, right away he began to tell me how he thought that human beings were better off living alone, like a lone wolf. We talked on this subject for the remainder of our meal and throughout our walk in the garden, which we took to digest our food better. Though it was green all over, the garden didn't really make anyone feel more peaceful or anything.

"Look," said Osman, pointing to a plane in the air. "It's as if it's suspended in mid-air."

This was an unexpected move. I didn't know what to say. "Yes," I mumbled, "because it is very high up there."

"What time is it?" he asked.

I looked at my watch. "It's five past one," I said. "No, actually exactly one, because this watch is five minutes fast."

"Shall we go back?"

"Yes; let's."

We went our own ways once in the cafeteria. I bought a cup of coffee and a bar of chocolate. The first thing I did was to check my inbox again. I had received a mail from a college friend. He wrote that he was happy to hear from me, that he was in the States. *As one ages, it becomes harder to form close friendships,* he wrote. *This is a perfectionist country anyway; the competition is fierce! Maybe that's why people lack intimacy.*

Replying right away, I asked whether he planned on returning to Istanbul, and in which country he would like to spend the rest of his life and other similar stuff. Then I bit off a piece of my chocolate bar and took a sip from my coffee. This calmed my nerves a bit and I was able to get back to work.

In order to uncover the Remote Meter Reading market, I tried locating some articles on the Web. I looked at the pages of the State Institute of Statistics. It wasn't easy, getting direct access to information. I could infer some figures by checking the amount of electricity used in factories and the average number of counters per consumer perhaps, but I wasn't sure if I could access that data either. The results' precision was open for debate anyway. My legs had begun to tremble again.

It seemed like the easiest way was to conduct espionage by determining the companies that had a hold on the market. I could pose as a complainant or –better yet– I could say that I was calling from The Scientific and Technological Research Council of Turkey and was conducting some research.

I thought of how I could sound credible. I recalled the politicians I had seen on TV the other night. At least half of them were lying but none of them showed it. I felt fascination towards them. Perhaps the best way to lie was to believe in what I would be saying first.

I work at The Scientific and Technological Research Council of Turkey, I thought to myself. *I'm a senior researcher at the Energy*

*Institute at the Marmara Research Center! We are trying to man-
ufacture a fully local, national, superiorly optimized energy counter. In order to put together the project proposal, we require information on the national Remote Meter Reading market. That's
why we decided to apply to the number one counter manufacturer
in the country, InterCounter for instance.*

It was a realistic story; I found it credible, I could believe in it.
Although I was deep in my thoughts, I felt somebody approaching me from the back. Then I heard a high-pitched male voice
saying, "I heard you're selling your car."

I turned behind to look at where the voice came from and
said, "Hi Gürsel. How are things? Are you interested in it?"

"Could be. What're you asking for it?"

"Have you seen the car?"

"Yeah, I saw it. There's a crack on the front window."

"Yes, I'll get it changed. My insurance covers such incidences
once a year."

"Nothing else wrong with it, right?"

"A few tiny scratches here and there; you must've seen them."

"Those aren't important, they can be patched up. No major
accidents though, right?"

"Nah."

Haggling like this bored me. Even though I was in sales per-
force, I really didn't like negotiations. Of course, Gürsel was asking the questions out of obligation too, he didn't want to be
bamboozled.

"It got serviced just recently," I said. "They were going to pay
nine and a half if I sold it there but you mark it a figure higher in
the second-hand market as you know."

"We'll call it ten then, eh mate?" he said coldly. Maybe he
thought I was lying to him and he didn't know how to react. He
was trying to fix a rigid and hard-bitten look on his face.

I didn't know what to say. Upon seeing me undecided, "Why are you selling it?" he asked. In doing so, he must've been out to hear if the car had a hidden malfunction, a curse, or a disease of some sorts.

"I need the money," I replied, insisting on telling the truth.

He smiled indistinctly. He probably felt he could keep the price down this way. I was so nervous I could break down in tears. In fact, it wasn't only my nerves; I truly needed the money.

"Why?" he asked.

"It's a personal matter!" I said.

"What do you mean? Are you getting hitched?"

My patience had come to an end. "Let's talk later, eh," I said. "I have a deadline to meet."

"Fine," he said. "You think about it, your money is ready the next day, ka-ching!"

"All right," I said. "You think about it too. I told you the figure I have in my mind out loud since we know each other. Look around. If you find the same features for a lower price, I'll sell it to you for that."

"All right," he murmured.

There wasn't anything left to say.

"Good," he said, "See you around then."

"Sure. Take care."

I checked my inbox before proceeding with my work. Another virus-laden spam mail titled *I love you* had arrived; I deleted it without opening. Then I started to write something to "her" but quickly decided against it. Holding my breath, I began to work.

***

I was sorry to leave my trustworthy car in one of the vacant lots remaining from the demolished buildings in the back streets of

24

Üsküdar, now used as a parking lot, and began to walk towards the seaport. The sky overhead was blanketed with dark clouds, as if concealing the infinite void of space. A wet cold slapped my face in waves. It'll snow soon, I thought. My anxiety was building up. I began to imagine the worst possible cases. Although there was nothing I could do about the situation, it seemed as if I could cross off some of the possibilities, just by guesswork. Though I knew it to be absurd, I couldn't help but hold this line of thought.

I crumpled up the page on which I had written the day's chores and threw it into the first trash can I came across. I had initiated the first phase of my last mission, after all. I despised myself. *Drifting, still drifting* I thought. Unconsciously I began to mutter an old song under my breath:

Everyone's at home, keeping to himself,
Serene in peace, cheerfulness abides,
Only I insomniac, only I in dire straits,
Only I desperate; only I alone, without you...

I must've been trying to torture myself...

Come ask me what I'm going through
Tell me where I can possibly go, Tell me what I can do.

As I could not see the sea from where I stood, a freighter moving down the Bosporus seemed to be wafting in the middle of the city. The traffic had congealed badly at the red light crossing the coastal road; I meandered around the cars. Although the angry bursts of car horns pained my ears, I enjoyed the heat of the engines. The road must have been clogged for some time or this was a particularly troublesome path as peddlers had surrounded the cars, trying to sell knick-knacks like lighter cables, flowers and bagels. There were also mendicant gypsies who had brought their kids along. "No jobs," said one. "They don't give us jobs, Hon." She had rolled up her sleeve and was showing the bruises on her arms to the drivers and their passengers.

As I arrived at the port, I checked the timetable immediately. The Beşiktaş ferry was about to depart. I hurried towards the counters. Tired crowds drifted by.

As I bought a token, gypsy kids sidled along and asked for the small change leftover from my purchase. The older one was crying out, "Hey my man, hey, hey!" The younger immediately began his belly dancing routine. The cashier at the counter was about to chase them away, but smiled faintly when he saw the little one. The youngster took this as encouragement, though it was clear that he wouldn't last long. The cashier was to scold him badly very soon. I took the token, gave the spare change to the kids, and ran towards the boat.

I passed through the dilapidated port building and went outside before the doors closed. The sea had a metallic, greasy smell to it. Mingled with diesel, the sea smelled of seaweed and fish; I liked it.

I was able to jump onto the deck of the vessel just as the ropes were collected. I climbed the steps and looked for a place to sit. Fortunately ships destined to the European side were far less crowded at this hour. The heat inside also felt good.

Suddenly, a metallic but polite woman's voice was heard over the speakers: "Distinguished passengers!" The usual expressions of gratitude followed, thanking us for not giving heed to the peddlers of knickknacks and the emotional blackmail of beggars.

I must've been fairly warm by now as I felt like going out onto the deck. Thinking I could shield myself from the cold with a warm cup of *sahlep,* I walked towards the ship's canteen. The men in white smocks at the counter were hooked onto a TV show.

"Man, look at those broads!" grumbled one.

"Women are far more cruel, I tell you," answered the other.

"Excuse me," I said.

"Yes sir?"

"May I have a cup of sahlep?"

"Of course."

The man who spoke to me picked up one of the cups lined on the counter and poured some sahlep into it, after which he sprinkled some powdered cinnamon on top before handing it to me. I paid the man and thanked him, going out onto the deck as I had planned.

Almost everyone outside was smoking. The wooden floor rotting from the sea water was littered with cigarette butts. A man from the canteen was busy collecting the tea glasses and the red and white saucers, on which the tea fees lay. He had a bit of a humpback. He was masterfully carrying the aluminum tray that jingled with the empty tea glasses crammed to the hilt. In the meantime he hollered out: "Yes, anyone for tea? Gentlemen; need any tea? Would you like some tea sir? Tea, tea, tea! You need tea sir?"

Under the pale glow of the caged deck lamps I looked for a place to sit. Eventually, I dropped myself onto a vacant wooden bench. As I sipped my sahlep, I watched the impending European coast and the Bosporus.

As we further approached the open sea, the waters became darker. It was as if there was a huge, dark snake lying between the two glittery sides of the city. The land across looked full of glamour amidst this darkness but I felt afraid of the journey ending as well. I had found a temporary refuge on the boat.

As I heard the engines come to a stop, I felt my stomach churn. The sahlep had begun to grow cold anyway. The boat sidled towards the Beşiktaş port and I saw the city growing larger and larger, to a proportion that could gobble us all up. Officials had started doing the rounds, waking up those asleep and the homeless who wanted to remain on-board. I left the sahlep cup on the bench and set off down the stairs.

***

It was pleasant to see the flowers in the office. When I reached out to touch their petals though, their paper-like texture gave away their artificiality, which unsettled me. The source of the pleasant smell then had to be different, some sort of spring scented room spray I presumed. Maybe it was the perfume the man across me was wearing. Indeed, with his dyed hair saturated with gel, his clean-shaven smiling face and smooth suit, he looked like a stick of apple candy himself.

"My name is Koray Ergülen," he said, smiling. "I am the public relations director of the Compassion Institute." He moved onto a quick introduction of himself, replete with his duties and references, much like as if he were giving the mandatory warnings during a medical advertisement.

"I read your pamphlet," I said.

"Where did you get the pamphlet? From the Net?"

"No! They were distributing them at the entrance to the chemotherapy clinic... You claim that your fee is lower than the cost of the treatment but the actual price is not listed. What is your price exactly? How many years of chemo treatment are you comparing it with? With which drugs? Different figures can arise depending on the circumstances as you know."

"Of course, you're correct. To be honest with you, we calculate our figures with acute cases in mind. Hibernation is, in the end, a last resort. Unfortunately, it's not easy to give an exact figure; it all depends on the individual's health condition, the options they may prefer, and their characteristics."

"I had given you information about my condition," I said. "I believe you should be able to give me an approximate figure."

Instead of answering, Koray Bey eyed me from head to toe and began typing on the computer in front of him. Eventually he asked, "Are you considering full-body hibernation or only the head?"

"Has there been anyone who has only frozen their head?"

"Yes, there has, though I don't advise it."

"Why not?"

"Developing the technology required to implant your head onto a suitable body may take much longer than the discovery of a new treatment. As you know, risks still remain and the guarantee we provide decreases the longer you postpone your revivification. Moreover, you may have adaptation difficulties once revived. If you can afford it, I would propose you to let your whole body hibernate. I'd urge you to try and push your financial limits, though it's up to you of course. You can be sure that our surgeons are very successful in head removal as well. You used the term "freezing" a while ago, but as you know our method is called hibernation. Instead of cryogenically freezing the body, we replace the water and oxygen in your body with chemicals. Therefore water crystals that damage cells do not occur. Freezing is pure quackery. Those frozen bodies can never be brought back to their initial condition; they're conning people."

"Yes, yes, I know... It's just that we generally hear it spoken as freezing..."

"Ok, we're on the same page then... I'm calculating your cost now. It'll take a few seconds."

"Fine, I'm waiting."

As he calculated my cost I went back to examining his office. The wooden table had a red tint to it. Was it the wood that gave it its' color or the varnish, I wasn't sure. On the large LCD screen next to me, flocks of birds flew over a forest steeped in fog. My concentration was scattered, to say the least.

"120,000 dollars!" he said finally.

"What if it's only the head?" I asked, my voice quivering.

"It'd roughly be half in general. So about 60,000..."

As I remained silent, he began to cite the reasons of the cost.

"It is a new technology in the end! We import the chemicals employed in the process. The risk we undertake is high; we cannot determine exactly how many years we will be caring for you. You will have to be kept under particular conditions for preservation. There are of course, other institutes that provide cheaper options but their methods are not sterile. Our price is quite reasonable if you ask me. The reason being that the demand is not high. Let me be frank with you: We have entered the Turkish market only quite recently. People hold biases. So we want to advertise ourselves more. This is a great opportunity for patients with acute cancer cases. If you don't have private insurance... You don't, do you?

"Unfortunately not! Well I used to... Anyway, no I don't."

"The money you will have to invest in chemo... You know they charge 1000 TL just to insert a needle. The prices constantly rise to boot! Why? No reason! Completely unclear! A surgery today would cost you thousands of dollars! Never mind what the doctors want for themselves! Moreover, it is up for debate whether the treatments are successful. This chemo center of yours, I'm sure you've noticed, you see the same people go in and out, have you ever seen even one person who has gotten better? Oh by the way, I forgot, terribly sorry. Would you care for something to drink?"

"No, nothing, thank you! I'll be trying to sell some of my possessions in order to pool the money... If I can't, is it possible for me to give them over to you according to their market value? Do you accept such deals? There is very little time, in the end."

"I can't say anything for sure, now. I'll have to speak with our accountant, then I can inform you better. By possessions, what exactly do you mean?"

"My car and such..."

"I see. Ok, I'll ask, I've made a note of it. You can also pay in installments, you know... If you have a relative you trust... Though I don't advise it. Life goes on, in the end. The best would be for you to pay the whole cost up front."

"Do you have the means to invest the money well?"

"We work with the best investment consultants and banks. You have nothing to worry about!"

I was sick and tired of talking about money. "Anyway..." I grumbled as I took out my list of questions from the breast pocket of my shirt. "I have a couple of technicalities I'd like to ask you."

"Actually..." he said, "I wanted to show you around the hibernation rooms. You would like to see them, right?"

"Of course!"

"Then without further ado, let's go. You can ask your questions along the way."

"All right."

Both of us got up. After he rummaged through his pockets and gazed aimlessly around the room, he moved towards the door and I followed. We went outside and began to walk through a glass tunnel that joined the two buildings of the institute. I was able to catch a glimpse of the tree-laden garden. In this valley that had recently been converted from a forest, between the borders that separated the city from the trees, they had created a paradise, or a purgatory to be exact. The valley was built to conceal it from the outside and gave the impression that the whole world consisted of these gardens. I brought the list closer in order to read out the first question under the pale light of the tunnel. Once I deciphered my handwriting, "Koray Bey!" I called out. "Once the electrical activity of the brain stops, doesn't amnesia occur?"

"Don't worry! Only your short-term memory is connected to the electrical activity you mention. Your real, long-term memory is processed in the form of temporary molecules and structural modifications in the brain. None of these are damaged during the hibernation operation."

I chose to take his answer as true and moved onto the second question.

"In the freezing operation..."

"Hibernation."

"No, I was going to ask something else. You mentioned that because the ice crystals that emerge during the freezing method harm the cells, nobody could be reanimated with the current technology. What could be the reasons for not being able to reanimate somebody who has undergone hibernation?"

"We know that the chemicals we use are able to preserve the brain's structure perfectly, however, there could arise certain unanticipated effects if the same chemicals flow out of the body. We haven't completely overcome this issue. In the majority of animal tests we have obtained satisfactory results, however with higher mammals we still lack the desired results... Biochemical poisoning can occur... Let me tell you something to put you at ease... Perhaps you did your own research as well: Organizations like NASA and ESA plan to send their future astronauts to other stellar systems using the hibernation technique. There is also talk about how orangutans hibernated in military labs have already been reanimated."

We had arrived at the end of the tunnel. The automatic door slid open, greeting us with a pleasant lady's voice that wished us well. A wide hall with laminate wood floors appeared in front of us. I think this was a waiting room of some sorts. Suddenly, the concert piano sitting in the middle of the hall began to emit a dithyrambic classical tune. The piano's keys went up and down, as if played by an invisible pianist.

"These sections," began Koray Bey, "were designed to fully withstand earthquakes and fire hazards."

Together we walked towards another mysterious door at the far end of the room and with the polite drawing apart of the automatic door, we found ourselves in a whitewashed room. Inside were a few large metal cylinders that reflected our images like mirrors. On each of them were grey sets of keys, cables and indicators. Among this color-deprived atmosphere, a bright red trash bag immediately caught my attention. I shuddered. Was hibernation in fact a bloody process? Gulping I asked, "do you keep them in here?"

"Not every one," answered Koray Bey. Meanwhile, he had begun to twiddle some of the knobs on one of the cylinders. "Only samples are kept in this room." Some of our initial patients accepted being displayed as samples. We of course give them a discount in return."

Suddenly the face of a sleeping young girl appeared on the screen attached to the cylinder in front of him. She was shaven bald and swam in some kind of dense, pinkish liquid. Apart from her face, her knees were also visible; she must've propped her legs up onto her body in the fetal position.

"Look how peaceful she is!" exclaimed Koray Bey. A few seconds ensued, in which we both stood silently watching. I was at a loss for words.

"Yes, that is the impression," I mumbled. "But what if it isn't as it seems?" I asked. "What do they really feel? How will I feel? If I hibernate I mean..."

"Our MD's describe the process as being akin to dreaming. A sense of infinity of some sorts... Of course we can't say for sure, but..."

"How can you be sure that I won't be feeling pain? It will be impossible to have myself heard, to ask for help, or to even commit suicide to put myself out of misery! How horrible, think about it! It's like being in hell!"

"Don't worry! We constantly monitor brain functions using sensors. During hibernation we have had none of our clients showing brain activity."

"But what if one day you do?"

"The possibility is minuscule. I wouldn't fret about it."

I stopped insisting. I had begun to perspire despite the cold room.

"Then," I said, "It is wrong to call it a dream, right? It's a type of death. Though temporary, one gets a taste of what death feels like in a way. Although, the word taste may be ill-chosen of course!"

Koray Bey's head bobbed up and down a few times, as if he really didn't understand what I meant. He went on giving me technical information on the metal cylinders.

"There's a built-in camera, resistant to the chemicals inside. That's how we get the visual. Apart from this, the person who hibernates is completely shut off from the outside world. There is an impermeable, vacuumed zone in-between the inner and outer walls of the cylinder. Just like a coffee thermos!"

I looked at the list I held in my hand that I had unknowingly crumpled.

"The pamphlet says that the hibernation cannot begin prior to the patient's death! Is this true? For instance, I feel fine now but I have a disease that progresses rapidly. If I hibernate straight away, won't it be easier to reanimate me later on? In fact, if the disease progresses to the point of killing me maybe I will never be able to get treated later on!"

"Unfortunately the Ministry of Health's legislature on

patient's rights states that *under no condition, even medical, can the right to life be waived.* So even if it is your personal request, ending a life is strictly not permitted. Thus, if we were to let you hibernate before your demise, we'd be committing murder."

Hearing all this brought in me the desire to weep in sadness and fury. I clenched my teeth and gulped, trying to hold a poker face and insisted, "But do they want us to suffer? Do you see the oddity of the situation? If I were to invest in hibernation I would have to stop my treatment as well!"

"You can open a court case," mumbled Koray Bey.

"Against whom?" I asked, "Say I managed getting the money together, can you see me dealing with lawyers, going to courts in this condition? Should I even try?"

I guess the man got a bit disturbed thinking he was being accused, as I was talking to him. "There is nothing we can do, unfortunately," he responded, "But even if the disease progresses to the point that it kills you, you can safely believe there will be a huge possibility of your being cured one day. You will not die. That, we will not permit!"

"There you go! This is not murder!" I burst out. "Homicide may be illegal but what you do is hibernation!"

"As the reanimation technology hasn't been developed yet, helping a live human hibernate is legally considered murder... But don't you worry! You will be doing the right thing by choosing hibernation. The process may not be seen very positively due to societal taboos and such but in the future it will be regularly practiced, I am sure of it! You do not have to die!"

After some silent thought, "Fine," I said. "Will you give me a discount as well? If I were to accept being displayed as a sample I mean?"

***

While in college, there were times when I felt the need to be alone. Once the last of my roommates had left, I would feel the sweet silence inside spread from my ears towards the very depths of my mind. My solitary home also gave off this bizarre serenity at first. Perhaps it was also what I thought I would find there that would excite me. The darkness I would sink in throughout the day would turn into a cheeky hopefulness towards the evening and I was able to convince myself that as I approached my street, I would be reunited with something I had long yearned for again.

The house smelled of bleach. I had forgotten that the cleaning lady would be coming and remembering this fact made me happy. The place was in tiptop shape, my clothes all ironed. A stranger had been popping in and out of my house but I hadn't even seen her face. This struck me as odd, when I thought about it. As I hadn't had much to eat the evening before, I felt famished. After I took off my coat and hung it on the hanger I opened the fridge door. The first things that caught my eye were the black nylon bags whose content I had completely forgotten; I didn't want to confront rotting, moldy food so I couldn't bring myself to check and see what was in them. I should pick them all up in the morning and throw them out, I thought.

I took out a slice of toast and began nibbling on it as I sat in front of my computer again. I was obstinately trying to write. Though I didn't want to waste my last days in this way, perhaps putting a full stop to my endeavor might give me some consolation.

As the computer lit up, I heard the lady next door scream at the top of her lungs:

"Look at him! He's smashing the lamp! Heh! You're a man now, eh?"

Doors were slammed, maybe the man left or the woman, the whole thing was depressing. The dispute was over, noise from the building had ceased but I still had trouble concentrating, giving full attention to my writing. Something preoccupied me, in fact, it was hurting me. Focusing on the noise, I noticed it was the call to prayer. The noise was a gut-wrenching wail that echoed throughout the street. It was extremely destructive; as if the call wasn't for the ritual prayer but to an impoverished past summoning the whole city. Then another mosque began sounding its prayer, and another one followed suit. Soon the numerous wails weaved into one another, turning into a disorderly canon.

I stood up. My eyes downcast, I began to strut up and down the house. I was preoccupying myself with trying to walk parallel to the lines on the fake wood flooring. I noticed I wasn't going to be able to write anymore tonight. I turned on the TV and dropped myself on the comfy sofa in front of it. The remote was on the other chair though. I sighed in pain. Getting up and fetching the remote, this simplest of acts suddenly seemed impossible. I felt like I had to change dimensions or move at light speed. For some unknown reason, I achieved the impossible and returned back to my comfy sofa in gasps. A few seconds later after I caught my breath, I lifted the remote with difficulty and finally turned the TV on.

As tension in the Middle East was again on a sharp rise, the news programs drew my most interest. The Turkish government had deployed fifteen units to the Syrian border as a precautionary measure. I found myself getting excited. Even I could not understand this feeling of excitement, for back during the times when I feared I was about to be drafted to the military the risk of war was as terrifying as death itself. The screen was alit with state-of-the-art tanks and planes, accompanied with fervor-raising battle songs. I thought how, even on the news, we get to watch what we want. It always struck me as amazing how the human brain is able to generate visions that do not exist, yet this electronic box sitting in front of me was also stuffed with things that we were shown only because we enjoyed watching them.

The tension between the nations had also drastically increased acts of terrorism. As a consequence of the counter-attack operations against mounting conflicts, eight terrorists had been "captured dead" –meaning they were found dead in some cave I presumed– and three soldiers were martyred.

The funerals were broadcast. A mother was lamenting in mourning:

"Oh my child, my son, oh my son. This pain, this pain is too much to bear. Oh you, my son, who passed away without having seen your child!"

By swaying to and fro and extending her syllables in a kind of melody, she was trying to purge the fire that burned inside, to alleviate, even if for a bit, the unendurable pain she felt. Listening to her, the elderly father of the private kept slapping his cane over and over on his face, worn out of fatigue and despair.

The anchor-man, who had introduced the news story and video with a sad demeanor and husky tone, suddenly pasted a smile onto his voice and exclaimed, "And now, let's turn to an interesting piece of world news!"

Up next was a video showing the amazing buffoonery of a talented ape. This switch left me puzzled. What were they trying to do, I wondered, allay our sadness with a touch of comic-relief?

Sports and the weather report were to follow, but first the commercials! The volume of the TV rose in an effort to force us to hear what was being said. The commercial opened with a soothing view accompanied by a provocative heroic melody. A team of horses were galloping in stormy weather. I zeroed in. A new bank was entering the Turkish market. The music came to a climax, as if an historical moment was in the making, a legend heralded, as if some very important bullshit was in the making!

Following these scenes, other jovial commercial ensued; my ears and eyes were being lambasted by pretty people with smiles doused in make-up, skinny bodies and voices echoing a manic glee–maybe right now, a few of them could actually be weeping, or had already fallen dead in an armed conflict. Of course, the point was just to sell me something.

The big news of the day was the coming international soccer match. We were about to enter into a battle of life and death with France, after which our fate in the team groupings was to be determined. The discussion moved as to whether or not our team would take to the field in our new turquoise colors. This story got my full concentration. As France was vetoing our accession to the EU, the game was exceptionally significant.

"We want to make our citizens happy," said the soccer coach, "They deserve only the best!" This made me proud.

Once the sports newscast was over, commercials followed, after which a science-fictions series that claimed to have based itself on mysterious files yet unsolved by the FBI. I think it was about aliens that secretly plotted to invade Earth but as I was being overtaken by the need to sleep, I wasn't really able to follow. I rose from the couch and switched off the TV. The room descended into pitch-black darkness. I went to the bathroom groping around for the light switch. I turned the light on and shaved, hoping that this way I could wake up a bit later than usual the next morning.

Taking to my bed when I was very sleepy was extremely pleasurable. I thought about how death in the form of sleep couldn't be that bad–though who was there to say for sure that death resembled sleep anyway?

I hugged the pillow, but just as I was about to fall asleep, I heard a distant shriek. I couldn't really make out the sound, which seemed like a cross between a child weeping and a dog howling. I did recognize, however, that whoever or whatever was screaming was enduring extreme pain. And then I thought that I may actually just be dreaming this scream. Still, my body trembled from the horror of it. I tried to convince myself that it was only the cries of seagulls calling out from the neighborhood rooftops.

I dreamed that somebody was telling me, "Hold on for a minute, you... You're dead!"

I was having none of this. "Stop!" I uttered my response, "There's still work waiting for me to do! Let me finish this first..."

Suddenly a happy melody began to chime. It was my cell phone's alarm. It was still dark outside. I had grown cold as I had somehow kicked my blankets off. I had been terrified because the dream had seemed so real. I loathed the idea of getting up. I imagined I had gone to the bathroom, washed my face, got dressed and ready to go. I truly made myself believe all this. I was astounded at how easily I had slipped my socks on. The truth was, I hadn't moved an inch. I became aware of the reality once the alarm sounded again. Forcing myself to sit up I though, *how nice this is going to be. I'll go to sleep and never have to wake up again.*

3

Gürsel approached my cubicle and said, "I heard that they are going to be transferring you to Sales too!"

"That seems to be the case," I replied in a listless tone.

"Dude, you're being promoted, don't you see? They might even make you the team supervisor of our branch in Russia."

"Really now? So it's like being appointed Tsar!"

"What tsar? You'll be spending half the year in Russia. You'll be in heaven don't you get it? The women there are hotter than the sun! Once you see the place and those women and then have to come back here, you'll be scared shitless by what we've got here!" he chuckled. "They're great in bed too, of course! It's not fair! I want to be our man in Russia!"

Selim, who worked in the cubicle next to me called out from where he was sitting: "Can't find what you want in China, Gürsel?"

"Dude, of course I get what I want but..." mumbled Gürsel.

"How much do they pay you?" I interjected.

Gürsel pulled himself together at once, all serious.

"I can't tell you. Don't get me wrong. Wouldn't be able to tell you even if you were my best friend. It'd get me fired immediately."

"Man, imagine finding a position in Russia!" said Selim. He was transfixed by the idea.

"I'll manage to secure a position there though! Gürsel seemed to be almost spitting out his words.

"What position?"

"Wha?"

"Tell us man, what position?"

"I'll let you know."

"Tell us now, whats the big deal?"

"Dude, people who can't speak a word of the language go there with the idea of trading! I recently met some guy from the Black Sea at the hotel. He had sold all his possessions and then just set off, but it's obvious that he doesn't know jack. It's either balls or stupidity," he laughed. "We met during breakfast, 'Are you from the Black Sea?' I asked him directly, 'Yes,' he says, 'how did you know?' 'Instead of pulling your chair up to the table, you pulled the table up to your chair, thats how...' I said. Hahahahaha!"

I had already heard this story of his before. In the previous version though, it was someone else who noticed the guy was from the Black Sea. Gürsel found it fit to place himself in the starring role this time it seemed. Perhaps now, he even believed that this was the case.

"Tsk tsk tsk!" said Selim, disapproving the Black Sea guys behavior; he obviously wasn't listening to a word that was being said.

Gürsel's cell began to ring. The young salesman checked the number calling him, cursed under his breath and mumbled, "Now why in the hell is he calling now?" Nonetheless he took the call and politely replied, "Yes, Fikret Bey?" "Of course sir, don't you worry!... Of course, I understand. I'll send some people over. No, don't worry, we won't leave you in a rough spot!" As he put down the phone, he began cursing again.

"What's up?" I asked.

"Nothing. A scratch on one of the boxes... The work these Chinese do... He wants 10 bucks per piece as well. I guess they're not starving anymore..."

Ibrahim Bey sidled by and interrupted our conversation: "Having a meeting lads?" Laughingly he added, "Sorry about the beating from our guys, Selim, by the way, haven't been able to mention it since Sunday!"

"Anyway, it's Europe we have to concentrate on!" said Selim, annoyed.

"Doesn't matter if you win the European Championship; we beat you! What's done is done. Hope you aren't suffering too much!"

Ibrahim Bey was known to be a hard-core Fenerbahçe supporter. Being a fan was a great part of his persona. Although that's the way he liked to present himself, I somehow guessed that he didn't care that much about Fenerbahçe when he was without an audience.

Silence ensued; Selim and Gürsel asked for our permission to leave and I ended up alone with my manager. They left and his artificial smile returned to his usual grim, expressionless frown.

"How is the market research coming along?" he asked.

I reported the day's efforts. He was far from being satisfied.

"Things aren't looking good Adem!" he said. "Our department didn't issue many invoices this month. We're recording losses. There might be some cutbacks. Finish this quick; I want to be able to tell the suits upstairs some good things about you."

"Well, actually, sales are pretty good, aren't they?" I asked.

"Yes, but our profit margins are very low. Would you believe it? The medical department has the company's lowest sales, but also the highest profits.

"Yeah," I mumbled.

"Sometimes I think you're just killing time. For instance, I think you should be dropping the finalized report I asked you for at my desk tomorrow morning."

His words were polite but the way he uttered them stung my ears.

"I'm trying to do so," I said. "You never mentioned a set deadline."

"Do I really have to? I'm guessing that you're still at square one. This is your job after all. Shouldn't you be a little worried? Look, I'm wasting valuable shift time talking to you, but am trying to ascertain whether or not it's doing any good."

"I understand, Ibrahim Bey." I had begun to clench my teeth again. "I'll try to have it finished by Friday evening."

"What do you mean 'try'? That report has to be on my desk by tomorrow evening!"

I didn't want to reply, nor did I think a reply was necessary. As I fell quiet, total silence ensued for some time. Together, we listened to the endless sounds of keyboards clattering and telephone chatter. Gürsel had moved over to the cubicle next to me and was talking to a young engineer. Together we unwillingly eavesdropped on their conversation.

"Well, who told you to go get married and have a child right away for godssakes?" said Gürsel jovially. "Didn't you know that you wouldn't be able to get any sleep?"

Ibrahim Bey just stood there without saying anything for a few more seconds then took off without a word. Finally alone, I was able to turn my attention back to my computer. Tapping my fingers on the table anxiously, I tried my best to continue with my research.

Just then, an e-mail arrived. It was an advertisement for a seminar on spirituality: "A group voyage to our inner self in order to reach the freedom and happiness that is our birth right." The ad went on to claim that we were going to be able to contact our higher self and by pondering on the meaning of life, find the occasion to discover the pure, loving being that lies within, full of peace and joy. By balancing our inner energies, we were to heal all pain, purify ourselves of negative emotions and by evolving, achieve miracles. We could increase our awareness and experience the love that bursts forth from within. The path we tread on would be a spiritual journey more meaningful than the actual destination we hoped to arrive. Being there was more important than attaining the target. The seminar that would be taking place at the Princess Hotel on Sunday would cost just 850 TL. The price included lunch, coffee breaks and unlimited tea and coffee. In order to confirm one's reservation, a down payment of 150 TL was required.

The cell phone of the engineer sitting in the next cubicle began to ring. I overheard him speaking to his wife about their new furniture arriving in February. For them, February was a close enough date; as for me, I wasn't sure I could stick it out until then.

Osman came by and asked if I wanted to go to lunch.

"Yes," I said, "Let's go."

We walked towards the cafeteria side by side, passing through the same corridor. The same sentences were inscribed on the walls:

We are a big and strong team that protects the interests of both our institution and staff!

We are constantly contributing to the increase of the quality of life of our society.

We adhere to ethical mandates in all our activities.

***

"I've been summoned to save the nation. My name is Suleiman, no? I am Suleiman the Magnificent! I told them, but they don't listen. They tell me, 'Let's take you to a hospital.' They're working behind my back. Obviously they saw the lion roaring in me, they're casting the evil eye now!"

"Why are you telling me all this?" I asked.

Suleiman lifted his head and peered into my eyes with a heart-broken look.

"You're Mustafa!"

"No!" I said, "I am not Mustafa."

"Yes, you are!"

"Jeez, no, I am not Mustafa!"

He didn't respond and I stopped insisting. He thought I resembled somebody and had no doubt he was right. Had I contradicted him further, I might break his heart, even lead him to get aggressive.

"May Allah help us all!" he began anew. "My arms are rotting... At nights... The doctors don't say much. Just like in the TV series! It's a fucked up situation! I think it's the weather. A snow blizzard is a-coming. Then there is the trash that stinks. That's not good! Like a rat for instance... I lock my door but the damned parasite still finds a way in! Anyway, whatever happened, happened there. Old memories. Nostalgia. A sweet moment in time, when young... Happy times at the pretty house in Karşıyaka! I saw the happy brother. Did I or did I not see, he said; what am I to do with him now anyway? Then I think... I guess something happened, maybe she cheated on me, right?"

Then Suleiman went silent, as if he was expecting a response. He continued to stare into my eyes. I felt like I had to speak.

46

"I don't think she cheated on you," I said. "Where did you get that idea from?"

"The neighbors' door is always open!" he said. "But whenever I arrive, it shuts. The family is like an atom...an indivisible whole, isn't that what they say! Life is so tough! She was sick there; her too. Do you know her? Don't you ever go and tell her I love her very much!"

Suddenly he began to wail and turned his back to me. He began to weep.

"Touching me!.. A hand is touching me! Save me! Save me!"

Gulping, I anxiously asked, "Who's touching you? Where? I can't see anyone."

"His eyes aren't in their places! He's all white, with a funny toupee! Like a furry dog's head!"

He had begun to survey the dark road that separated two buildings across the street.

"There!" He yelled. "He's waiting for you to leave! Once everybody leaves he comes back! He comes back and then he gets into me!

His face was stretched back with fear, his jaw kept moving whilst he spoke. I wasn't sure what I should say or do. Suleiman took a few steps back without removing his gaze towards the space where he thought the creature lurked. His step caught on an upturned rock, he stumbled. Straightening up, he turned around and ran away limping.

I stood there for some time, watching him run along the street until he disappeared out of sight. Then I remembered what I had been busy doing and continued to walk towards my apartment. While walking, though, I kept one eye peeled on the spot Suleiman had indicated. I hurriedly entered the garden and shut the thin, steel barred gate–as if it could protect me from any danger.

The old lady living on the ground floor had again taken up her place on her balcony. I had never actually seen the face of this head-covered woman, for she always faced the opposite direction, but I had gotten used to spotting her here most evenings after work. I noticed that she would frequently raise her arm and check her watch, as if she were waiting for something. Maybe dinner, the call to prayer or a TV drama to begin...

I walked quickly by the steel barred windows of the ground floor, towards the entrance at the side of the building. The wooden window frames were rotting; the paint had peeled off and the frames had taken up a grayish hue. Even the windowpanes looked like they had lost their transparency due to the soot. Behind these blurred windows and filthy curtains lay imprisoned dismal and bizarre looking plants. I would see a cat every now and then as well. The kitchen window was ajar. An old tune could be heard from inside. I think it was Zeki Müren singing.

Is this longing?
Is this love?
Is this life?
The heart in pain, the world in dismay, the eyes full of tears!

At the outer door, as I was rummaging through my pockets to find my keys, I suddenly jumped when a hand touched me my back. My heartbeat began a drumroll.

"Sorry, my friend!" said the apartment super. "I didn't startle you, did I?"

"No, it's okay. What's up?"

"I just handed out trash bags to each apartment. I was going to give you a few too, but you weren't in so I figured I'd give them to you now."

While talking, he handed over a bunch of black plastic bags. I took them and tried to stuff them into my pockets.

"All right, thanks a lot."

"You're welcome, good evening to you."

"To you too."

As he turned and walked back towards the yard, I finally managed to open the door and enter the building. The entryway had a faint odor of mildew, but the warmth felt good. Before climbing up the stairs, I peered into my post box out of habit. I expected it to be empty as usual, so when I saw the white of an envelope I was surprised, even a bit excited. I used my entry key to turn the lock of the box, retrieved the envelope, and looked at the return address. It was from the Office of Military Recruitment. I immediately opened it and began to read the contents. It seems that I was being summoned to the center next week Wednesday at 08:00 to pick up my conscription papers. The notice particularly emphasized that I had to bring my identity card and my military service book documentation. (I had no idea what a military book documentation was.) The letter went on –in a very polite manner– to say that if I did not show up on the date assigned without providing a prior reason, I would be prosecuted as a DRAFT EVADER. They were obviously unaware of my medical condition. I realized that I was going to have to document the illness with an official report. Meaning I had to go to a state hospital. I had been postponing this for some time now. Should I first apply to the local recruiting station I wondered? To stamp out the flames of my dread I took a deep breath. Then I began my long, daily trek up the stairs to the top floor.

The concrete steps spiraled upwards. Residents had placed flowerpots on the landings. The large sunlight on the roof let in plenty of light so the flowers were able to survive. Slowly I climbed the steps, never looking up but always ahead, inspecting each step I took. Otherwise the height I had to climb could easily discourage me. I was panting now, and my lungs were flaming. I thought maybe I had caught a cold on the ferry the other day.

All I wanted was to take refuge in my apartment as quickly as possible.

Once I had reached my floor the neighbor's door swung open. Necmettin Bey was spying on me again. "Good evening," he said with his polite and clammy tone of voice. The rakı odor I smelled was either really there or I was just making it up, thinking it had to be there. "I'm sorry! It probably seems like I was spying on you but..."

"Not to worry!" I replied, "Good evening!"

"I'd like to meet with you sometime. There are certain things I wish to discuss with you."

My reflex kicked in by trying to make up an excuse but my efforts proved unsuccessful so I mumbled, "Ok... I'll... I'll try to find some time."

I suddenly considered that the sooner I got this new task out of the way, the better it would be, so I said, "You can tell me now if you wish."

"No. This is not a matter I wish to speak about on the run."

"Then why don't you come in?"

***

"There was some noise last night," said Necmettin Bey. "I'm very sorry. The walls are thin. You must've heard it."

I presumed he was talking about his fight with his wife.

"I didn't hear much really," I lied. "No harm done." In the meantime I turned on the TV in case we ran out of words to say.

"In any case," he insisted. "We disturbed you."

"These things happen in marriages. Don't worry about it."

"You were married once as well, weren't you?"

"Yes I was; we got divorced a few months ago."

He felt sorry for me for a moment, or feigned to do so.

"Recently," he continued, "it has become a bit more difficult to manage relationships. Almost all the young couples around me are getting divorced these days. I hope you get over it without much damage."

I thanked him and then found myself at a loss for words. For a while we both stared at the TV screen. Then, "Was that it?" I asked. "What you were going to tell me; the noise I mean?!"

"No!" he said. "That's not all... Another thing... Well I see you're a bit under the weather recently. You look pale and you've lost weight. Is everything all right? Is there anything we can do to help?"

"I'm fine," I said, smiling. "Thank you."

I didn't want to tell him about my illness for some reason. It felt inappropriate. Besides, it wasn't like it would do any good I thought.

"You must still be sad, of course."

"Perhaps, yes."

Commercials had begun on TV. The advertisement underscored how quite attractive and cheerful ladies would reward a man who chose to shave with a certain razor. Many times!

"Have you got anything planned for New Year's?" asked Necmettin Bey.

I was a bit disturbed by the question as it sounded more like he was interrogating me instead of giving me an invitation.

"No plans so far," I mumbled. "I'll probably have a couple of friends over..."

"Really?" he said. "That's nice! We'll be at home as well. If your plans change, we'd be very happy to have you over with us. Nagehan has wanted to meet you for some time now. I've been telling her about you, you see."

"Thanks!" I said, trying to politely avoid his offer. I had first felt denigrated, after which I felt guilty for thinking so; yet I really didn't want to greet the New Year alongside two middle-aged people and their first grader son. I'd much prefer to be alone. So I smiled.

"In any case, I wouldn't dream of coming without a personal invitation from Nagehan Hanım. I don't want to risk a beating."

He chuckled.

The commercials had ended and now it was time for the *advertorials*. I took the remote control and began to zap through the channels until I came across a soccer game. For some unknown reason, watching people run around to and fro across a green field comforted me.

Didn't Necmettin Bey perceive my lack of interest? Perhaps I couldn't recognize another's lack of interest either, perhaps nobody did.

"Are you hungry?" I asked, since I had begun to grow hungry too.

"No, no!" he said. "I'll be leaving now. And you'll have dinner."

"Let me offer you a drink then. What would you have? Coke? Beer?"

I was making such an effort to be polite –either as an apology or to hide the thoughts that ran through my head– on the other hand, it couldn't be said that I was totally insincere.

"I don't want anything," he said. "Thank you. I'll be leaving now. I've already bothered you enough."

The team in red was beating the team in white, 4-nil.

"Not to worry!" I said. "Stay a while longer."

"Ok, I'll stay for another minute or two then... How is your book coming along?"

"Not bad. Slowly but surely..."

"Do you have anything else you've written? I'd like to read them."

"I've written some short stories."

"I'd like to take a look at them sometime, if you don't mind."

"Sure, sure," I said, clenching my teeth.

The game on TV had ended and the commercials had begun again. A music channel showed a group of girls in mini-skirts who had turned their back to the screen, had bent forward a little to display their buttocks, and were spanking themselves in line with the rhythm.

"What are you doing on the weekend?" asked Necmettin Bey. "Do you have any plans for Saturday night?"

I was really getting tired trying to make up excuses for this man. Why didn't he just leave?

"Nothing so far," I grumbled. "Why do you ask?"

"The international game is on Saturday... Why don't you come over to our place to watch it? Do you follow soccer?"

I could get out of having to spend New Year's with them at least, by using this opportunity to fulfill this now mandatory visit to the neighbors. "Could do," I replied. "I could come... I don't support any specific team but I do watch the national team when it plays."

I wanted to sleep. *What if I just drifted off right here,* I thought. He could continue to sit here if he liked. Then, in order to behave more properly towards him, I began to ponder the ways in which I could make Necmettin Bey useful to me. Maybe I could use him in creating a new character.

"All right then," said Necmettin Bey. "I'll take my leave now. I already wasted plenty of your time."

"Not to worry," I objected. "It was nice of you to drop by."

He apologized over and over again, perhaps because he wanted to hear me say over and over "No, please, oh come on, not to worry," and the likes. If my departure were not so eminent, I would've probably started to see my neighbor as a critical obsta-

53

cle and begin to plot precautionary measures that I could use to ward him off.

However, once I saw Necmettin Bey out, I was overtaken by a strange sense of guilt. Perhaps I had hurt his feelings. I concluded that he had indeed been hurt, but was trying not to let it show, just as I was trying not to let my own anxiety spill out. The worst was that I had lost my desire to write. Or maybe I was just being lazy.

What sort of man was I, too lazy even to dice tomatoes? Dinner was simple and quick. I heated the canned beans in a pot and sprinkled on several spices to make the dish more edible. One thing was for us, I no longer needed to worry that I would get cancer from eating canned food. Besides, I needed to be thrifty these days.

4

I was on an island that saw the mainland. A boat had dropped me off, leaving me stranded. I busied myself by meandering on the shores of the wide strait that separated the two continents. Suddenly I noticed how insurmountable the foaming waters that flowed in front of me were. To return was nearly impossible. There was only a very narrow, wooden plank that could be used to cross over. Afraid I would fall off, I gripped the plank and tried to cross over by crawling. When I woke up a cry had swelled up my throat.

In order to calm myself, I hummed a melody and went to the bathroom to have a shave. As I hurriedly got dressed I tried to overlook the physical changes my body had been undergoing. Later I checked each room to see whether any lights or the gas were on, after which I sealed the apartment in its desolate and dark state and went out.

The nighttime cold still lingered and the air reeked of coal smoke. I looked for my car trying to remember where I had parked it. It pleased me to find it waiting for me right where I had left it. I caressed its chassis and opened its door, sat in the drivers seat and started the engine. I didn't both putting on my seatbelt. I just didn't feel like it.

While trying to get onto a main road by maneuvering through the city's narrow streets I thought, *she doesn't call anymore. She probably found someone else; maybe there was someone else all along.* I was surprised that she never worried about me. I couldn't understand what lay behind such a drastic, sharp change in behavior. Though when I had mentioned to her that I worried about her, she had told me that that kind of curiosity had something to do with pity.

The sides of the road were lined with various life-like statues of animals; goats, sheep grazing... Artificial palm trees bedecked with lights of various colors had been positioned at some spots along the motorway.

I was suddenly swept with the notion that something horrible had happened to her and I was swept with a feeling of anxiety: It's cold outside I said to myself, it's cold, because she's gone. Why did I enjoy torturing myself? I concluded by thinking that I'm becoming a bit paranoid; once the anxiety had dissipated, I slowly returned to my usual lusterless, apathetic state of mind.

The traffic between Kadıköy and Üsküdar was a snarl. I had guessed that there would be some stalling due to the on-going construction of the underpass, but I didn't expect it would be this bad. Something out of the ordinary must have happened. Whatever the problem was, of course it had to coincide with my passing! Convinced that somebody out there was trying to pit obstacles against me on purpose, I found myself getting angry.

I wasn't the only one angry. Drivers unabashedly tried to cut each other off, trying to squeeze into any space they could find on the road. Profiteering risk-takers had already fully invaded the emergency lane.

My inners were being torn apart by the noise of insistent car horns. Causing pain, after all, must be the underlying aim of those who were pressing their hands down over their horns. The sounds of blaring horns were suddenly pierced by the sound of ambulance sirens. Angrily I thought, *something always happens to someone when there is a traffic jam.* Instead of feeling sorry for the ambulances and their passengers, I had begun to harbor suspicions. Perhaps the drivers were frustrated as well, and were feigning an emergency, or a businessman or someone of that sort had paid his way to gain this priority to save time. Rumors of such instances had circulated around the city and there really was nothing to hinder these types of possibilities.

Yet in about fifteen minutes, I passed an accident that justified the ambulances' blaring sirens. The road was strewn with the debris of burned and crashed vehicles. Both the drivers and passengers seemed to have shared the same fate. It seems that there had been an explosion of some sort. Police were screaming, "Don't stop! Keep moving!" The moment I found my path open, I stepped on the accelerator and raced away.

I knew of a car park near the local recruitment office. As I did not want to search street by street for a parking space I immediately pulled into the lot. The price was fixed and they wanted it up front. Although I tried to explain how short my business was, the man in charge wasn't convinced, so I had to pay up. As I walked towards the office I thought how I had paid all that money for nothing, but as I came closer to the building, I understood that I was the one who had come out ahead: Hundreds of people were lined up in front of the office.

Instead of getting in line, I tried to get information from the private at the gate. "Do we have to get in line to get a medical report as well?"

He said nothing. After eyeing me in an annoyed manner, he motioned with his head to get back to the end of the line. So I walked past the youngsters lined up against the concrete walls of the garden, came to the end of the queue, and began to wait for my turn.

I had brought a book that I had squeezed into my jacket pocket. After gazing around for a while, I took it out as if it were a flask of liquor and began to peruse its pages. The author was a retired psychiatrist. While he used hypnosis to make his patients recall old memories, he had noticed that he was able to reach far beyond, to earlier lives, even the transitional periods in between reincarnations. The book consisted of records he had kept during these sessions of hypnosis. A patient, who had come to the doctor for an incurable sore throat for instance, had apparently died by an Indian arrow in the throat in a previous life. In a similar vein, there were patients killed in the world wars, or as samurai, fallen with a sword in hand.

From what was written in the book, the conclusion was that at the time of death, our souls –easily– shot out from the top of our heads as a glittery being. Once we passed onto the other side, we were no longer bound by the laws of gravity and we could move as we pleased. We watched our bodies from above and felt sorry for those we had left behind. Patients recounted how at a height not so far up the ground they felt suspended for some time, after which they began to be sucked upwards by some gravitational force. They would gravitate towards sources of light and colored clouds. As they were released from physical pain, they began to feel freedom and serenity. They heard small wind chimes and string instruments sounding around them. According to these people, death was actually the easiest part of life; death was not darkness but light; the other side was orderly and held great plans for us. We were to meet with the already departed in magnificent palaces. Friends that awaited us at a table would quickly come and greet us. We were to return home at long last.

While reading I eavesdropped on the conversations between the young men around me. One of them finished his cigarette, flipped the butt on the ground and after viciously crushing it under his feet, said:

"When I asked him if he hadn't broken up with that girl, he said he had and when I asked him why, he said she was just too immature for him. But then again, that's Tolga for you..."

Another guy in the line who was swaying to and fro, either out of boredom or the cold, cut in: "He's a grown man, let him do whatever he likes!"

"Tolga ain't a grown-up! I told him that since they were lovers, it wasn't right of him just to leave her like that, but he said that they never did nothing. He said that anyway she had started it, but I don't know, 'It's a real shame!' I said."

The two suddenly stopped talking, as did everyone else waiting in the line. I looked up to see what had caused this change and saw that some staff persons had arrived and were climbing out of a van. The staff of six, most of whom were middle-aged women, passed by us with denigrating looks and entered the yard that was out of bounds for us. I checked my watch; it was almost 9:00 AM. I tried to focus on my book anew.

Why did the scenes from the patients' past lives always resemble those from a film? Why did they always mention Samurai, Indians and whatnot, and not unknown histories and tribes with unknown and unknowable names? After all, most of human history still remains unknown. Where were the unexpected though reasonable details that allow us to believe the story, even if it's fiction?

"She gave me hope, don't you see? She can't deny it! She gave me hope!"

Suddenly I noticed one of the youth remove a white booklet from the inside pocket of his jacket.

"Here's how it goes!" he said. "Now you're applying to go in February... For July, it won't work. It'll already be late!"

I lifted my head from the book and asked, "Is that a Military Service Book?"

"Yes!"

"Do you guys have any idea where I can get one too?"

"At stationary stores. But they ask for a photograph too!"

"Does everybody need one? I'm here to get a medical report..."

Their heads bobbed right and left gesturing negatively. Then the one wearing a hoodie grumbled: "Why don't you ask the soldier at the gate?"

"Nah!" I said. "He snaps back! I already tried."

They laughed. So did I. I caught myself laughing like this every once in a while, as if all had been forgotten.

"What's wrong with you then?"

"Never mind that. It's not contagious though!"

"Are you trying to dodge the draft, then?"

"Not at all!"

"I've got Hepatitis B, but I'm not telling them. If I do, they won't draft me."

"So you want to go do your service?"

"Yeah. Can't find a job until I have done it."

"Don't they give you an 'unfit for service' report for hepatitis B?"

"Nope. They just make you wait."

A bespectacled boy behind me cut in and said, "I've already done my service. I'm trying to get my discharge papers."

I thought it strange that once you had completed the service, even that wasn't enough, you still had to wait in line to get papers to prove you had served. The other young men waiting in line began to ask him about where he had done his service and how it went and so on. This way we all learned that he had served as a ranger and listened to him talk of his memories a little. He told us stories that were so out of this world yet were suffused with such suffocating details that none of us doubted their reality. He spoke with a placid, odd tone of voice. I noticed that he kept his hands in his pockets at all times. Maybe he had lost his hands, or his fingers.

"They say the friends you make there are for life, but that ain't true!" he said, finally. "Anyone falls sick, yeah, everyone rushes to their aid but once you're out, that's it. Nobody calls. I don't want to call anyone either, so I don't."

We all became silent. I opted for some introversion. I felt like a scarecrow about to topple down. I went for my book and tried to pick up reading where I had left off. They asked me what I was reading. I tried to give them a summary. My voice did not sound very persuasive. In response, one of the boys told me about a book he had read on Atlantis.

"Apparently there used to be a great civilization way before ours," he said. "Then back to square one!"

"Could be," I managed to say.

Every hour, they would let 20-25 people get in the building. In this way, slowly but surely, we approached the gate. Our lunch consisted of some sesame bagels or sandwiches procured from street vendors nearby. A deli close by was available for beverages.

Finally, as it began to grow dark outside, I heard myself being ordered inside. Inside was a cacophony of conversations, yelling, coughing and sneezing. As my part in the line was on the steps, I tried to rest my legs by leaning against the railings. After some soldiers shoved us around to pass by, as if we were useless animals, they escorted a man approaching the end of his middle ages. He was wearing handcuffs. A tall sergeant who obviously had some sort of seniority and was guarding the office entrance barked out:

"You can't escape from the State! They'll find you even in the depths of hell!"

He acted like he was part of some drama or another. A soldier yelling from upstairs also injected its own theatricality to the situation. I thought how they might be trying to intimidate those who were about to join, or about to evade. Perhaps they had even been ordered to act this manner.

After waiting for another hour on the steps, I finally was able to reach somebody to whom I can speak about my business here. I handed my documents and with the politest tone I could muster I said, "I am a cancer patient, but just received my draft papers. I guess a report from a government hospital..."

I stopped talking. The lady wasn't listening to me. She turned her back to me and began chatting with her colleagues. For some unknown reason, after a bit, she turned around back to me and said, "We're having a chat here! Go ask over there!" they chuckled. I didn't know what to do. Then she put on a strict, serious air and said "All right... What's the issue here?"

"I am a cancer patient," I said, my voice trembling; "But I received a draft notice; I'm guessing I have to go to a government hospital and get a report."

She took the documents I had handed her and after perusing through them for a while, "Ok," she said. "Go sit over there. We'll fax a notice to your hometown. After we receive a confirmation, we'll prepare your papers for the hospital."

I thanked her and drew back. There weren't any vacant seats so I stood there waiting, not too far away from her desk. I was a bit more relaxed now; at least I had gotten the ball rolling. I went back to my book.

"If death really meant the end of everything that we are, then life would truly be meaningless," was written in the final chapter. This was like saying, "if life were meaningless, then life would be meaningless." It didn't add anything new, didn't give hope; only sorrow...

* * *

When I arrived at my apartment building, I saw that the old lady was nowhere to be seen. For a moment the thought crossed my mind that she must have died, but I was relieved when I saw her in the corridor.. She was complaining to Necmettin Bey's wife; I think it was about the building manager.

I bid them good evening as I passed them by and headed for the staircase. There was something in my post-box again. I fiddled with my fingers and was able to draw it out without using the keys. It was an ad for a newly-opened pizza parlor nearby. It began with *Dear Adem Bey,* and ended with a photocopied signature.

Just then, the conversation in the corridor had come to an end and Nagehan Hanım had begun to walk towards the stairs behind me. I turned around and looked at her. She was carrying numerous shopping bags and was barely able to walk, bumping them this side and that. "Let me help you," I said. She objected out of politeness. I insisted and she eventually gave in. We began to walk up the steps together. For some time, neither of us said anything. Then I quietly remarked, "You've done quite a bit of shopping," trying hard to smile. She got nervous.

"If its too heavy for you..."

"No, no! That's not what I meant. I'm fine. I need to exercise more anyway!"

She laughed.

"I bought a bunch of toys for the little one again. I just can't stop myself when I see them. Such things they come up with nowadays... I didn't forget myself either of course."

I smiled in response. "It's snowing," I added.

"Has it really begun?"

"Yes, just as I entered the building."

Amidst the darkness seen from the glass pane above, we could faintly see the falling snowflakes. As Nagehan Hanım opened her door with the keys she never let go of, she said, "I hear Necmi invited you over for Saturday."

For a second there, I felt this was a fait accompli and thus became a bit nervous.

"Yes," I said, "if it's all right with you of course, I wouldn't want to bother you."

"No, no," she objected as she took off her shoes. "I've been wanting to meet you for some time as well. Please do come."

I gave her bags back and smiled. "Ok then. See you on Saturday."

She thanked me and closed the door. I turned around and headed into my own apartment.

After I made a kind of salad out of some diced vegetables and feta cheese, I turned the TV to a station that was screening a wildlife documentary and sat down to my desk. I couldn't do anything for some time though. Writing felt meaningless, which was as difficult for me to handle as surrendering after a defeat on a battlefield.

I could hear a little girl crying in the apartment below. Her sobs and gasps came from deep within. This brought "Her" to mind. I really didn't like just sitting there doing nothing but didn't really know what exactly I could do in the first place. In this way, I became indifferent to the suffering of a person, who was at the most three meters away from me. 30 cm thick walls were enough to stop gigantic worlds from mingling.

Then, unable to resist, I did something foolish: I picked up my cell phone and called "Her." No one picked up. I went breathless. *It shouldn't have ended like this*, I thought to myself. A dark hand seemed to press on my chest as I tried to string together a logical sentence in order to continue writing. I began to grow afraid as sweat poured out of me and I breathed with difficulty. There was no way out, no way to salvation. I thought about dying. Besides, I needn't just disappear as I had a ticket to an adventure full of possibilities.

Suddenly a text message arrived. My heart was about to leap out of my chest from the excitement. I thought that she might've written a few sentences explaining herself; that she was in a meeting and couldn't respond to my call. However, the message was from a newly opened massage parlor. As if launching a gamut of swearwords, the text delivered me the message that the New Year's special offer was only 90 TL for a body peeling session on a waterbed.

I got up and walked around the room like an asthmatic trying to catch his breath. Then I made myself some coffee and sat back down to propel my story onwards, hoping that the few cups I had downed would give me the necessary vigor. I was busy describing people who were forced to live in houses made of glass. When mistakes were made, the glasshouses would burst into pieces, along with their residents.

I wrote non-stop until midnight. Recognizing that I could not go on any longer I turned the computer off and got up from my desk. I parted the curtains and peered outside for a bit. The snow was still falling. It wasn't sticking to the ground, even though roofs were icing up. I went to the bathroom, then slipped into my pajamas. As I crawled into bed, I thought to myself, *if it snows like this all night long, in the morning everything will be covered in white.*

I dreamed that I was racing to and fro along Istanbul's tangled streets, looking for an exit. When I woke up, the clock read

3 AM. I had a fever and was aching all over. My head felt like my nerves were being squashed and yanked apart almost to the point of tearing. The pain was a kind heretofore unknown by me; I had no idea as to how to combat it, or whether or not it would eventually end. I got up and paced around, but to no avail. When I lay back down, the pain got even worse. To distract myself, I turned on the TV. I began zapping through the channels with the hope of finding something interesting that would distract me from the pain.

The news channels were broadcasting news of the accident I had passed by the previous day. They were calling the incident a terrorist attack–or at least claiming as such. Similar attacks had taken place at separate times in other districts of the city. The news anchor described how the panic-stricken public had been trying frantically to get home amidst the stalled traffic. The word "home" brought back warm feelings. Years ago, during a semester break from school, I had been caught in a snow blizzard on a bus while trying to make it back to my parents. There were two wonderful women at each end of my route who were worried sick about me. Those were the days! From a hospital bed a soldier who had lost his legs in a terrorist attack was saying that he was in pain but that he was happy, as it was for the realization of a sacred cause.

Another channel featured the telephone numbers for a sex hot line. Text scrolling across the screen urged viewers to: "Call Right Now for Good Company." The text was soon replaced by a cartoon figure of a girl who was pleasuring herself with her thin fingers. In the meantime, websites and phone numbers where one could purchase dildos and sex dolls also kept popping up on the screen.

The pain just wouldn't subside. I turned the TV off and tried this time to take refuge in the silent darkness. I looked out the window. The snow had subsided. I began to moan a little. For some reason this alleviated the pain, though I also tried to keep it low, as I knew my voice could be heard easily in the dead of night. For a moment I almost wished there was somebody with me, though I quickly decided that this wasn't really the case.

I swallowed a painkiller and lay on my back on the bed, cupping my eyes with my palms. After about 5 minutes my heartbeat began to calm down. The pain began to transform itself to a heavenly feeling of serenity. I couldn't decide whether it was the position I was lying in, or the painkiller that did the trick. The next time I came across such a predicament, I would have to try both together. Calming down, I slowly drifted off to sleep. This time I dreamed of pleasant things. Things that hadn't happened; things that would never ever happen... For a while I believed in them all. This made me feel better, until I woke up again.

5

There were certain faces I saw each day on my way to work. I would pass them by with a downturned gaze, saying nothing. I didn't want this instance of greeting to become a reciprocal obligation. I presume they also silently agreed. That morning though, there wasn't a soul that went by without a good morning from me. They were dumbfounded; they faltered a bit, trying to respond with a smile. Some didn't hear a word I said.

As I approached the door, the smart building greeted me once more with its warm female voice.

"Good morning, Adem Bey! Welcome and I hope you have a productive day!"

I reached the office passing through automatic doors that swung open like loyal servants. As if trying to stifle my troublesome disposition, I greeted my colleagues with hearty "Good Mornings." Then I went to my desk, turned the computer on and began perusing the papers on the Net while having breakfast.

The political tension was cooling down now that the parties involved had begun to negotiate, which in turn made the politics page all the more boring. I checked the other sections. A

world-famous illusionist had arrived in town. The paper was saying that he could pass through walls, make objects disappear
then reappear in front of the cameras. He had stated that he was
no wizard or sorcerer but that he tricked the human eye. A father
continued marching towards the capital, protesting the traffic
accident that had killed his son. I checked my horoscope: My
dreams were all to come true next year. My emotional and famil-
ial matters were to come to rest on more solid foundations.
Moreover, until June, as Jupiter was in Cancer forming a square-
like position with my sign, I was to receive good omens concerning real estate. As my fortune was to turn out well, I should leave
all worries behind, wait for the right opportunities to appear, and
then to seize them when the time came.

I had just quit reading the paper when Ibrahim Bey appeared
right behind me and grumbled: "Not really the early bird, are we
now?"

I slowly turned towards him and said: "Good morning. What
can I do for you?"

"I was just worried. All sorts of things come to mind. Anyway...
Have you taken care of your business with the military?"

"Yes," I replied briefly. I did not add that I had to go the hospital. "I was able to postpone it," I continued. "If I hadn't
checked in, they would've put me up as a draft-dodger. I waited
in line practically the whole day; it was dark when I was finally finished."

He looked at me in a strange way. I guess he was trying to
ascertain whether or not I was lying to him.

"All right! I hope you'll finish that report I'm expecting you
to hand over today!"

"Don't worry, Ibrahim Bey, I'll get it done by tonight. If worse
comes to worse, I'll stay overtime and send it to you at night."

"Night? What night? What did I tell you? Didn't I say

evening? I guess I'm not making myself clear! I have to send that report to Rüstem Bey ASAP!"

"All right Ibrahim Bey! It'll most likely be finished by evening anyway."

The fact that I continued to speak in uncertain terms must've really made him angry, even though he stopped insisting. This time he took it upon himself to criticize the way I dressed. He told me that since I was now a part of the sales and marketing department, I had to pay more attention to my appearance. "You have to remember that you are face of TeleTurca," he said. "Get your act together!"

The ringing of my phone came to my rescue and my director took off as if he was waiting for the cue. I picked up the receiver and brought it up to my left ear. Somebody from Pakbank had come to visit me. He said that he was here concerning the credit card I had ordered the day before and that he was waiting downstairs. This angered me. I had rejected their offer of a credit card but apparently this gentleman had not been informed of this, and could I just spare a minute or two, since he had already come this far to see me. I clenched my teeth, stood up, and ran down to send the man away as soon as possible.

The salesman was sitting on the leather chairs in the lobby, waiting for me. He was wearing a nicely pressed dark suit. As I drew closer he got up to shake my hand.

"Welcome!" I said, out of breath.

After greeting me, he began to pour out the details of the credit card they were offering.

"Sorry to barge in, but..." I barged in. "I really am not considering purchasing your credit card. You shouldn't waste your breath telling me about it."

"Do you have a credit card?" he asked. "No," I said, taken aback. This time he began to tell me why I needed to have one.

"Look, I have personal reasons," I said, "for not getting one, that is."

He couldn't make heads or tails of my last remark.

"It won't take a minute!" he said, ruffling through his brief-case. "We fill the application form for you."

He took out a lengthy form full of pages. As he took them out and placed them on the plastic table, his hands were trembling. I wondered what his motivation could be.

"I'm sorry," I said. "I really don't want a card and I really do not want you to get upset about this. I do not have the time, nor any business with a card, believe me. There's a report I have to complete by tonight."

"But on the phone you said that you were interested, that we should visit you."

"I did not say such a thing." I said. "I can't recall what my exact words were, but there must've been a misunderstanding."

After mumbling something incomprehensible to me, "All right!" he said. "Since I've come all the way over here though, can you at least give me a few names of your friends that I can talk to?"

I was taken aback. I felt as if I were forced to give names during an interrogation.

"I'm sorry," I said. "I don't have any friends."

This time it was his turn to be dumbstruck. I grabbed this opportunity to shake his hand one last time and, after bidding him good day, ran back to my office, fleeing the scene.

In the meantime Gürsel had stopped at the cubicle next to mine and was busy giving Soner his advice.

"Call him 'Sir!' he said. "Offer him a ciggy or two, engage him in some small talk, he'll like that!"

I passed them and started to arrange my desk, preparing what I needed to take with me. On the shelves were the monthly

TeleTurca magazines. I briefly thumbed through the pages. *Between Us* was one of the titles of a section. *Advice of The Month*, *Best Team of The Year*, company trips and other social activities crowded the pages. In a tree-planting ceremony, both employees and supervisors were smiling together to the cameras. TeleTurca's contributions to sports and the arts, rewards, grants, sponsorships, contests had all been written up with the utmost pride.

Next door, Soner's cell began to ring.

"Worst part of marriage!" grumbled the young engineer. "The phone rings every two seconds!"

"And the kid!" added Gürsel; "Just when you thought you solved one's problem, the other's will begin!"

Rüstem Bey arrived; they went looking for Osman. There was an emergency. Osman was nowhere to be found.

"We pay an engineer, but then he's never around when we need him!" grumbled the General Manager.

I came across the folder on business conduct that had been given to me on my first day at work. When I glanced at the index, the clause on death caught my eye; I immediately opened the page to read it: *In case of death, the contract between employee and employer automatically becomes null and void.* I chuckled.

After tossing all these documents into the waste basket, I began to collect all my old mail. I wanted to copy them all onto one folder and transfer them onto my computer at home. This mail folder was one thing I wanted to take with me onto my long trip. My gaze unavoidably drifted onto some of the sentences. They were full of forgotten details. All those words of love felt artificial, even those written by me. I recalled how "she" had said that even if she harbored suspicions, she could act as if all was going well. This had disturbed me, I had told her that I preferred honesty but maybe I was the true liar here.

***

As there was a Beşiktaş game in the evening, I decided to avoid the crowds by using the Kadıköy-Eminönü line to pass the Bosporus. I climbed to the top floor of the ferry and found a place next to a window. As I was on the brink of tears, I had my face turned towards the window, facing outside as far as I could. On the badly washed window, there were round blotches and melting snowflakes. I was able to see both the outside and the inside of the ferry without having to turn my head, thanks to the reflection on the window. Most of the passengers hadn't found themselves a seat yet. The reflection of the port lights in the sea disappeared one by one among the dark waves as the ferry further set out.

"Dear passengers!" said a polite voice. "For your own security, please refrain from accepting food or drinks from those whom you do not know! Please do not give your pocket change to the beggars!"

We had exited the bay. Now I was able to make out the Marmara Sea. Billions of snowflakes were dropping down into this abyss that stretched downwards into infinity. I tried to engrave onto my mind the things I saw. A ferry official wearing a white uniform jacket walked down the corridor, trying to sell the cups of sahlep he was carrying. An old flower seller had also begun to do the rounds among the passengers.

The couple sitting by me began to chat enthusiastically.

"Nazan didn't really want it, you know?" said the girl.

"Of course she didn't!" replied the young man, "Who'd marry Özcan to begin with? He doesn't have one K in the bank! Spent all that he's made, has no investments... 'Get your act together,' I told him! 'You're right!' he says... Everyone wants to get married sooner or later. Don't you?"

"I have always admired Nazan for being such a hard worker."

"She's nice girl, but a bit insecure."

"I don't have things like that."

"I know."

The flower seller came and stood right in front of them, insisting they buy a bouquet. They refused, but this interruption had served to sour their conversation.

I opened the book I had carried with me and started to read. It was a novel I had stopped reading some time ago. It had been sitting in a corner for a while and now I felt the need to go back to the fantastic world it described. The setting was a planet in which men and women lived freely, without any possessions. The female protagonist who lived with a hard working man struggled with this difficult situation and her effort was being glorified. As usual, I tried to locate sentences that would legitimize my own behavior. Perhaps I was just seeing in the book, things that really weren't there. Even so, certain contradictions jumped out. While on the one hand it was claimed that those seeking possessions eventually ended up solitary and dying alone, on the other hand, an eternal bond between the minds and bodies of two people was being praised. Whatever the case may be I had grown fond of the characters in the novel. I yearned for a life lived through emotions; a sense of loss difficult to counter began to fill me. I tried to convince myself that I wasn't leading an unrighteous life, that things could not have been different.

As I continued to read, the white pages full of strange shapes began to take the form of a cinema screen. The printed words left the pages, leaving behind visions in my mind. Thus for a short while, a completely different planet had replaced the one I presently lived on. Then the engines of the ferry came to a halt, only to rev back up anew. I flinched. The ferry was maneuvering to moor. I had returned to reality, having brought back nothing from the time that had passed. I felt a rebellious cry surging up my throat akin to the one Jesus had on the cross: O Lord, Why Hast Thou Forsaken Me?

I looked out the window. Sarayburnu was now visible. The clouds reflected the lights of the peninsula, creating a roof of orange hue up on top. Passengers had begun to stand up and queue alongside the steps in order to get off the ferry as quickly as possible. I made a move and got in line as well. The cold air outside had seeped into the corridors. When I felt a tremor, I knew that we had docked. With small steps, I followed the crowd to the bottom deck and made it on land using the gangplank.

The cold was excruciating. The smoke from cigarettes, lit impatiently by those getting off the ferry, once exhaled, mixed imperceptively with the rest of the passengers' icy breath. Street peddlers pushing wooden carts mounted on rubber wheels were lined up to greet us at the space between the port and the boule-vard. Mimicking the rough voices of the peddlers, I ordered a plate of chickpeas and rice and used the plastic spoon handed to me to dig into it then and there. Arabesque melodies poured noisily from the cassette peddlers. Amidst the sounds of boat engines, somebody was singing, *it was a lie it seems;* another screamed *my loneliness is frozen, I daren't say a word!* My appetite was long gone.

On the billboards behind the cassette peddlers were pictures of smiling youth, doing somersaults and jumping up and down. They were supposedly hopping from joy upon learning about the new opportunities that one bank was offering.

***

"I only want my head to be hibernated," I said glancing at the landscape paintings hung on the wall.

"Sure!" said Koray Bey. "It's up to you!" Then he pulled out some forms from the bookcase behind him and placed them into the printer feeder, albeit with difficulty. "Economically speaking, it's definitely more viable. I think you've made the right choice."

I nodded. It pained me to watch him force a smile. I guess he was trying to inspire me with hope and courage, but his timing was completely off kilter. Because he wasn't the one undergoing hibernation, he wasn't able to fully grasp the fact that the process was not unlike death and that my chances of being revived were extremely small. He should be looking sad but clearly could not play the part and was not able to conceal his insincerity.

"I mentioned before that I didn't want come back until the technology for reanimation had reached full maturity, even if a cure for my disease were to be discovered," I said. "I'm not sure if you included this in your notes or not. Can you add that into our contract?"

"Of course!" he replied, hurriedly typing something onto his computer. "I do recall your words. I'm preparing the papers right now. It won't take long."

"How will I make the payment?"

"You were to pay cash up front, right?"

"Yes, that's how we calculated the price."

"Well, we have a blocked account that you can wire the money into. As long as you're safe and sound, neither you nor we can touch the money. After your demise, it becomes unblocked for us to use, to cover our expenses."

"I see."

"We use the TahSys 802 standard collection system. Our people in accounting have access to its interface. Once you deposit the funds, your form will be activated."

"Great," I mumbled.

"Excuse me?"

"Nothing!" I said, "Sounds good."

"Yes, it is indeed a good system!"

After fiddling with his computer for a bit longer, he removed a backpack from the lowest drawer of the closet behind him and placed it on the table.

"You can use this for the things you want to take with you," he said. "We unfortunately don't have a lot of room! Use this for items you value the most. We do provide special chemical protectors for sensitive items like photos, letters or a diary and such. The goal here is to preserve your belongings as long as you're alive."

In the meantime the printer had come back to life and had begun to print out the contract the man had been busy preparing.

"I don't think I'll be taking a lot with me," I said, trying to smile. "I don't want my grave to be pillaged!"

He made a gesture as if he disapproved of my last comment. Then, drawing out the printed pages of the contract from the machine, he looked over them one more time and turned them so they face me.

"Here you go," he said. "Go over it please. Don't get tangled up in the details; most of them are mere formalities. This is our standard contract. It is the same text that all of our patients have signed so far."

I stifled my reluctance and began to read the text. The typeset was extremely small and I felt the need to fully understand each and every sentence. As a result, my reading the contract took about an hour. The institute had taken into consideration every minute detail they could to protect themselves. For instance, according to the text, by signing I was agreeing to the fact that there was no guarantee for the hibernation process, that there was a giant percentage that it wouldn't work. I also was agreeing that in the case the institute's activities were legally hindered, I was to be abandoned to rot.

As I was in no condition to challenge or change anything in my circumstances, I merely asked him where I should sign. He indicated the spot and I put my John Hancock down. Then I completed the payment in the way he had suggested.

"Congratulations!" said Koray Bey.

"Congratulations!" I reiterated; "Let's see what happens!"

I stood up and held out my hand.

"I won't take any more of your time."

He stood up as well and said, "Please, sir, we are always at your service here."

"How will you be informed?" I asked. "About my death, I mean."

"Do you have the number of a relative that could let us know?"

"No. Maybe I can give you my neighbors' number though."

He reached for a pen on the table: "Ok, tell me the number."

"I don't have it memorized," I said. "I'll call and let you know. May I have your cell number? If my condition worsens, perhaps I could call and let you know. Please excuse me but I would like to know a way I can reach you anytime I need."

He hesitated briefly and then said, "Of course! Are you writing this down?"

I took out my phone and recorded the numbers he gave me. Then I thanked him and quickly asked if I could leave now.

Koray Bey also made a move to see me to the exit.

"Don't bother!" I said.

"Let me see you off... Do you know the way out?"

"Yes, I do. I learned it the last time I was here. You really needn't bother."

"Well, all right then. Until the next time Adem Bey. Take care of yourself!"

"You too! And take good care of me too!"

"Don't you worry about that!"

Upon leaving the office, I began to look for the exit among the silent, carpet-covered corridors. My mind seemed to have leaked out of my head. There wasn't a single thought going through it. It was quite pleasant actually. In a few minutes I reached the elevators and pressed the call button. Suddenly a piercing noise began to sound from one of the rooms towards the back of the corridor. I went next to it to see what was happening and peered through the little window on the door.

The walls of the room were almost child-like with their strong colors and selection of cheery pictures. At the far corner stood a bed, upon which a thin man sat with his back to the door, as if he were cross with someone. He was tightly hugging a big, furry toy. He was entirely oblivious to the alarm, leading me to believe that he was perhaps deaf. I wasn't sure of what I should do. As I looked to my left and right along the corridor, I noticed an official approaching. He was holding a toolbox.

"The alarm is ringing!" I said.

"I know!" he replied.

"Aren't you going to do something about it?"

"I am."

"What's wrong with him?"

"He's dead. Nothing to hurry about... We were expecting his death."

He passed beside me and entered the room. I began to watch him. Like a doctor, he dropped his case of equipment onto the bed and turned the corpse of the man around, tearing the teddy bear out of the man's grip and tossing it onto the floor. The patient had blotches all over his face. The official removed a box of powder from his case and began powdering the scarred face.

***

Having boarded the last train of the day, I got off at Karaköy. The snow had subsided. With the empty backpack they had given me at the institute slung over my shoulder, I used the underpass and emerged near the port. All the stores along the way had closed. Bits of rubbish were swaying to and fro with the wind over the checkered pavement and vapor seeped out of manhole covers like specters. I saw a young man with a guitar inspecting the space below the staircase of the entrance to an old office building before curling up for the night.

The bakery opposite the ferry port was still open. Standing in front, glue sniffing street urchins were soliciting change. One was shivering, or was feigning to shiver. I went up to him and handed him my cap but he refused.

Those waiting at the port to board the ferry at this hour were almost all drunk. A few Beşiktaş supporters were screaming their guts out: "Long live Beşiktaş! My life is yours, nothing can change my love for you, Beşiktaş!"

At the entrance to the port, a one-eyed peddler whose face looked like a fox was busy picking up his display of porn magazines that he had laid on the ground to sell. Every now and then he would stop to take a drag off the cigarette that hung between his lips.

Passing through the ground decks of ferries moored one against another, I boarded the last one that was waiting for its turn to depart. The ferry's lights were on. It was to move according to the schedule, regardless of the number of passengers. It would not run late, nor disappoint... I liked the ferry. I went into one of the halls at the ground deck, sat next to a window and extended my hands onto the warm radiators. Resting my head against the windowpane, I once again began to watch both inside and outside.

The passengers were all half-asleep. The old man sitting opposite me had his eyes shut and his head was tilted back. His mouth was open but he wasn't snoring. A bottle wrapped in newspaper was propped next to him. On the row behind a young, sleeping couple leaned on each other. Their heavy coats had somehow got tangled into one another, morphing into one big mass.

The darkness of the sea both frightened and beckoned me at the same time. The Maiden's Tower was decorated for New Year's. The lights strung on the first Bosporus Bridge kept changing colors. An effort to ward off suicide attempts I decided. Sleep slowly engulfed me; I let myself go.

When I opened my eyes, amidst the darkness beyond the window, I saw white dots that seemed to be aligned along a path. When I looked closer I was able to make out the seagulls that slept in unison on the windbreak. We were approaching the Kadıköy port.

The man across me had also woken up. He cleared his throat with a cough, looked around trying to pull himself together. "See!" he grumbled to himself. "Winter's here! I'll call Hüseyin now!" He raised his voice, changed his tone, and began talking to himself.

I sat there for another minute listening to what he was saying, after which I took my bag and walked towards the door. I got off the ferry but couldn't exit the port as they had locked the steel barred gates. One of the drunkards impatiently went up to the glass pane of the management office and began banging on the window. "Heeey!" he yelled, "Are you trying to imprison us here?"

An official wearing gloves yelled back, "Hold it," and came running towards us. He shoved the drunkard around a bit, scolding him. "Who gave you the right to bang on the State's windows, huh?"

81

He unlocked the gates all the while grumbling: "What's your hurry? Maybe there's a PKK terrorist inside and we've locked him up. Ever considered that?"

As we were dispersing into the Anatolian shore, he continued to grumble and curse behind us.

"Off you go now! Can't handle your drink! Off you go, dog! Are you fucking from the PKK too, eh?"

The drunkard tried to mumble something back but unable as he was, he looked even more pitiful. I worried that he might go home and take it out of his wife and kids – if he had a family that is.

I got into one of the cabs waiting outside and gave him my address.

"Which way do you want me to take?" asked the driver.

"Whichever way is shortest!"

"No, you tell me first, so I don't have to hear you complain about the route I took. People don't know their way, and then start complaining that I took them for a ride."

"I don't know which way is shorter," I grumbled. "I place my trust in you."

So off we went.

"Beşiktaş won," I said. "Do you know the score?"

"2-0!" His face lit up a little as he said this. "Are you a Beşiktaş fan too?"

"I used to be. I'm no longer a real fan of any team."

For a while, we drove in silence. The radio was playing an arabesque tune.

Where are you?
So I'm to forget you?
Where are you?
This is not up to you.
Where are you?

You think it's that easy?
You think it's that easy to make me holler thus?
Tell me, where are you?

I felt a bit stifled. The driver asked for my permission to smoke, and after offering me one, which I refused saying I didn't smoke, began to smoke while lost in thought with the window rolled slightly down. Then he changed the radio channel.

A fairy tale, all those past years
How many leaves are we left holding?
Love was a dream, now I'm awake.
Only its name remains.

Eventually he gave in and began to talk.

"Solitude is for Allah only," he said.

"Yeah," I said. "He created us to flee His solitude."

I think he didn't quite grasp what I had said. Suddenly with knitted brow, "They talk of some evolution!" he lunged. "Do you think it's true?"

"This doesn't have much to do with the existence of Allah, but..."

"Of course not," he barged in. "Because Allah exists!"

"But evolution is a fact!" I completed my sentence.

With a condescending gaze, he asked: "Are you a student?"

"No!" I replied. "I work."

"Where?"

"At TeleTurca."

"Is that why you're the way you are?

"Yes, they brainwash us at TeleTurca."

"They haven't washed it man; they've bleached it!"

We drove on in silence, then stopped at a red light. A blind beggar –or maybe feigning blindness– was meandering between the cars. He was brushing his hands over the hoods of the cars, trying to locate the windows and talk to the drivers. I didn't want to give him any money as I thought he was lying. The light went green; the blind youth noticed this as the cars began to move. With a perplexed gaze he stumbled onto the sidewalk, almost falling. That's when I realized he was truly blind and felt terrible for thinking the opposite.

As we approached the last bend, a gigantic woman wearing a bikini and lying sideways greeted us with her silky skin. She eyed us invitingly. We drove passed her and she turned back into a rusty billboard.

***

As soon as I walked in I sat in front of the computer. I first checked my e-mail out of habit and was surprised and excited to see there was a message for me, as I really hadn't expected one. However, it turned out to be nothing more than the summary I had sent myself back at the office. I dismally opened the letter and burned a CD of the file I was contemplating taking with me.

Just as I had opened the file that kept my short story to continue writing, my cell phone began to ring. When I looked at the screen I didn't know what to do with myself; it was "she" who was calling! I held my breath and brought the gadget up to my left ear and said: "Hale? How are you?"

"Did you just call me?" she asked with a soft tone, though not without a sense of anxiety. "I was in the bath. Somebody called."

The more I listened to her way of speaking and her words, the more I felt my pain being relieved, as if I were swimming in a lukewarm, silent environment. As if I had returned to the womb.

"No," I said, "It wasn't me. But good thing you called. How is everything?"

Her tone changed immediately and she brushed away my

question coldly: "Well, then! I just wanted to ask whether it was you who called. See you later."

I was confused. After remaining silent for a few seconds, I was finally able to say "All right! See you around." She hung up.

I wondered if she had thought I had pitied her due to her nervousness and thus became upset? Then another suspicious thought crept up. Perhaps she was expecting somebody else to call. If I hadn't called, she would've understood it was "he." Perhaps this was the sole reason why she called after all those months! In any case, I was suspicious that there was somebody else she was seeing, even if she had tried to deny it.

I looked for a way to escape all those thoughts whirling in my brain. Writing seemed like the best refuge. At least when writing I could make myself believe I was up to something meaningful. I began working. In the first good sentence I wrote I found some comfort–albeit insignificant. I invented imaginary characters and objects whose verisimilitude to reality were as close as can be, and entertained myself among them for some time. I took up different roles, spoke and laughed at myself. Even though I was completely alone, it felt like the whole world was present in me for a short while. Maybe it was the thought that others might eventually read my writing that gave me that effect. Then again, I might've been confusing fact and fiction as well. The world in my writing engrossed me in such a way for a while that I had forgotten my predicament and Hale. She detested the way I would exclude her from my head when working. Once upon a time... Befriending imaginary friends, in effect, was an indication of the deepest loneliness; a man could suddenly be faced with the most dreadful silence.

Time was running late and I was tired. I decided to rest a little and got up to turn on the TV, planting myself in the armchair in front of it.

The singer on the screen was saying:

You think farewells are easy
Let's see when you're alone
I took the memories
Then what will you lean on?
Stop saying there's a woman
Who loves you; she's gone
The knots in me are left
Untangled, let them be.

As the music videos continued to play, the bottom of the screen was given over to messages and photos sent by viewers: *I'm a cheerful, 26 year old, dark-haired, young man, 1.80 cm tall, wanting to meet like-minded girls... My name is Leila; if you'd like to do it with me, this is the price, and here is my number... Nobody's calling girls, come on, here's my number... I'd like to meet girls living in this area. Ladies, do call me if you're seriously interested... Pretty and free girls of Istanbul... Attractive ladies...*

Unable to stomach any more of this stuff, I switched channels. As it was now past midnight, a fashion channel was showing models with their breasts exposed. The cameras all focused on the swerving hips as if the models were parading on the catwalk of a lingerie show. After watching these shots for a while, I changed the channel again. There was a TeleTurca ad on. The ad claimed that the company brought and bound citizens together. The half-robot, good-natured mascot and a group of cute little children sang songs loaded with messages of friendship and love. Models with training in acting were feigning to be TeleTurca employees and jovially working for the good of humanity. Some of them even had white coats on, as if to underline a clean, scientific approach to things.

I switched off the TV, undressed, and got in the shower. I had

PARADISE IN RUINS

to take a bath or else I'd start smelling soon. First I masturbated fantasizing that I was with a hooker. Then I left the bathroom and immediately lay down, trying to fall asleep. Just as I was about to nod off, I heard somebody yell, "He's here!" Scared, I pricked my ears to hear more, but nothing else was heard. This must've been a hallucination. I had never had this happen to me before; I wondered if I had finally gone insane.

The books on the bookshelves slid down and fell on the floor. The wind was wailing outside the windows. Engines echoed in sounds that resembled screams of wild animals. Then I heard sounds of whistles. As I drifted off to sleep I thought aliens were descending onto the city and the night guards were trying to warn us, but I didn't panic. When there is truly nothing, dreams and visions bubble up but with the faintest light, all ghosts flee.

87

6

"Love is sort of overrated," I said as if atoning for my sins. "I mean to say it's not a port to take refuge in; it's only a fragile, chemical condition. For a while you feel high on drugs, up in heaven, but then you eventually come crashing down."

I must've looked very strange in that room. Although I felt in control of the topic we had begun to speak about, the fact that the psychiatrist sitting in front of me was trained to read behind the human mind made me uncomfortable. I could turn out to be an extremely ordinary case that could be defined in the flash of a moment. My dark moods may just as well be delusions and I could just be a problematic personality. I was terrified that I would suddenly find myself guilty as I continued to speak. I tried to look at ease but the doctor was probably able to deduct that I was in fact extremely vulnerable. His expressionless gaze looked down, as he constantly took notes on the pages at the table in front of him. I went on speaking.

"Most people don't love each other. Though they try to act like they do."

Barging in, "Why do you think they do not feel love?" he asked.

"That's the way I see it and that's the way I feel," I said. "The other day I asked myself how many friends I am truly concerned about, and couldn't come up with a straight answer. We have a good time when we get together, when we got together that is, but I don't think they really care about me either. Why is it so? Is it always like this?"

"Why do you think they don't care about you?"

"Because for the most part, I don't care about them."

"But you can't blame others for what goes on in your head."

"Are we really that different than each other?"

"Of course; each individual has certain unique particularities."

"I even asked myself whether my love came from fear or dependence," I continued; "I told her this. I asked her: 'Are we staying together because we're afraid of remaining alone?' We have to know the answer to this question,' I said. How dumb is that?"

"It's not dumb at all. But wording it this way may give rise to misunderstandings."

"That's exactly what I meant when I said it was dumb. When together with someone, we should make sure that we are not trying to hold on to them solely because of our own interests, right?"

"Relationships should not be experienced as a mutual dependence of course. Love should go hand in hand with the honest desire for the other to grow, to flourish. A love that embodies repression always contains selfishness. I think you're trying to be honest beyond the point of necessity. Some things should remain unspoken. You don't always have to tell the truth. In fact, you're opening up to relieve yourself, which is also a bit egotistic. We live among others and have certain responsibilities towards them.

We can't just let everyone know what transpires in us every moment; moreover, we have to accept and live with this fact."

"So you say we should deceive each other from time to time..."

"Well, no, that's a negative word to denote the situation..."

"Hale also told me to deceive her if necessary."

The psychiatrist sat silent. Maybe this was just a cue for me to go on.

"I worry much about her," I said. "She has to live in this city as a solitary woman. I want to protect her. When I see a lonely kitten on the road, I feel so sorry for it, I don't know what to do."

"You're worrying about yourself, actually," replied the doctor.

Suddenly I felt as if I had come face to face with something terrifying. Could what he said be true?

The shrink went on: "You should back off! People can protect themselves. You're using that premise as an excuse."

"You also think that my love, or my display of it, springs from weakness, right?" I interjected. "Is that what you're implying?"

"That's not what I said! Once again, you're presupposing that she feels the same pain you do. After all, wasn't it she who ended the relationship? That's what you told me."

"Yes, but we came to that point together."

"You have to define yourself as a separate subject. You can begin a new life. You're still young. However, you are undoubtedly depressed and have to get over it. I also see other psychological conditions that seem to be triggering each other."

"What sort conditions are you talking about?" I asked.

"You seem to be a bit obsessed. You compulsively get stuck on certain issues. I also think you're a perfectionist." He glanced at his notes, trying to make out his writing.

Did he add the 'perfectionist' part to soften the adjective 'obsessive,' I wondered? Perhaps he also thought I was paranoid but wasn't sure if he should articulate it. So maybe I really was paranoid!

"Actually," I said, "I don't find it very healthy to smile as if everything was hunky-dory."

"Why do you think that everything is not right?"

"Just take a look at the world around us!"

"Adem Bey, the world is not as bad a place as you may think it is. Perhaps you choose to see it that way so that you can comfort yourself by shifting much of the responsibility related to your troubles. You may find something to hold on, an anchor as it were, in an attempt to change the world, however, no one has asked you to do this. These are issues you must confront."

I was terrified yet again. "Do you think I'm deceiving myself?" I asked. "But you were just telling me that I was over-realistic."

"You see, one has to find a balance in all things. You, on the other hand, wander around extremes."

He asked me how my stories were going. I talked a bit as if I weren't even there. I felt like I didn't really communicate anything at all. It was as if I wasn't writing, but all of this was a game, or maybe a sham. I thought that writing was only a refuge and felt that he also thought the same. I began to panic. He feigned to be interested and told me that having an occupation would do me good. He didn't add that the whole thing might be another obsession; he probably didn't want to push me any longer. I was on the verge of giving the whole act up anyway.

His glance shifted towards the clock on the wall, our time was coming to an end.

"I'll write out some pills for you," he said. Then he started to scribble the name of an antidepressant and some other drugs. "These will help you out in times like these. They'll help you relax."

I felt that he hesitated for a moment, as if he wanted to say one other thing but decided to keep it to himself. Then he picked up a card from his table and handed it over to me.

"Actually," he began, "if you continue to feel down..." I took the card. "I have a psychotherapist friend who does regression therapy. She used to practice the profession she was trained in but now her business card has spiritual advisor on it. As you know, we aren't allowed to practice hypnotherapy. However, I do believe it can be beneficial, if carried out by an expert. It can easily dig out old traumas. She's been quite successful with a few patients who had lost a family member; in fact these patients came back to life. Maybe she can be more efficient in motivating you towards healthy behavior."

I thanked him, put the business card in my pocket, paid the man, shook his hand and got out of there as fast as I could.

***

The Tibetan Doctor Whatshisname and mystic Hosmar Anechtaiduthuzam were able to listen directly to human spirits by way of drilling a hole on the side of the skull and thus shed light onto the meaning of our lives. They had already begun to deliver their superior knowledge, their ground-breaking truths that would shake the world, using an American woman as a medium. They heralded the advent of the supra-consciousness. I was surprised and regretted that I had not caught wind of this information before. They also hadn't forgotten to thank the three djinn that had lent them a hand in the writing of the book. In the introduction, they wrote that they loved us in all sincerity, without any concession as we weren't separate from each other but were a part of the same whole.

Another book written by a woman, who had had a near-death

experience and had returned, caught my attention. The back cover told how a bright light would greet us once we had passed over to the other side. With an implosion, our soul would be sucked out of our chest. There was to be no pain though; we'd be floating in bliss and limitless freedom. The shelves were stocked with thousands of books. Suddenly the thought occurred to me that so many books meant as much loneliness and I sidled quickly onto other sections.

The souvenirs and greeting cards all had clichè sentences of love and compassion written on them. Then I found myself at the children's section, looking at toys. An automatic crib kept rocking to the tune of songs celebrating the New Year. I presumed that it was designed to begin to move when it detected the sounds of a baby lying inside. Then I had a bright idea: The mini-robots were on sale; I could buy these for the whole family!

On the shelves were dolls that could talk, laugh and weep. Right next to them sat hairy dolls with giant heads. Then I saw the *Pepero*s. These were colorful toys with wheels, about 20 cm high. They reminded me of Lego characters. The document that cited their technical specifications wrote that they were able to recognize and speak a number of words. The price was also quite affordable. I looked around for someone to help me out. There was a young man not too far away, whom I took to be an employee, as he was wearing a neon shirt and a nametag around his neck. He was busy trying to explain something to two middle-aged women. I walked towards them.

"What is your name?" grumbled one of the women. "I am going to file a complaint. This is no way to treat a customer."

I waited for the crisis to subside and the women to part. Then I began by saying, "I'm interested in the Peperos."

The young man nodded, trying to squeeze out a smile. Then we walked towards the toys section together. I continued:

"Can you show me how they work? A demonstration, like. I'm thinking of buying one as a gift."

"Of course."

He picked up a yellow Pepero from the shelf and pressed a button, then put it on the floor. The little robot first looked around for a while, then decided to move randomly to and fro. The employee bent down to show his face, then pet its head.

"It recognizes faces," he said, "and responds when petted."

The robot swayed a little and mumbled out noises denoting its pleasure.

"Come!" I said. The robot immediately approached my feet. I bent down as well. It looked at my face as if it was trying to inscribe what it saw onto its robotic mind. "How's it going?" I said with a smile. I held its tiny hand.

"Hello!" it responded. "My name is Pepero!"

"Nice to meet you, Pepero!"

"Who are you?"

"I'm Adem."

"Adem!"

"Yes, exactly!"

I couldn't think of what to say next so I turned it off for fear off upsetting it.

"All right!" I said to the employee. "I'll take this one. Can you gift wrap it for me?"

After I handed the toy to the young man so he could send it to the cashier, I began to wander around the store, this time solely for pleasure. I felt relieved. Maybe I could buy myself a gift too. I went to the DVD section. As I entered, the New Year's songs were replaced by serious movie soundtracks. I felt like a character from a movie. I began to examine all the films from A to Z, trying not to miss a single one. I began to collect the films I had chosen in my left hand. As I arrived to F, I felt the usual anxiety and dismay. Trying to force myself a little longer, I was able to move up to M. I examined a teen movie whose sleeve was cracked. On its cover, the actors were all smiling in glee. However, they looked a bit too silent. I froze right there and then, stuck in limbo for a while. Then it felt like everything I was holding began to scatter and fall to the ground, the DVDs, the shelves, the store; the whole world began to melt. I was being siphoned towards empty space, towards nothingness.

I couldn't bear standing there any longer. I left the DVDs I had chosen on the shelves and fled towards the cash registers. They had already wrapped the Pepero and had put it in a plastic bag. As I didn't have an ExtraXX card I missed the giant reduction in the price but I still paid the money and hurried out.

As I left the store, I saw that the display that was prepared to greet the New Year looked different to me again. I imagined the employees being forced to finish decorating either in the dead of night or early in the morning. They would be busy placing the artificial snowflakes, candles, Christmas trees and smiling Santa Claus figurines. None of them were smiling though. As I walked the streets of the city, I tried to grab hold of something, step on something steady but to no avail; everything I passed by melted into dust.

***

It was like any apartment in the city: rectangular in shape, long and narrow, feeling smaller than its actual size. The even narrower corridor was decorated with mirrors; no doubt to try to give the impression that it was wider than it looked.

As it was raining fiercely, the drops falling on the window on the roof made quite a ruckus. So when the residents invited me in and shut the door, a pleasant silence ensued. "Come in to the living room," said Nagehan Hanım, "Please have a seat." They gave me a pair of slippers, which I put on, then followed them inside. Then I gave them the present I had bought, "This is for both New Year and as it is my first time here..."

"We've been neighbors for months now," said Necmettin Bey. "What can you do? Big city life, right?"

"You shouldn't have," said Nagehan Hanım as she took the bag from my hands. "You shouldn't have gone to all this bother."

They opened the gift. Suddenly in the corner of my eye, I felt a slight but nervous movement near Necmettin Bey. I glanced to see what it was; it was their little son. He was trying to squeeze through his father's legs. First his head popped out; our glances met. "Tee-hee!" he laughed. I smiled back.

"Berkay, look what Adem Bey has brought you," said Necmettin Bey. "You remember Adem Bey right?"

"Of course he does," I said. "We've been neighbors for months, haven't we? After all, neighbors need each other, right Berkay?"

Pepero was out of the box. I picked it up and introduced it to the family. Then I turned it on and placed it on the ground. It began to stroll around the house and entertain the family members with its speech. Berkay, in particular, seemed especially fond of the toy. He hugged Pepero passionately and held it against his chest.

"If you don't play with it..." I continued. "It gets upset apparently. It begins to grumble..."

"Just like our little one!" responded Nagehan Hanım. Then she invited me over to the dinner table. I sat down. It had been a long time since I was at a family dinner and I enjoyed it.

"How have you been?" asked Necmettin Bey as he spooned soup into bowls. "I hope you're feeling better."

I don't know why I kept hiding my condition. The more one

hides something the more it became difficult to explain it. I felt like I needed to share it with someone. "Actually," I began. "I have cancer." Quickly I followed up to soften the dramatic effect the sentence would cause: "But it's a mild case!" I said, "and at an early phase. They're treating it with medicine right now."

They looked at each other, speechless for a while.

Then Nagehan Hanım said, "Really sorry to hear that! I hope everything goes well and that you'll recover quickly. We really didn't know. And you're so young!"

Necmettin Bey didn't say anything. He looked at me as if he was trying to gauge whether or not I was joking. Maybe he was so upset and surprised that he didn't know what to say.

"Yes," I said. "I'm sorry to blurt this out so suddenly but that's what is mostly on my mind these days."

"Of course you should say what you like," said Necmettin Bey. "We're neighbors after all."

Berkay hadn't come to the table yet. Her mother yelled, "You'll go to bed hungry if you don't come here right now!"

The kid shuffled over with a frown and sat down at the table.

"We were supposed to go to the movies," said Necmettin Bey, "but didn't. And that's why yours truly is putting on a frown."

I suddenly occurred to me: "Is it because I was coming over?" I asked.

"No not at all, it was because of what happened in the morning."

"Oh."

"It has nothing to do with the movies!" responded Nagehan Hanım rather harshly. "He's in love with that girl on the phone! I-girl or whatever she's called. Now he's mad because I don't let him play with it."

"Who's I-girl?" I asked.

"It's a virtual woman," explained Necmettin Bey. "A Japanese invention. She blows kisses. If you buy her a gift she gets happy and chuckles. Of course the girl is virtual but the gift is with real cash."

I laughed, thinking about all the pretty girls in cartoons I had fallen in love with when I was young.

"That's too bad!" I said, "Berkay, you and I should go and have a drink together to drown our sorrows."

Although Necmettin Bey chuckled, Nagehan Hanım did not look very pleased. I felt ashamed thinking I had committed a blunder.

We slowly sipped on our spoonfuls of soup.

Then they began to mention alternative therapies. "They say holly works wonders. Soy beans, sweet potatoes..." They continued by talking of relatives in similar predicaments. I listened to them without feeling any sympathy for their troubles.

"Never mind!" I said finally. "Thanks a lot, but the treatment is going fine. Let's talk about something else."

"Oh!" exclaimed Nagehan Hanım, "my TV drama is about to begin!"

She ran over and turned on the TV, switched to the channel, turned up the volume, then came back to her seat. We continued with our supper, watching TV at the same time.

"Well," said Necmettin Bey. "Maybe our guest doesn't want to watch your program."

"No, no!" I barged in. "Please, we can watch it together. I don't mind."

The screen was covered with familiar faces. Nagehan Hanım's face was wreathed in smiles, as if she were seeing some of her close friends. The good, in solidarity, kept up their struggle against the baddies outside. The influential and reputable businessman performed his duties, interrupting his meeting and jumping on a plane when his pretty beloved was in need of him.

After soup we went on to the main course. The food was accompanied by rakı, as well as the tiny plates of standard rakı fare. I didn't have much of an appetite and kept playing with the food on my plate. Nagehan Hanım had also mentioned that she was on a diet and wasn't going to eat anything else. Anyway, all her attention was focused on the TV and her drama. My legs were restless and kept twitching.

"I read your stories," said Necmettin Bey. "I liked them. I think you write well."

Turning her head towards me Nagehan Hanım also approved: "Yes! I read a few as well. They're quite absorbing."

I thanked them. The whole scene was actually quite bizarre. Once silence settled in, I opened the subject of our neighborhood's mental case, Suleiman the Magnificent. This could attract everyone's attention.

"I know," chimed in Nagehan Hanım. "Such a shame! He's actually quite a nice-looking boy. He can get scary though. They say that he had an unrequited love and something happened and whatever that was turned him into what he is now."

"Doesn't he have any family?" I asked.

"I guess not."

"I sometimes wonder if he goes hungry. Perhaps we should give him some food every now and then."

"Then he might get used to it and come every day."

"I haven't seen him for a while; I wonder if they took him away."

"Could be. Maybe somebody complained. People with children may feel threatened."

"And I thought I was the neighborhood nut!" chuckled Necmettin Bey. "There goes that title as well!"

I laughed. "So you were the one who filed the complaint! You must have gotten jealous of him. And just think, the poor man meant no harm to anyone."

He burst out in laughter. "There you go! Without a laugh, one can't go on living!"

"You're right. Although laughing doesn't solve everything, but still..."

Once the subject on Suleiman had drawn to a close, "Well," I said. "At night, I sometimes hear somebody screaming. Do you have any idea who that could be?"

Necmettin Bey seemed poised to respond, but his wife darted a look in his direction and he closed his mouth.

"What do you think?" I said. "Is there a Frankenstein's monster in the neighborhood?"

They tried to smile. "No," said Nagehan Hanım. "We hear those screams too. You're right about that, but I don't know where they're coming from."

"It could be drunkards yelling," said Necmettin Bey.

"It sounds more like somebody's in great pain."

When they both fell silent, I stopped insisting and let the topic lapse.

"The other day," Nagehan Hanım began, trying to change the subject. "I dropped in on Hanife Hanım. You know, the old lady that lives on the ground floor?"

"Yes," I said, "I saw you together."

"She's got troubles of her own too, just like everyone else. Her eyesight has been failing. Apparently she tried to cook some food the other day and burned it. The poor thing just dropped down and cried her eyes out. I've decided that I should visit her every now and then.."

"Doesn't she have any children?" I asked.

"She had a daughter who passed away. She lives through photos, the poor thing. You should see her flat, photos everywhere. Really now, say her daughter were alive, does any child help their parents nowadays? She said, 'Check on me once in a while.' She's afraid she's going to drop dead and stink before anyone finds her."

"She's also got that cat," added Necmettin Bey. "If that cat gets hungry she'll eat the poor woman up, I tell you!"

"Necmettin!" exclaimed Nagehan Hanım. "Such words!"

"But it's true! Cats eat corpses!"

I laughed.

"You're doing the right thing," I said to Nagehan Hanım. "We all should follow your lead."

"Right?" said Nagehan Hanım, pleased with my approval. "It's difficult to be thinking about all this though. I worry myself over little things a lot; I like looking at matters from all levels."

"Check on me once in a while as well," I said.

"Oh come on, don't talk like that. You said your treatment was going well, that's great."

"You know, nowadays people speak negatively about marriage but I think it's a good thing for two people to be on the lookout for each other. Take you for instance; nobody would worry about you because you've got Necmettin Bey. They'd think if something bad were to happen, Necmettin Bey would let people know about it. In the same way, you watch out for him."

"A real watchdog, that's for sure!" said Necmettin Bey. His wife didn't laugh at this joke so all I could do was twist-out a broken Mona Lisa smile. Nagehan Hanım had this way of seeming angry even when being polite. She would get lost in herself every now and then. Then after I spoke, she'd change her expression and smile once again. This began to get me on edge a little.

Our meal had finished. They brought in dessert. Berkay got up from the table and tried to get our attention, running frantically around the room. "I'm the Super Captain!" he yelled with his shrill voice. He climbed on the sofa and jumped down. He played with an ashtray a bit as if it were a plane or a spaceship. The sofa had become a mountain, which his toy hovered over.

"Put that down!" yelled his mother, "You'll break it and then cut yourself!"

Although he whined a little at first, he put the ashtray back where he had found it, then came next to me. He began describing his adventures as Super Captain. His logical way of speaking was intriguing, I liked it. Suddenly I turned and grabbed him.

"They've got Super Captain!" I said. "Captured by the neighbor!"

He giggled nervously and tried to break loose. His body was so soft and supple. I wanted to squeeze him tighter. Then, out of fear of being misunderstood, I let him go. He ran away.

The father watched his son. Taking a giant gulp from his rakı, "Some people," he said, "love, but can't show their affection."

The TV drama had come to an end. We got up and cleared the table together. We put the tea on to brew, then came back to the living room and sat in front of the TV. We all heard a text message being delivered to Necmettin Bey's phone. We watched him in silence. The old man read the message on his phone's screen and laughed out loud. "It's from the insurance company!" he grumbled. "They're wishing me happy birthday."

"So today's your birthday?"

"Not even close! They'll probably wish me happy mother's day soon as well!"

Smiling, "Which insurance company?" I asked.

"Solidarity Insurance!"

I nodded.

"They cancelled my policy last year! They dropped me and now I have to pay for my treatment out of my pocket."

"Why did they cancel?" asked Necmettin Bey in surprise.

"I was insured through my wife's company," I replied. "Once we got divorced, her human resources department immediately stopped paying my premiums."

"Didn't they inform you?"

"Nope, I only found out after one of my medical appointments. I tried to sign up for an insurance policy on my own, but a month had passed. Apparently after a one month grace period, all my rights were automatically cancelled."

Of course, there was negligence on my part as well, though I didn't let them know of that. I didn't inform them about all the details that would make me look bad.

Necmettin Bey let out a loud curse and said, "You should've signed up with another company."

"I tried all the insurance companies I could. They work together anyway. Once I was diagnosed, all the companies excluded cancer treatment from their policies. They even dug up other problems. Apparently I was unaware that I have so many health risks."

"You shouldn't have told them about your illness. This is what happens when you're honest."

"I didn't tell them, but they caught wind of it from the hospital. As insurance companies are their best customers, hospitals never conceal any information from them. The insurance staff people were sad too, to tell you the truth, but all they said was that their hands were tied."

"But..." said Necmettin Bey with a scowl, "the people are to blame as well. We run to the doctor at the slightest problem. So liabilities pile up and they go berserk!"

"It's not only that though," I objected. "Medical science is advancing rapidly, new drugs are being invented, and hospitals are purchasing new equipment and then the management pressures doctors into writing more prescriptions, and using this equipment. It's the insurance companies that pay in the end! Prices are off the wall in the industry as you know, and when people are holding on just to survive, they don't care much about money. It's simply a matter of supply and demand!"

"As you get older, they mark up the premiums as well, no matter what!" added Nagehan Hanım. "The more you use insurance, the more you pay!"

"Then what's the use of having a policy, right?" I grumbled.

The game began. Nagehan Hanım got up and brought our teas.

"So you got divorced," said Necmettin Bey. "Well, hope it all turned out for the good! Nothing much to do about that kind of thing. Have you been coping well?"

"I guess so," I responded while taking the tea that Nagehan Hanım offered me. "No matter what though, you get this lingering feeling that you have left your child behind somewhere."

This seemed to leave them both at a loss for words. Berkay was running around the chairs. He bumped into his father as he was trying to pick his glass, spilling tea all over the floor.

"God damn you, child!" screamed Nagehan Hanım. The kid ran away to his room in fear. His mother followed him but quickly dove into the kitchen instead. I presumed she was going to fetch something to wipe the stain on the carpet.

Necmettin Bey was saved from having been scorched only because he managed to move his legs out of the way in time. "I swear I saw it coming!" he said. "So I moved away."

Once his wife had come back to the living room and was trying to wipe the stain off the carpet he muttered something that sounded like, "We have a decent marriage, touch wood." He praised both himself and his spouse for having found just the right person. Nagehan Hanım in return made a gesture that indicated she found his words nonsense. Or so I thought at least. I just kept bobbing my head up and down.

"Does your ex-wife know that you're sick?" asked Necmettin Bey.

"I haven't told her," I replied. "I figure she might think that I am just looking for pity. And this may even get her angry."

Both national teams had waltzed up to the pitch and the anthems were being sung. We all had our eyes glued to the TV set. The players took their places on the pitch and the game began with the ref's whistle. For some reason I found it relaxing to watch a group of men run around passing a ball between them on a wide field. I didn't fixate on why this – silliness really – was somehow comforting, but rather just let myself bathe in this warm feeling for some time.

Nagehan Hanım got up and went inside, while Necmettin Bey and I continued watching the game and voicing our own running commentaries on the match. At that moment we joined the majority of the country as we focussed our attention on the same small ball. The sports announcer gave a running play-by-play summary of the action, all with a voice that beamed with excitement and optimism. I decided that his descriptions tended to be over the top and he must have been acting a lot of this seeming enthusiasm. Nagehan Hanım must've been busy with housework inside as I heard sounds of things being pushed and pulled. This is what having a woman in the house feels like, I recalled.

Suddenly our team scored a goal.

We stood up. Necmettin Bey screamed in joy and raised his right arm, showing his palms to me for a high-5, which I duly obliged. It was strange to partake in a bonding of delight with someone I barely knew.

"Goaaaaal! Goaaaal!" screamed the anchor. "Atta go boys! You're great! This is it! This is Turkey! Unbelievable, ladies and gentlemen! This is how you write history!"

7

The washing machine had finished its wash cycle and from the noises it was now emitting, I understood it had begun to dry the clothes inside. This persistent, soulless sound was the only thing that broke the painful silence at home.

Although I would have liked to call someone and chat a little, eventually I decided that I didn't have the right to bring others down with tales of my tragic condition. In any case, I was no longer able to conceal this morbid tone and they would at once realize that this friendship would be disadvantageous to them. On the other hand, as I distanced myself further and further from those around me I also knew that I was actually breaking even the faint bonds between us.

This won't work, I thought to myself. Writing about this is not going to make this any easier! I had always thought that the very act of putting my thoughts to words could alleviate a burning, spiritual pain and that I could find relief. But now I was even losing my faith in writing. In fact, all I was doing was packing my problems into a chest and closing the lid. It may be true that I needed these short-term escapes from reality, but I also knew that eventually the lid was going to pop open and my troubles would bubble back up, this time as an even louder, maddening crowd of jumbled thoughts and anxieties, pressing down on me.

Perhaps it was the illusion that I had established a relationship with writing that comforted me. I was also aware, however, that my writing was not a means of communication, as everything I put down on paper was taking the form of a monologue. As I killed time talking to an imaginary reader, my actual readers would only be hearing an artificial intelligence that consisted of a copy of my contemplations.

Even though I had conceded that writing was insanity, I stubbornly clung to this gambling-like habit whose outcome was opaque. I told myself that I should stop, that I should realize what has been happening. I should stop madly persisting in this game whose original reasons had already putrefied. I had become a kind of animal being driven by instinct instead of reason. I had to stop. If I could, if I wasn't completely hooked; if I had any other choice, any choice at all.

I turned off the computer and got up. The trash had been in the house far too long. As I filled it very slowly, it had accumulated and had started to spread an odor of decay. I tied the ends of the trash bag and took it out. I dusted here and there a little. I cut my fingernails. I applied some silicon around the leaking tiles in the bathtub. The large bottle of drinking water was on its last dregs, so I ordered a refill from the local water supplier. Seeing anything coming to an end, even if it were drinking water, was enough to summon a lump in my throat.

The door rang. I got up and looked through the hole. It was Necmettin Bey. I didn't know what to do. I felt like I was caught naked. Finally I decided to act like I wasn't home. I just stood there motionless, as if a wild animal was up against my door. The more he pressed the doorbell the more I curled up in silence, my heart beating like a drum. Eventually the predator gave up and left.

I had begun to run a fever. I looked out the windows. The city's buildings were a jumble with roofs resembling the choppy waves of a rough sea. And just like watching the sea, watching the city was also distracting. The evening was drawing to a close. I liked evenings. I liked the settling of darkness and the protection and concealment it afforded. I liked being unseen, invisible, in its cloak.

I decided that I would spend the last of my days doing whatever I wanted to do, whatever I could. I decided to play some video games. I enjoyed how as I entered into war at the head of a medieval army, all my advisors praised my strategy. I didn't want to think that they were all sucking up to me, or indeed that they were non-existent. Then I turned the TV on and sat in the sofa in front of it. The dark glass pane began to emit colorful worlds. Twenty-some frames per second went shooting past me; this was enough for me to feel like I was indeed in front of tangible, moving objects.

I watched the new version of *Before Bedtime*. A virtual hologram of the late Adile Naşit continued to tell fairy tales to children. Then I switched to a Brazilian soap for a while. I caught myself grinning idiotically when the characters chatted with each other in convivial words of passion. I wondered how Ricardo was going to escape the difficult predicament he had found himself in.

Once the soap was over, I switched channels, finding myself watching a station known for its conservative stance. The talk show host spoke with religious pundits. He and his guests chatted in a calm and respectful manner, full of courtesy and veneration towards each other. Ramadan had almost arrived and an increasing feeling of security stemming from the spirit of congregation was well reflected on the screen before me. In the news, positive national developments, the successful endeavors and international achievements of our paternal leaders were constantly listed.

I checked the movie channels and started watching a sci-fi flick. The pretty girl was reluctant to let her man go fight the aliens. Although the man in question was also rather unwilling, we the viewers cheered him on, hoping to see a good old fight scene. The whole film was polished with an exuberant score and lots of bright lights. Plenty of special effects were employed.

The film ended and I had to once again face my miserable life, feeling heavy at heart. Strange, for just a couple of seconds earlier I had been swept into the illusion that as an invincible Space Knight I was making mad love with beautiful women.

Now my fever had gone up quite high and my body began to ache all over, as if it had been beaten to a pulp. All I wanted to do was just lie there with my eyes shut. I tried to lie down and sleep. Insistent blares of car horns ripped through the night. There must've been either a wedding, a team that won a soccer game, or some young lad being sent off to the military; in any case whatever the affair was those blasting their horns were certain that it deserved everyone's attention. Shots were fired. The distant sounds of a drumbeat also pumped into the room. My chest heaved uncontrollably, letting me breathe. It was an automatic gesture, but when I became aware of the struggle, it began to stall so it was best not to ponder upon it.

8

"What brings you here?" asked the woman. She smiled. I guess she was trying to show me the universal love she harbored inside.

"I don't really know," I said. "For some relief... some distraction... I've got concerns and can't quite contend with them."

"You said you had cancer."

"Yes."

"Cancer stems from a torn chakra. Now our objective here is to help you heal naturally. Your physical health is not the only thing that matters; your spiritual health is as important. In fact, the two are interconnected. I am explaining all this so you understand the process. I will use my hands to heal certain layers of your aura and energy field. This is not quite like drug therapy. Medical drugs may damage the spiritual field. This might be the case with you. Your healing may take one session, or I may have to call you back for a few more. The chemotherapy may have blocked all your energy fields."

"I haven't had chemotherapy."

"That's great!"

She handed me a tissue, which I accepted without asking why.

Then, indicating the therapy bed that was not unlike a table, she politely asked me to lie on my back.

"Where are you coming from?" she asked. "I'll try to keep it short so you're not late."

"Don't worry!" I said. While I enjoyed the fact that she was concerned, I also thought that this might be an excuse to shorten the session. Touching my shoulder, she placed a pillow under my head. Then she placed colored crystals on my arms and torso. In her hand, she held a stone that was larger and brighter than the ones she had placed on me.

"These are quartz crystals," she explained. "They generate a lot of energy. Their stable vibrations will align your energy field and have positive effects on mental confusion and pessimism. We will clean the unnecessary deposits in your aura. Please close your eyes now!"

I did as I was told and thought I caught an illusion of light in the darkness that ensued.

"I will work on the different layers of your aura," she said. "First, I'll work on your lower field, that is your physical body, after which I will begin to move up. This way I'll analyze the general properties of your energy system. If there are problematic regions I will try to heal them by cleaning away the harmful deposits. I might have to touch your neck, stomach or chest in the meantime. If it disturbs you, I can try to evade doing this as much as possible.

"It's not a problem!"

She murmured to herself: "Let me be a channel to share the universal love and truth that heals!"

Then –presumably to increase the density of the luminescence– she cupped her palms like radar dishes and began to move her hands over my body. For about five minutes the only sound I heard was her deep nasal breathing. Every now and then she would also ask me to relax my feet or to bend and straighten my knees.

Later she made me lie facedown, saying that she would clean my spine. To feel comfortable I had to place my head into the hole at the tip of the bed. In that position I lay, watching the patterns of the rug below. Then I closed my eyes again.

"Yes," she said. "A vortex of your solar plexus chakra has been torn, the protective layer has been damaged. This in turn, hinders the natural cyclical movement."

"So what do we do about this?" I asked.

"Don't worry!" she consoled me, "It's repairable. I'm cleaning it now, but we have to stop it from being damaged again. The underlying causes are important."

After that, she remained silent for a while and began speaking: "We choose everything you know. If we fill ourselves with dark thoughts and anger, we eventually enter into darkness. One has to think positively and look for beauty. Sometimes falling ill may be a result of these thoughts; in fact some even see illness as a refuge. It all really stems from the illusion that we are separate from the whole. We shouldn't build a wall up between the whole and us. We have to discover our walls and tear them down. Try to talk to them and overcome your energy blockages. The success of the therapy also rests on your effort, on your willingness. Lower your shields a little. You're always on the defense. Relax a bit."

"Are you telling me that I created my sickness?" I called out. My voice reverberated under the table but probably only reached her as a muffled murmur.

"No!" she objected right away. "You must think that the illness may be trying to tell you something. The illness brings a message with it! You may be confronted with a difficult lesson you may be forced to learn."

She kept on talking in a calm tone. In the meantime, her hands were over my body as if I were a lover or a friend.

"Then what is the lesson?" I inquired.

"We can't know this for sure at the moment. Neither you nor I; you will learn in time! All I can say to you right now is this: You can do far more things that you can imagine. This includes conquering your illness! Do not forget: The darkest moment comes just before dawn."

"You speak of how everything is guided by fate but also add that there are responsibilities, things to do, duties to complete!" I grumbled.

"These are actually intertwined in a balanced way," she said. "They do not exclude each other. Though they seem contradictory, they are not. As our perception of things is narrow, we come to false conclusions. We have limits. This we must accept."

"What do you think of the afterlife?" I asked impatiently.

After a period of silence, she began: "At the time of death, we enter the spiritual dimension bringing our knowledge with us. All that happens is that we pass into another type of structural organization. There is a brighter, lighter life there, full of love. But first we must strive to stay alive and live a good life!"

She massaged all along my spine with her two hands. She placed one hand on my back and the other under my stomach and rested there for a while. She asked me to imagine that all my troubles disappeared, that my body fully healed and had begun to fulfill its function in the best possible manner.

"You are being enveloped in a golden, healing light; you look vibrantly happy and healthy... Think of yourself as being a perfect, divine being; the illness has no power over you! Don't think of the illness; don't provide it with any energy! Now I will place my hands on your back and stay there awhile. In the meantime, my spiritual guide will work through my hands and if necessary, heal those areas that I haven't been able to reach."

She placed her hands on my shoulder blades and stayed there for quite some time, as she had said. Then she switched positions and held my feet in her two hands. She pressed her thumbs on the soles and began to rub them as if in a massage. I realized that this was the first time this had been done to me since childhood. Then she held my ankles and knees, trying not to lift her hands up during the transition from one point to the other.

I looked at myself from the outside. It felt demeaning for a moment, lying there destitute, having relied on such a sèance. The woman's touch was relaxing, but painful as well. Tears began to well up in my eyes. I wondered whether the tissue that I had crumpled in my right palm was for this purpose?

***

I was ascending stairs made of stone. The thousand feet that had trodden on them had polished the steps; their corners were rasped and had become round. When I looked up I saw old buildings that had merged into one bizarre looking giant structure. Mothers at windows, where clothes in tatters hung limply, were calling out to their children who played outside, kicking tin cans instead of balls. Their hollering echoed in the silence of the evening.

Suddenly –for the first time while walking, and not in bed– I was overtaken by the fear of death. I became conscious that I would disappear. Trying to think of other thoughts, as fast as I could, I was able to divert the relentless terror I felt, though my heart went on beating like a drum for a few minutes longer.

I pulled myself together and, worrying that I might get lost if it became dark, I began to walk downwards, following the incline of the street. Though the progressing heaviness of traffic indicated that I was close to the center, I stopped and asked a man the directions, partly so I could just speak to someone. I understood the directions he gave immediately, though I wasn't really listening. The man was happy that he could be of help.

A street peddler on the sidewalk was tinkering with the electronic gadgets he displayed. He kept turning on the toys that played infantile tunes over and over. He had focussed on them solely, as if he had forgotten that they were there to be sold.

A police van was full to the brim with bagel stands. A middle-aged man holding a lottery ticket in his left hand sat on the sidewalk and was covering his face with the other. A young man lay on the ground as if dead; I passed him by, believing him to be feigning.

Suddenly, I thought someone was waving at me from a bus. When I turned to see who it was, I noticed it was only a woman trying to rub out the fog on the window. Although the crowd got thicker, there were no familiar faces to be seen. I felt completely alone, in an indifferent, even hostile world.

A dark claw had once again gripped my mind and was squeezing it to the point of bursting. I tried not to show my pain. In order to alleviate it, I began to image that I was a character in a novel. This way I could see myself from a distance, my life and the pain I was enduring took on some meaning. It was as if I was being heard, pitied and thus consoled. Like a sick child deserving his mother's attention, or a martyr who bore her suffering, I too was deserving of God's tenderness. All until I noticed what I had done and deprived myself of this one refuge.

I saw a pharmacy on the way. I entered the shop and ordered all the drugs that the doctor had prescribed. I hung onto their boxes as if they were my gates to salvation. They could've very well been just placebos, just candy, but I shouldn't think like this, I thought; then they wouldn't work at all.

I walked down to the Beşiktaş ferry station and passed over to Üsküdar on a boat. It was evening, the clouds had passed and the sun shone on the earth with an angle that tinted everything with a golden hue. The wide concrete deserts on the two sides of this valley were invisible and could be easily ignored in this time of the day.

Once I reached the Asian side of the city I began to walk towards the Karacaahmet cemetery. I tried to find my mother's grave amidst the muddy paths of this bizarre marble labyrinth strewn with cypresses. A small mosque stood in the center of the labyrinth. A green hearse had parked next to the cubicle where they washed and bound the dead. A sad-looking or seemingly sad crowd had amassed in the middle of the space. In their attempts to bury their dead according to the traditional rites, they seemed to me to be playacting children.

Some of the relatives of the deceased and the regulars of the mosque were taking their ablutions as the imam droned on with his sermon. He was telling the crowd about paradise, how rivers flowed there and how pure wives awaited the dead, who had reached everlasting life. Every now and then he interjected bits from the Quran in Arabic. Though I didn't understand what was being said, something about the words was comforting.

I finally managed to find the grave. It had been neglected for quite some time. I began to tear out the weeds, walking around the marble walls.

My mother had told me that she was going to die soon. She was trying to get me to accept that she was ill and that I should act accordingly. But I didn't want to believe this to be true so I kept trying to give her hope. In fact, if I was fooling anyone, it was only myself as I was just too weak to acknowledge the truth that her life was drawing to a close.

Eventually she lost her will to wake up in the morning. "I can no longer bear this," she'd complain, "I want this to end one way or the other!" She said that if only she were braver she would commit suicide. "My death would be a blessing for us all," she had said. "You'll be upset for a while, but then you'll get over it."

She had always dreamed of being part of an extended family living together in a large house. She kept asking whether or not Hale and I were planning to have a baby. At the time, I resented these questions as I felt she was trying to box me into something I wasn't ready for. I told her that we were putting it off until we were financially secure. "But a baby is not such a heavy burden," she had said.

I remembered how she had tried to take her last breath and couldn't. When she died, a tear was left suspended in her left eye. She had clenched her two fists as if she was holding onto something, though they were both empty.

I couldn't stand it any longer and let my tears flow. I cried for some time. However, after I left the grave and began walking to the exit, my tears dried up in the wind. I was surprised as to how quickly I had reverted back to my insensitive self.

As I returned home by bus, I saw that a big moving truck had backed up near the entrance of the building. Some people were climbing in, as some were getting out.

And then I spotted Suleiman the Magnificent who was wandering through the trash.

"Glory be!" he began to report. "He's here! As well as the aliens! But they're keeping it secret lest the world panics!"

I really had missed him.

"Let's see them then, Suleiman!" I grumbled. "Damn easy to watch everything from up above! If they're going to stay invisible and not help out at all, I couldn't give a rat's ass if they exist! They could fuck right off back to where they came from!"

"I told them: America has 350,000, Japan 700,000, Turkey

35!" he replied. "If things work out this way, there could be a price increase of government bonds–I can reveal my sources if anyone's interested. Same shit! The stock market is on the move... All of this, is it real or not? I'm not sure anymore... But in savage times, I saw it all happen!"

9

When I woke up the next morning, I found myself immersed in a pool of anxiety in the silence of the new day. I did my best to hold on to whatever it was that was helping me stay glued together, but nothing worked. There seemed to be nothing left to clutch on to. I opened my palms and held them over my chest for a bit; then I moved them onto my face and behind my head. The healer had told me that it would do me good. As my body warmed, I really did relax a little. Then I became tense, again, thinking that all I was doing was touching and embracing myself. I was trying to draw strength from myself by tricking my body into believing I was holding a partner, or another living being.

I got up and turned on the TV and without having any breakfast, began to place the things I wanted to take with me into boxes. This was a nice distraction for a while. I glanced at the books in my library one by one. I picked out those that interested me and looked at the sentences I had underlined and the notes I had taken on the sides. In one of the books I read that God had created someone to love for everyone who struggles. It was followed by the sentence, "if this were not so, then humanity's dreams would carry no significance." The book advised how love should not distance one from one's personal saga. If the person in question felt hindered, then this was not true love.

Then I came across the novel Don Quixote, and read a chapter. In it, the antiquarian protagonist believes that a dust cloud rising from a herd of sheep is actually coming from a battle between two armies. So, to help the side that is losing he attacks and massacres quite a number of the herd, putting him into a difficult predicament. In fact, he imagines that he is valiantly fighting in the front lines under the banner of the brave Pentapolin and his knights, rallying them and proudly taking the kings' revenge on Alifanfaron from Trapobene. Of course, it is impossible for him to accept the hideous truth of the reality. Who could survive such a fall?

Another book advised on how, every now and then we must comfort ourselves by saying "I am a strong and creative being full of love." Apparently, we have to validate our beauty, the fact that we are loved and that we carry value by looking into our eyes in the mirror. We also were advised to imagine a virtual mentor for ourselves, embellishing it with an unusual and surprising sense of humor, an exotic appearance and a dramatic and flamboyant style. The book was like an introduction to schizophrenia. When in pain, the book advised us to conceive of our ailment as a colorful sphere of light of 1.5 meters in diameter, then imagine that we enlarge it then shrink it down to a diameter of 30 cm and then destroy it.

I stopped looking at the books and turned my gaze to other objects. Hale's giant teddy bear was sitting in one corner of the room. When she had first seen it, she had joyfully hugged it like it was an actual living being. She had embraced the teddy bear's large belly as much as she could, then had closed her eyes and rested her head on it. When she was moving out she came into my room and told me, very hesitantly and as though she was at a loss for words, that she wanted to take the desk lamp. I now felt sad for the objects I had to leave behind; the objects, however, were silent and indifferent, as expected.

I was beginning to feel hungry, so I stopped the search and began to brew a pot of tea. I had some bagels so I put some feta cheese on the table to go with it. When the water came to a boil I switched on the TV. A young man was walking in the middle of the highway in the middle of the night. The reporter was both trying to coax the man into getting off the highway and talk to the camera at the same time. Suddenly a speeding car rammed into the man, hurling his body up 3-4 meters into the air like a plastic dummy, before plummeting to the ground.

I impatiently poured the tea without waiting for it to brew completely. I hadn't had a bagel for a while so when I bit into it, its smell and taste brought back many recollections; both good and bad memories flooded into my mind with such force that I felt overwhelmed and felt like I was going to topple over. I frowned and stopped eating. I got up from the table and went back to preparing my boxes.

I knew that I had to do something with my diaries. I hadn't looked at them for quite a while. Hesitatingly I began to peruse their pages, reading what I had written in the past. Unawares, I ended up slowly crouching on the floor as I read, leaning against the radiator under the living room window. It was a personal history I was reading; each story could be considered almost sacred though I had forgotten most of them. As it passes, time buoys us like water filling a pool and we forget all the stories that remain in the depths. After a while we even forget what it was we standing upon, who we were, and who the others were. This was why we neither really value others around us nor ourselves. I thought how if we were able to remember the past, we probably wouldn't be distanced from anyone. Although it was all recorded on paper, it was never re-read, thus forgotten. And eventually, separation ensued.

If what we grab hold of in order not to topple down the cliff begins to hurt our hands, we end up having to let go. We know that we will fall; and that we will hurt more so when we do but we just can't stand it.

...

Separation is difficult... Casting out or being cast out, despite the love felt; now we must both end up happy, or else neither of us will manage... Can the day come when one becomes happy despite the other? (Perhaps it should be so!)

...

I awoke in the middle of the night feeling that darkness creeping on me again. As if I were to be executed that day... Even worse, as if I had killed a loved one and had woken up realizing the blood on my hands...

I couldn't write anything, any work I completed devoid of emotion, anything I did while forgetting her, would certainly cause me to be cursed.

Hale had stopped answering my calls. This was how the world was. Two people who had been making love the day before could end up so distant the next day that they would never be any more contact between them forever again. This happened even if there were no wars, deaths, and captivity. Or maybe they all existed but we couldn't see. We learned to live accordingly. If you can call this living!

"You won't be with me when I die, right?"

"Under different circumstances, I would, but no, I won't be by your side."

...

"There is no 'we' anymore Adem! It's high time you accepted this!"

...

They've hurt her so; I must've hurt her so that for a second it seemed like she laughed while I cried!

I began to slowly hum a tune that had caught my attention but it didn't comfort me in the least. There was a comedy show on TV. The bland, artificial laughs from the effects seemed to be on repeat. My hands had begun to shake again. I could've cried, though I would only go on for a few seconds, then return to my dry silence. A text message arrived on my phone; I didn't want to check it.

The contradiction between living for oneself and trying to conform to the wishes of others! The dilemmas of letting someone go free and holding onto them for dear life! Of letting one's emotions run rampant and trying to stay calm and collected! The contradiction between whom you love and what you believe in, or the contradictions among those you love.

Looking at myself from the outside, I saw that I was incredibly irrelevant. A huge vacuum existed where my heart used to be. The blood in my veins flooded this vacuum and all my strength drained out of me as if I were having a seizure. My mind was aflame and I lost sight of my surroundings. I couldn't focus and had lost almost all my will to fight. Gasping for breath, I tried to walk around the house, but to no avail. I couldn't find the strength to stand upright so I leaned against the walls of the corridor.

As fear and shame fed each other, my pain rose like an unstoppable giant wave. My brain felt swollen, pushing against my skull, almost to the point of bursting. I was receiving one sudden blow after the other. My head throbbed like a muscle whose strength was depleted but still tried to function. I was breathless, and started to moan in fits. This would continue, the pain would increase; there was no future to be seen. Depression was also physical pain.

123

Nobody would want to leave this world unless they were caught in the talons of an unstoppable terror.

Desolation, the fear that rises when one is stranded alone in a desert, our private ineptitudes, our woeful condition; these were all top secret, things we couldn't and shouldn't share with others. Once narrated, the loneliness came to an end and we forgot once again all that we had experienced.

Our sinister torturer scuffles away into the crevices like an insect upon hearing another human being's voice and once there are no more witnesses left around, would slowly show its legs from where it was hiding once again.

My mind had surrendered to a fiery flame; I wasn't thinking any longer. I just couldn't. All I wanted was to disappear. I had promised myself that I was going to die when I wanted to, so I didn't have to pass away in fear and pain. I went to the bathroom and rummaged through the medicine cabinet. I found the boxes of pills I had bought the day before and swallowed the lot, using a half a bottle of vodka to wash them down.

Then, gasping, I looked frantically for my cell phone all around the house. I felt like I was being gripped in a nightmare. Nausea had begun but I resisted the urge to vomit. When I found the phone I remembered that I had received a text message. I checked the message with my trembling fingers and read: "In sickness as in health, Keval is always with you. Spend over 300 TL at your local Keval Shop and win an Emergency Insurance Policy from us!"

Without losing any more time, I dialed Koray Ergülen's number. After a few rings, he picked up the call.

"Hello?"

"Koray Bey, isn't it?"

"Yes?"

"This is Adem speaking, I signed a hibernation contract a few days ago at your office."

"Yes, of course I remember, Adem Bey. How are you?"

"Not too good. I am committing suicide."

While talking, I walked towards the entrance and opened the door of my apartment.

"What have you done?"

"I am trying to kill myself! I am hoping not to survive. I will also call the police, so that you are not incriminated in any way. Please make the arrangements for my body. I am placing my trust in you."

In fact, I didn't have much trust to place in him. It would've been naïve to do so. I had already learned this. I just was unable to see any other way and figured that perhaps vanishing was the best option after all, so I was taking my chances. I wished God existed, but it seemed to me that he didn't; and that was so sad.

PART 2
PARADISE

*"If suffering is freedom
then we are both free*
...
*lies, all were lies
once there was something called love
now there is nothing."*

– Hasan Hüseyin Korkmazgil
Acılara Tutunmak (Clinging to Pain)

1

The smell of sweetgum trees and soap wafted up to my nostrils. I lay a bit longer, keeping my eyes shut, unaware that I even possessed them. It was silent; all I could hear was the trickle of water. I surmised I was alone. Although wrapped in heavy garb, I still felt somewhat cold, as thought I had been newly washed and dried.

Once I recognized I was in an unknown place, I tried to recall what had happened the day before and where I had gone to bed. As recollections flooded in, my heart began to beat madly; my eyelids popped open by themselves and gaspingly I looked around me.

I was in a cellar-like place with marble pillars, not unlike a hammam. Directly above me was a large cupola that emitted light from its small arch-like windows. The walls were decorated with blue-green enamel tiles and miniatures.

I was surprised to see that it looked as if time had not gone forward but actually had regressed. I got up to a seated position, letting my legs dangle over the side of the bed, which was decorated with ornamental emeralds and carved woodwork. Adjacent to my bed were sandals with pointy and curled tips, along with a turban and a copper washbowl.

I took note of the clothes I was wearing. I was dressed in a loose, collarless white shirt and a black vest ornamented with precious stones. Underneath was a pair of blue shalwars. I slipped my feet into the sandals and placed the turban my head. I felt as though I had dressed for a role in a stage drama.

The first thing that popped into my head was that I had not hibernated but had had my stomach washed and then had been transferred over here. I could have also been dreaming of course, but I felt awake somehow.

I started to check my body parts, touching my face, head, feeling my hair. Suddenly I remembered that I had only wanted my head to hibernate, so I looked at my hands and fingers as if they were alien objects. They didn't really look that different than my own, nor did they feel so.

To my right was a window covered with an iron grill that gave view to another room. I felt nervous, with the impression that somebody was watching me from that window. I turned around to see if the room had another exit. A bit further lay a wooden door with carved woodwork decorating its frame. It was wide open.

As I began to walk towards this exit, something quite large passed by the other side of the door. Whatever or whoever it was had moved so quickly that I hadn't been able to ascertain exactly what it was. I stopped, held my breath and waited for a few seconds.

My heart was beating violently, as if wanting to burst out of my chest. Then, rather out of obligation, I began to move again towards the door.

Outside was a spiraling stone staircase, which I began to climb frantically. The ascent was lit by lanterns hanging on the walls.

The shadows cast by their flames made the place resemble a shadow puppet stage set.

The staircase eventually led me to another room whose floors were covered in scarlet rugs. I could smell fresh air. Thick, black curtains made of rich material danced with a light breeze; I could hear the faint sounds of wind chimes. When I drew the curtains aside, I saw that they were hanging from doors opening onto a balcony. The door was unlocked, so I stepped outside. Who knows how long I had spent without any sunshine? As my eyes began to adjust to the light I started to make out what my surroundings looked like.

I was at the top floor of a large pavilion built upon a hill. Tall cypresses planted around the walls reached up to my feet. In front of me spread a grove of purple and green trees that led to a medieval city. Although the city was cut by a a navy blue strait, I couldn't be sure I was in Istanbul as there were a few small islands between the two shores. Bridges stretching between these islands connected the two shores. Boats of all sizes sailed on the water.

Near the pavilion were other tall, stone buildings covered in moss, some castle walls and a clock tower. I shivered, for looking at them made me realize how high I was standing. The walls of the tower were decorated with colorful mosaics in geometric shapes and wooden planks.

Had I somehow travelled back to the past, rather than the future? But, how could this have happened by sleeping? As far as I knew, from the point of view of physics, such a trip was not possible. I knew that the city I was looking at could not be the Istanbul of the past. However, it didn't look like its future either. Maybe I wasn't in Istanbul at all. In fact, I couldn't be sure whether I was in the same city, same country, or even the same world. I went back inside to find the exit. As I descended the stairs I tried not to make much noise.

***

A fountain decorated with golden lion statues stood in the garden of the pavilion. The clear, dense liquid that gushed out of the lion's mouths flowed into a river that ran towards the city. The liquid smelled pleasant; I dipped my finger in it and tasted it. The taste was one of sherbet with floral flavors. I bent down immediately and began to drink it deeply. I was famished, but the liquid only increased my thirst and hunger instead of satiating it. My body must have been starving for nutrition.

After I had filled my stomach to the point of feeling slightly satisfied, I began to follow the river of sherbet that ran through the flower groves. The earthen path that stretched by the river was covered in colorful pebbles.

As the grove ended and gardens full of roses and tulips began, so did the earthen path became a road of cobblestones. Eventually I saw stretching before me a neighborhood of large villas with bow windows and mansions lining the two sides of the valley that had been cut by the river. I also began to make out the sounds of human voices. My heart throbbed with excitement. As my steps got quicker I found myself in the middle of an abundant marketplace.

The streets were full of handsome people, all dressed in medieval garb. As I saw them, my pulse quickened and my ears flushed. The women who passed me by, eyeing me, had wet, large and sparkling eyes, beautiful faces semi hidden underneath their tulle veils, and wore colorful silken clothes that concealed swaying figures, figures that were somewhat too perfect. Moreover, they had another seductive quality, which I couldn't put a name to. Their aura had affected me in a way that made me feel almost inebriated. I had begun to stagger.

I looked up and turned around a few times to see the rest of the surroundings. Ten-yard high rose bushes and Judas trees sprouted out of the marble sidewalks and formed an arbor over the street.

The fragrance of spices intermingled with the aroma of bread spilling from the bakeries. I rummaged through my pockets, but they were empty. Following the beautiful residents of the city, I tried to ascertain what they did for food. I didn't see anyone paying for anything but I couldn't be sure.

Pensively I walked by the stalls with baskets full of fruits, nuts and seafood. Sausages and pastrami hung from the stone walls. As I arrived at the neighborhood square, I decided to brave it at a restaurant that showcased whole chickens roasting on spits. I entered their vine shaded garden and sat at the farthest table. For some time I just sat there, not knowing what to do. The seat I had chosen was shaded by two big sycamores.

Finally an old waiter came by and placed a dish of pilaf dotted with almonds in front of me. "Go on son!" he said, "Don't hesitate! Dig in!" His voice was hoarse but reassuring. After speaking to me he left quickly, his wooden sandals clicking and clacking after him.

Strangely enough, these were the first sentences I had heard in my new life. I thanked the man and hungrily began to devour the pilaf. When I lifted my head up from the plate, I saw that a large tankard full of a yogurt drink had been placed on my table as well. Everything was so delicious that I couldn't stop eating.

"Aaaah!" said a voice from behind me. I turned and saw that the speaker was a green parrot. After a moment of silence, it started to grumble, "What do I do? What do I do now?" as if it could imitate thoughts as well as words.

I had lived my whole life with a specific goal. I wasn't used to not having one as now. Ever since I had opened my eyes I was asking the same question that the parrot voiced: What should I do, where should I go now? The person I knew myself to be would have immediately begun investigating how he came to be here, where this place and what the date was, but I didn't want to be this kind of person any longer. After all, I could eat whenever I wanted!

I was about to burst from overeating. "You know what I'll do?" I asked the parrot. "I'll go to the bathroom!"

"Best choice!" it replied.

I was surprised but just laughed it off. I rose from the table and did what I had told the parrot I would do. Then I exited the restaurant, almost running, as there was no guarantee that the food was free. I came back to the square and wandered into whichever direction pleased me. In a few hours darkness would settle but I supposed I would eventually find a place to stay. If not, the weather being favorable, I could very well sleep outside.

Suddenly a girl on the street stared at me long with her large, auburn eyes. She looked pretty much the same as all the others but I caught a shadow of melancholy on her face. I was surprised to find anxiety and sadness in paradise. Although at first I didn't make much of it and continued to walk, I suddenly regretted that I had.

The indifference I had for some time had now left its place to a strange feeling of unease. I was cross with myself because of that, but to no avail. My battered self was also angry with me for letting the girl wander off. I turned around hoping to see her there but of course she had already mixed into the crowd and disappeared.

I came to a castle-like structure surrounded by high stonewalls. From inside I could hear noises of sword fights, horse's hooves and neighing, mixed with jovial sounds of loud laughter. I approached the building and entered using the first door I came by. The door led to a hippodrome surrounded by a marble colonnade. In the middle was a grass field on which a war game was being played out. I mixed with the crowd and tried to see what exactly was going on.

On the side of the field closest to me a troop of knights were seated on horses with their shining coats of arms and shields covering their dark robes. Scarlet cloth had been draped onto the horses for saddles. Some of the riders carried shields decorated with gold and gemstones. The knights started to holler and drawing their blades from their sheaths, spurred their horses and began to attack the right flank of the rival troops.

The commander of the team in white caught the move and sent a large group of pike men to counter the attack. Soldiers garbed in white, collarless shirts hurriedly rushed to the ordered location. Their beige pants had blue stripes running down the sides and their waists were bound with satin, navy blue sashes. Once they reached their targets they regrouped and formed a defense line. They resembled a giant hedgehog with 3 meter long quills. I was curious as to what was going to transpire next.

In a few seconds, the cavalry struck the defense line with all their might. I wasn't expecting what would happen and fell aghast while watching. Pikes were broken, horses fell, and infantrymen were thrown to and fro. All the while though, the whole crew were chuckling. As the attacking cavalry acknowledged their defeat, they began to retreat. Accompanied by great applause, those who should have been killed or injured also arose from the field with the referee at their side and joined their fans.

Thus the third thing I had learned about them: not only were they of statuesque beauty and beaming with child-like joy, they were also far from being fragile. The horses were all in one piece as well. Those that must have been pierced by pikes or must have had broken legs all got up and went back to their stables. They also received wide cheer and applause.

Then something even more surprising happened. The weeds on the field began to sway as if under heavy wind, carrying on their tips the weapons and pieces of armor that had been strewn here and there to the sides of the battlefield. The objects fell into the grooves on the sides and like billiard balls falling into the tables' pockets, disappeared out of sight.

Entranced, I watched a steel, seven-foot long spear slide rapidly over the weeds, as if carried by a set of hands. As the weapon reached the side of the field, it was sucked down, in front of an octagonal wooden gazebo. I suddenly caught my breath as I saw the girl I had recently seen on the street sitting in the audience. She had caught my attention as soon as I had gazed over at the crowd.

For a while I stood there, contemplating what to do, then slowly walked towards the gazebo. I advanced step by step, trying not to arouse suspicion though I felt or imagined that she was aware of my presence. I could have been mistaken but it seemed as though she was constantly watching me from the corner of her eye.

I swallowed hard, but did not avert my gaze when she suddenly turned towards me and looked directly into my face. Our eyes locked for several seconds–perhaps she was trying to figure out who or what I was. It was almost as if she were watching an exotic animal in awe, though I also felt that there was a feminine sense of challenge being directed to me. Her long black hair moved in the wind; I did not think my behavior was disrespectful in the least.

Even though I continued my approach I also saw that she had again turned her face to the field. As I neared I began to make out her voice. She was joyfully cheering with the rest of the crowd and commenting on the players. Her voice had the softness of satin and despite the crowd's roar it was easily discernible. As I drew closer, I was pleasantly surprised to see that there was an empty seat right beside her.

I didn't make the first move though. It was she who suddenly turned towards me and called out: "We have a visitor! You seem to have come from a long way!"

"Yes," I said, trying to stifle the violent beating of my heart. "A long and tiring way. This place isn't taken, is it?"

She moved aside a bit without saying a word. I sat down on the red cushion.

"Thank you," I said. "I see I got the best seat!"

"Why do you think it the best?" she asked. She either did not catch my hint or feigned not to, maybe trying to be sure of what she heard.

"Well, we're near the command center!" I responded.

"Oh!"

I returned my gaze onto the field, feigning to watch the game. The eyelashes topping her big blue eyes were highlighted with mascara. For some reason I had thought her eyes were light brown at first. Her full lips were pressed together. I could feel the heat of her slim legs under her shalwar pressing against mine.

"Is this a tournament?" I asked, just for conversation.

"No," she said. "A single match."

When we turned to each other, our gazes met at a dangerous distance.

"Who are the competing two teams?"

"The Cabbages and the Leeks."

"Cabbages and Leeks? What an unnecessary war!"

She laughed. There was an attractive oddness to her laugh whose reason I couldn't discern.

"That's what the teams are called," she said. "Cute, right?"

"Yeah, cute and funny. The black team are the cabbages?"

"No, those are the leeks... Are you from outer space?"

"Perhaps."

"You don't look like you're from here. Are you the Sultan or something?"

"The Sultan?"

"You know, they say that he wanders among us in disguise."

"Oh! Well, no, that's not me. Though I would deny it even if I were I guess. How about you?"

"I'm not the Sultan either."

"Can I trust you?"

"Yes, you can."

"Well, thank you."

A moment of silence ensued. I felt really happy just sitting there, serene and joyful at the same time. I had many questions in my mind of course, grand questions to be exact; but I didn't think I should be asking them. In the same vein, she didn't look like she was interested in the trivial details of my identity.

Suddenly she turned to me and tilting her neck slightly to the left, murmured: "Being a team is a good thing right?"

"Yes, of course!" I managed to say. I let the joy that arose in me turn into a wide smile. Just then one of the cavalrymen fell off his horse. The white-clad infantry swarmed him immediately, like a pack of scavengers.

"Oh!" yelled the girl. "Kasım has fallen! He's such a pretty boy, but look at how they're attacking him."

"Maybe they're jealous," I said, smiling.

She didn't respond; her eyes on the field, she went silent. I just couldn't control myself. Not only was I constantly making the kinds of hints and jokes you make to someone you've known forever, but now, I was also reproaching her.

Kasım pulled out a dagger adorned with precious stones in place of his fallen sword and valiantly tried to defend, despite the disproportionate number of men surrounding him. After a while, counted dead, he was removed from the battlefield and came next to us.

The girl wiped the sweat off the brow of her friend with a handkerchief she had pulled out of her pocket. "You were great!" she exclaimed.

I felt my face go yellow, just like when in pain.

"No I wasn't!" retorted Kasım.

His attitude was child-like and sweet. He was quite handsome with brown hair, green eyes and with caved in cheeks that suited his slim figure. He looked at me with an amicable and soft gaze.

"It was heroic," I praised him. "In fact, I'm jealous!"

After thanking me, "I haven't seen you before," he said. "But you supported us! I saw it. I fought for you too!"

I blushed.

The game was almost over. The girl –what was her name I wondered?– got up and prepared to leave.

"Why don't you come with us too?" asked Kasım.

"Where are you going?" I asked back.

"To the palace!" he said.

Then he turned towards his friend as if asking for approval. She stood silent, a bit shy, or perhaps brazen. I gave myself the liberty to intuit pleasant things from her attitude.

"Sure!" I replied. I had nowhere else to go after all!

They were overjoyed, or at least acted as if. We stepped outside onto the street passing under the colonnade that surrounded the field. I followed them as we headed towards the palace.

"Why are we going there?" I asked.

My voice sounded timid; they might not have heard it.

"We'll freshen up and eat," said the girl, not leaving my question unanswered.

"Oh, to be safe as well!" added Kasım. Then, with a mysterious tone of voice he shook his head and said: "You don't want to be left alone outside after dark!"

"Don't be silly!" retorted the girl, "Don't scare our visitor!"

Kasım chuckled.

"Do you live in the palace?" I asked. Then I turned to the girl and asked, "I know Kasım now, but... I still don't know your name?"

"What difference will it make?" she asked, smiling.

"You're right, it doesn't matter," I quickly replied. "I'm just curious."

"Leila," she said. "My name is Leila."

"I'm Adem. Pleased to meet you."

She nodded with a smile.

"We live in the palace only now and then," said Kasım. "Actually there isn't only one palace, but many here. We can go and stay at whichever one we like."

"I see," I said.

In fact, I didn't really, but I didn't want to prolong the subject. I hoped that one day I could ask them about everything, right from the start. I didn't feel up to the task of trying to keep in mind this new puzzle, whose pieces at the moment seemed rather disparate.

"So where do you live? Where did you come from?" they asked.

"I don't know," I said. "I think I was asleep in the past, in Istanbul. I must've stayed that way for quite some time. Then I awoke here."

"Very interesting! Like the Seven Sleepers?"

"Exactly! I'm a total stranger but I feel and act as if I am one of you, when by your side. This is your influence of course. Which is sort of strange!"

"Not at all! Nobody is a stranger here!"

As we continued walking, others joined us. Each could be a runner-up for a beauty contest. As one of the girls passed me by, she smiled, showing her beautiful white teeth.

"Hello!" I replied.

"Hello."

"How are things?"

She laughed.

"Fine. How about with you?"

"Fine here as well."

We walked along a marble road lined with trees on each side. The shadows of their branches blended with those of the buildings; evening was closing in. In a few minutes I saw the palace surrounded by tall walls. On two sides of the entrance stood rather awkward appearing towers with thick bases that narrowed as they rose. They reminded me of prison keeps. Then we entered a large courtyard amidst the castle walls. It created a sense of both safety and freedom.

***

The table was set in a hall that overlooked a grassy palace courtyard with a fountain in the middle. My newfound friends and I settled on the soft cushions lined alongside the table. I leaned back against the pillows behind me and drew a deep breath.

As the wide windows were open, the fresh, cool air, the fragrances and sounds from the garden all drifted inside. The floor was paved with wood, darkened with varnish, which highlighted the colors of the carpet that covered it. The long dining table was positioned in the middle of the hall, on top of one of these scarlet carpets. I could feel the soft touch of the heavy wool under my soles. For lighting, oil lamps were fixed onto the walls. The corner fireplaces illuminated the room with an orange hue.

For starters, the table was replete with a variety of small dishes and lentil soup in ceramic bowls. Small service trays with wheels whose handles were not unlike ears spun around us, serving hot bread.

I felt extremely hungry once again. Before I made a move to the silver spoon to begin my soup, I checked my hands; they were as clean as if newly washed. After all that walking, I hadn't even broken a sweat. I guessed my body was one that dirt could not adhere to. I shrugged with a smile and tried some of the soup. The taste was so delicious that for a moment, the pleasure made me euphoric. I also tried the ice-cold rose sherbet that smelled delightful.

Looking across at the blond young man in front of me, I asked: "Do you have a fridge? The sherbet is cold!"

Brushing off the breadcrumbs on his hands the young man replied: "There is no fridge. We keep the ice in the basement."

"Where do you get the ice from?"

"From the mountains."

"But why?"

"Because it's better this way! It's authentic!"

"What is all this for?" I asked finally.

Leila smiled and looking over the Nubian girl called Cheshminaz sitting between us, asked, "What do you mean what for?"

"I mean," I said, "I don't know what year we're in, but why do you live as if in Ottoman times?"

"It's nice, isn't it?"

"It is, but..."

Cheshminaz interjected: "You're confused because you've only seen this area. This is only a small part in the world. You're in Istanbul, in the future!"

Laughing, I asked, "But why does it look like Istanbul's past?"

This time, only Leila smiled.

"Each city..." answered Cheshminaz, "has been restored to its grandest time in history."

Hurriedly swallowing the humus with pastrami in my mouth, " Are you serious?" I asked. "That's lovely!"

Sitting on my right, Kasım intervened, "Actually, not only have the cities been restored to their past grandeur, but they're also as they figured in the imagination."

"There's an upcoming trip to Cappadocia in a few days!" said Leila. "You can come and join us. That place looks like a fairy-tale land for instance."

I could only mutter a bland "Okay." Then, as if to change the subject, "What else is there?" I asked. "Which regions enact which eras?"

"Well, in the West, the Greek Islands are re-living their mythology for example," jumped in the youth in front of me. He seemed like he didn't want to relinquish the pleasure of explaining this all to me to anyone else. "Mount Olympus now hosts all the pagan gods. One day we can climb up and see. The port is full of ships that sail off to the seven seas. But one must be careful! Each island has a different story; along with its delights, there lurks various dangers as well. Monsters, humans with animal bodies, animals with human bodies, and also evil, enslaved demigods. Nice, eh?"

"Yeah, nice," I murmured.

"The god Apollo swims in the Aegean in the form of a dolphin," said Cheshminaz. "Sailors catch a glimpse of him every now and then. He wanders alongside sea fairies with fish tails and mermaids. Sometimes, winged horses fly in the air. Troy, in all its splendor has been restored near the Dardanelles. Greek ships cluster constantly around its shores, waiting to attack. A passerby can see it all!"

Having turned my head towards Cheshminaz, who was sitting between Leila and me, I was desperately trying not to catch Leila's eyes.

"In the South, Egypt has been restored to the time of the Pyramids!" intervened Kasım. "With all its legends of course. In the southeast, the cedar forests of Lebanon and the Hanging Gardens of Babylon have been reconstructed. Baghdad lives in the time of the Caliph Haroon Rashid! Travelers to faraway lands return with new, amazing tales and exotic animals heretofore unseen."

As I listened, I continued to eat my soup. Suddenly my right hand hit the purple bowl full of sherbet and as I tried to grab it, a porcelain pitcher of fruit juice fell off the table and broke into pieces. Fortunately, the carpet –with great appetite– sucked in the stains and pieces of porcelain immediately.

"What year are we in?" I asked, as if nothing had happened.

"We've stopped counting the years," said Kasım, "Humanity has long since stopped counting time."

"When did this begin?"

"As we have stopped counting, we don't know."

They all chuckled.

I was amazed at what I was hearing.

"Why did you stop counting then?" I asked.

"They looked at each other, seeming puzzled as to how to reply.

"Well, when was the last year you know of?" I asked. "When did the clocks stop turning that is?"

"Why don't you try to guess?" said Leila, in a playful, child-like manner, trying to lighten up the mood at the table.

Then they began staring at me, anxiously awaiting my answer.

"Ten thousand?" I asked.

"Higher!" said the youth sitting across me.

"Twenty thousand?"

"Higher still!"

I was taken aback. I guess I had to up the figures a bit. "One hundred thousand?" I asked.

The young man smiled and murmured, "Higher!" They were enjoying my amazement at the situation. So the passion of telling someone something mysterious still hadn't died off after more than a hundred thousand years.

"Bullshit!" I said.

"Down!" they said. I laughed.

"Three hundred and twenty eight thousand," said Cheshminaz finally. "The clocks stopped in November, 328,000 C.E. It was the seventh day of the month, on Thursday. After then, as the seconds weren't counted any more and each day resembled the other, no one can tell if ten thousand or a hundred thousand years have passed."

"Why did the clocks stop?" I asked right away. I couldn't stop myself anymore.

The wall at the far end of the hall's windows had an automatic door fixed onto it. As each service tray sidled up, a revolving mechanism swirled it to the other side, after which it appeared back in the hall full of new dishes. Nobody had heard my question as our table waiters had passed to our side with large copper plates. A feeling of enthusiasm swept the table.

The plates' lids were lifted and under them, spicy meatballs, kebabs, pitas and fried game meat appeared. We were free to choose from whatever we liked. I repeated my question.

"I guess because things stopped changing," responded Leila finally. "Change had stopped for some time actually. Humanity had reached its desired point and history ended."

"Ancient people busy themselves with measurements!" said the youth in front of me. "We are a new generation. Perhaps due to our life of abundance we have no need or obligation to count anything!"

"We don't really know much!" admitted Cheshminaz. "We don't know any facts anymore. Whatever was known has been forgotten in time as well."

I found this to be totally unacceptable.

"But they must be recorded somewhere, right?" I asked.

"Of course they are! There are universities and professors on all subjects; and you can reach any information you want from libraries."

This comforted me a little. I cut a piece off the stuffed chicken on my plate and bit into it. The stuffing had rice with almonds, coconut and black pepper in it. Since the data was accessible anytime –and since the world had been the way it was for quite some time– I saw no harm in postponing my investigations a little longer. Moreover, there was no guarantee that I would like what I was going to learn.

"Why don't you tell us your story?" asked Leila with interest. "Where have you come from? We haven't had a visitor for a long time. Especially someone from the ancient people..."

"The ancient people..." I grumbled half-jokingly. "I must look like an ape for you people then."

They all laughed.

"Well, since you're able to express doubt on the issue..." said Cheshminaz, "I don't think you would qualify as an ape." She squeezed my left arm as if to say *just kidding*.

I laughed. "Yes!" I said, "I think I can notice myself in a mirror."

"Hey, don't skip over the question now," grumbled Leila.

"Oh yes, of course... It's a long story though. Besides, I don't know much about it. Like yourselves... I just found myself here one day. The past is not so nice anyway, maybe I can tell you about it some other time."

They did not insist. As nobody spoke, silence ensued. We con-tinued to eat. Now only the noises of cutlery and chewing were heard. I suddenly became aware as to how much I had missed having such a dinner conversation. I tried to hide my trembling hands, which had actually been the cause of my dropping the pitcher. I felt a secret joy from being seated with Cheshminaz and Leila, talking to them.

"Who prepares these meals?" I asked more out of admiration than curiosity.

"The kitchen does!" said the blond youth across me. "We can cook as well if we want to though!"

"I can't," I said. "Even if I wanted to. I could at most fry an egg."

He laughed. "That's fine. Whatever makes you happy."

"But it wouldn't taste very good."

"Well then we won't eat it."

"Ah, but then you'll break my heart!"

We all laughed together. The service trays now brought us our desserts. Decorated with exotic flowers the trays carried baskets full of desserts made with milk or dough, syrupy pastries, melted halvah, Turkish delight and all sorts of fruits, nuts, giant melons stacked one on top of each other. Coffee was also served.

I began with the halvah. It would go great with fresh bread. However, just as I reached for the first bite, suddenly all the lights in the room went out. As the hour was late, we were all left in the darkness. If the others hadn't responded with applause, I might've become nervous. Kasım, sensing this, bent down and said, "the Karagöz shadow play is about to begin," to clarify the subject.

I nodded and smiled. A white curtain was draped in the mid-dle of the hall, lit from behind, turning it into a shadow-play screen. Tambourine sounds indicated that the show was to begin shortly.

On the screen was a house with a bay window. Hadjivat entered the screen from the right and began to complain: *"Oh Lord, grant me my beloved!"* he said, *"Send me a princess, lest my soul perish! Oh dear Lord, everyone has a soul mate, I just wish I be granted one!"*

"Lord grant me one who longs for a good bashing!" said Karagöz from the bay window overhead.

There were small giggles uttered here and there.

"Every demeanor delicate," said Hadjivat. *"Her conversation, her conduct sweetly doth taste..."*

"Are you back here again, you spinach-face?"

We all laughed together. Cheshminaz opened her arms to each side and shook her head left and right, saying, "what's with this spinach-face!" In the meantime, Karagöz and Hadjivat –their paper replicas to be exact– had begun a fierce skirmish.

"Brother, stop!" cried Hadjivat; *"You're tearing my beard out!"*

"And you've broken my nose!"

"Brother, you're going too far! Leave my ears be!"

"Take your ears, give me back my beard, kiddo!"

Karagöz fell out of the stage, Hadjivat escaped. We applauded.

Then another Karagöz came on stage. Everyone was surprised. Silence ensued.

"What the?.." uttered the first Karagöz. *"I'm going to go crazy!"*

"I'm going to go crazy!"

"Who are you?"

"Who are you?"

When the two of them could not decide, Hadjivat was called to act as judge.

"My dear Hadjivat!" asked the first Karagöz, *"Am I the Karagöz of this stage or is he?"*

"*My dear Hadjivat! Am I the Karagöz of this stage or is he?*"

"*Dear sir, that is Karagöz...*" said Hadjivat. "*And you are Karagöz too!*"

I laughed at the fact that Hadjivat wasn't surprised.

"*All right, I get it,*" insisted Karagöz, "*but which one is the real Karagöz?*"

"*All right, I get it, but which one is the real Karagöz?*"

"*You are the Karagöz of this stage!*" answered Hadjivat.

"*You see, rascal? I'm the real Karagöz!*"

"*Get out of here, you! It's me that's the real Karagöz!*"

Leila chuckled. "Finally he said something different!" she whispered. I liked the fact that she had seen this. I also joined in laughing.

"*Hadjivat, what do we do? Do we fight 'til the morning comes?*"

"*Hadjivat, what do we do? Do we fight 'til the morning comes?*"

"There! He's parroting him again!" I said.

After the first Karagöz beat the other out of the stage, Hadjivat grovelled, "*Good riddance, Karagöz! That was close!*"

Besides his grovelling, it was clear that he was, in fact, aware of the complexity of the situation. We laughed.

Then Karagöz, after strictly advising Hadjivat not to interfere, began to tell him a recollection of his. Hadjivat however, just couldn't keep from jumping in.

"*Didn't I just tell you no to interrupt me?*" retorted Karagöz.

"*Okay, okay why so cross brother? I won't open my mouth again!*"

"*What if you do?*"

"*May you go blind then!*"

"*Hadjivat, better not swear!*"

We laughed. Whether it was all the food and drink, or just fatigue in general, but my eyelids began to get heavier as I watched on. I couldn't follow the play anymore. I could only catch bits and pieces of dialogue.

The last things I heard were Karagöz's ramblings.

"...*got on a dolmuş,*" he said. "*Straight to the port! After I paid the fare, looking back and forth...*"

"*After contemplating the surroundings...*"

"*Fluttering eyelashes and heaving cleavages... You'd drop dead if you shut up right?*"*

While the others laughed wildly, I had begun to miss all the connotations.

Then I felt like many hands were softly carrying me. Maybe it was just a dream.

"Let him sleep!" said one.

"He'll get cold..." responded another, "He should be wearing pajamas."

I was softly put onto a comfortable bed, had a quilt draped over me and I think somebody briefly caressed my hair.

---

* Karagöz Shadow Plays, The Garden Play, Act II (Dialogue).

2

I awoke to birds singing outside. Before I got up, I turned left and right, without opening my eyes. With every turn I felt the discomfort of the previous position I was in fade away, leaving behind a great relief, as if I was fleeing my body. I didn't need to get up and get back to life yet.

Then I was startled when I heard a door slammed shut. Suddenly there was only silence. Even the birds had stopped their chirping. It was as if somebody had left, violently slamming the door shut. I opened my eyes in dismay. I saw that I was covered with a purple quilt dotted with pearls and that my head rested on a red silken pillow. The linen was of the same color as my pillow and of satin. So this was the soft touch I had felt while sleeping.

I stood up and sat on the bed, my feet dangling over the side. Then I took a deep breath and got up. A chair had been drawn up next to my bed, leading me to guess that someone must have stayed with me throughout the night. I walked towards the windows. When I drew back the curtains light flooded into the room. I must've been at the second or third floor of the palace. I peered down into the garden, but there was no one about. The city seemed abandoned. I shivered. Then I turned to my left and came face to face with a giant, wooden wardrobe that took up half the wall on that side of the room. After just standing there and staring at it for some time, I grasped the two handles of each wing and opened the wardrobe. The doors creaked as they parted. Inside were various colored clothes, all nicely washed and ironed. I chose a collarless white shirt and a dark colored pair of pants, and dressed after removing my pajamas.

Even though I had no idea where to go, I left the room and found the corridor. Just as I was about to shut the door from behind I caught a glance at the room and in surprise, saw that my pajamas had disappeared and my bed was made. I rushed back inside and quickly inspected the wardrobe, its drawers, under the bed and carpet but couldn't see anything. Maybe it was the bed that made itself and the pajamas perhaps got up, folded themselves and went into a separate drawer. Such a long time had passed since my era that all of these seemed possible.

I shrugged and went back out into the corridor. From there I ran down the marble staircase to reach the ground floor. When I reached the courtyard I began to make out the distant sounds of a crowd, so I set off in that direction. On the narrow but tall stonewalls of the garden was a large, wooden door, strengthened with iron girders. One wing of the door was open, the other closed. From the one left ajar, I could catch a glimpse of a colorful marketplace. A bazaar must've been set up right outside the castle walls. I hurriedly passed through the door and joined the throng.

I soon came to a narrow street covered in grapevines and tenting canvas. In front, as the road curled to the right I could see the large stone dome of a mosque. I passed by the sweet-smelling stalls of flower sellers and looked at the azaleas arranged upon carpets. For breakfast, I grabbed a sesame bagel from a baker I passed by and continued my way, biting into it. I was on my way down towards the coast.

The through to the bazaar brought me to a busy harbor. The numerous boats in different shapes and sizes tied to a long pier resembled a windy and naked winter forest with their masts swaying to and fro. Low waves were slapping the purple rocks covered with moss lying underneath the pier. The sun, just visible above the hills covered with thick woods on the eastern side of the Bosporus, reflected on the water, and this reflection resembled a sparkling bridge connecting both sides.

"Helllooo!" said somebody from behind me. I turned around to see Leila approaching! The beating of my heart changed immediately. Nevertheless, I was able to hold my breath and say "Hi!" back and smile. For a while, neither of us spoke; this reciprocal hesitance actually pleased me.

"What are you up to here?" she said eventually, with a hint of compassion in her tone. "We were wondering where you were, as you weren't in your room..."

I didn't know what to say. I was feeling mixed emotions. "I didn't see anyone when I woke up," I mumbled.

She laughed jovially. "So you march off to the coast when nobody's around?"

I laughed as well. "Yes!" I replied, with a mock-seriousness in my tone. "It is a primitive urge drive we Ancient People have. When left alone we go to the closest seashore."

She laughed as well.

"When you disappeared," she continued, "we thought you really might be the Sultan. I thought you might've tested us and left."

"I'm no sultan, ok?" I said. "I wish I were, but I'm not, you hear me? I'm not!" We chuckled again.

All I wanted was to make her laugh. I was more than willing to spend all my time and energy in making her laugh. Her deep dimples appeared as she laughed, which made her look like she was laughing three times over.

"Actually..." she continued. "I do understand you. Sometimes I too enjoy being on my own. I feel refreshed when doing so."

"Exactly!" I agreed. "It gives you the time to take a disinterested look at things, right?"

We stood silent for a bit. "You woke up early," I continued. "I was the first to dose off. But everyone is awake before me, I see."

"We need much less sleep than you do," she replied.

"It was obvious that those living in the fast-lane were going to survive anyway," I grumbled.

The situation was a bit odd. I noticed how fidgety I was when speaking. She in turn, mimicked my movements. When I noticed this reflex mirroring my enthusiasm, I tried to stifle it and she –perhaps because she caught on– also held herself back.

"Where were you headed?" she asked.

"I don't know?" I said. "How about you?"

"Just wandering."

"Shall we wander together then?"

"Suuure," she said in a coquettish manner.

We walked side by side to the south, following the coastline. That moment I thought how everyone should be aware of us; that everyone was watching, as it was a significant relationship we had. I felt as if two people, who were meant for each other, had come together. I could even go as far as to say that it was destiny that brought us together. How else could be bumping each other in such crowded areas otherwise? I had the tendency to interpret these affairs as signs. Love, in the end, could draw one into religion just as it could lead one out. When we become extremely afraid or when we desire something strongly (after all, these two are not so different) superstitions are hard to supress.

A ship's crew and some dock workers were loading newly picked vegetables in hay baskets onto a ship. Some had climbed up on top of the masts and were busy getting the sails ready, which made me presume they were getting prepared to depart.

"People are working!" I remarked. "And in tough jobs!"

She smirked. "You think they're obligated to, that they're slaves, right?" she asked.

Although I liked the way she read my mind, what she said hadn't quenched my curiosity. "I saw people working hard at the bazaar as well," I said. "Why don't you people work? Or do I need to work as well?"

She smiled as if she had found my words cute.

"The people you see here working," she said," do it with great pleasure. They get bored of constant leisure. They want to be a part of life; whether that be selling fruit at the stalls or being part of this ship's crew. Without being a part of the picture, neither the bazaar nor the port can truly be enjoyed. We could also begin working anytime we want, then go back to resting and relaxing at our whim."

I was confused. "Well, don't businesses suffer when everyone only works when they choose to do so?" I asked.

"Definitely not!" she answered. "For instance now, I want to wander around with you, but the minute I feel like I want to grow something in the fields I can work for hours or days with great pleasure, to the point where you couldn't stop me!" She laughed. "There's always somebody who's willing to work anyway."

"Don't those who work get disturbed by thinking that they are acting as servants to those who're at leisure?"

"Not at all. We *love* each other. Does a mother get tired of serving her children? No, she derives pleasure from her work. As I said before, everyone takes turns anyway!"

"I don't know," I said. "I guess it's possible. But it's quite interesting!"

"It works," she interceded. "Believe me! Perhaps you're confused because you're thinking with respect to the conditions of your time. Nothing is difficult for us anymore. Everything is made easy. All elements of nature, the earth, water, ships; they are all our helpers. We take the seeds from the silos, plant them in the earth, rain falls, trees grow rapidly."

What she was telling me resembled a beautiful dream more than anything. Actually, I worried that I was perhaps only dreaming this entire scenario, but I didn't want my mind to go into that direction of thought. Apart from the excitement I felt from what I had been hearing her tell me, I had also turned towards Leila, and was pleasantly watching her movements, her attitude as she spoke. I liked her seriousness, enthusiasm and her efforts to convince me. For a moment I thought of her as complete purity and a smile rose up in me. As I was busy with these thoughts at times I missed what she was saying. I think those who say that to listen to someone intently is a sign of love are perhaps misguided.

She stopped speaking and glanced at me, smiling. She again probably had read my mind.

"There are secret robotic systems everywhere, right?" I mumbled, "My bed made itself after I got up this morning for instance, then my pajamas folded themselves. Nano-technology or something of that sort I suppose! Well, never mind!" I continued, "Whatever!" Going into details like these made one feel distanced. I stopped speaking as I felt I had begun to ruin the magic of the moment with my curiosity. I smiled widely again and she laughed in return. She really looked like she understood me all the time.

"Come on!" she said and motioning towards the sea with her head, began to sprint towards the shore. I couldn't budge. She stopped, turned to me and asked: "Aren't you coming?"

I turned my palms upwards as if saying *Dear Lord* and shook my head, then began to run after her. She jumped onto the deck of the largest ship in dock. It was a gigantic galleon with huge sails. A behemoth fit for battle, the thing was 130 yards long and got fatter towards the bottom like a roly-poly toy. I enjoyed seeing such a vehicle with my own eyes. I was surprised for some reason; it was different, yet familiar at the same time.

Together we began to climb its highest mast. The crew didn't pay any attention, as if we were kids playing games around them. I was as agile as an ape. When we reached the top, "Let go!" said Leila and pointed at the waters of the Bosporus, which looked even calmer from up here. She held my hand, I didn't object nor ask; we dove in together. Right at that moment, a strong wind blew and carried us up in the air; we began to fly and hover downwards towards the sea.

"Look!" she said, indicating the east of the city, where there were fields and forests. "That's where we will be headed! First thing tomorrow!"

"All right!" I said nodding. "Sounds lovely!"

She laughed. "We'll also go hunting!" she said. "The place is full of weird animals and monsters!"

"Fine by me!"

We landed softly on the port. We straightened up and looked at each other. Then, "I have to get going," she complained. I was upset; *we were playing so nicely*, I thought.

"Come to dinner again tonight!" she said, "at the same place!"

I was relieved as if I could breathe once more. I nodded in acquiescence and smiled.

She waved at me in joy. Then she began to run towards the seaside mansions with colorful bay windows and disappeared from sight. Once again, I thought that I must have been dreaming.

She had sought me out, had spoken to me, and laughed with me. Was she really interested in me? Although I knew I had to be wary of such assumptions, I felt it was true. Her words, her glances and something else I couldn't name, or articulate, indicated so. I was also afraid to ponder too deeply on this possibility. I was happy right now just busying myself with sweet possibilities. In this world, one which was full of uncertainties, some things could remain the way one imagined them as long as one didn't articulate or scrutinize. I continued to wander on the shore in shock, my hands trembling.

* * *

Anxiously, I wandered around the winding streets and narrow paths of the city until the evening. Having so much leisure time on my hands, not being obligated to work was already difficult for me. Laziness was oppressing, as if tons of work were waiting for me. I still had problems accepting the idea that I wouldn't eventually have to go back to work. I worried that the dream would soon end and that I was becoming late for something, but I couldn't figure out what that something was.

Leila's image accompanied me throughout the day of course. I couldn't help imagining her as a being much more wondrous than she looked and my insides knotted up whenever I thought of the melancholy in her gaze. Somebody like her just shouldn't be upset I thought. She shouldn't, because her dismay may become unbearable; it could turn into a profound and insoluble grief. Slowly a yearning had begun to grow in me, like a tiny, pleasant ache. I was anxious to see Leila again. However, I was also afraid of this, as I may not be able to withstand her not smiling, or the tiniest disinterestedness in her gaze. We had to at least be friends, or like siblings; we just had to, otherwise living might become insupportable for me.

This time dinner was served on the top floor of the palace, in a hall with high ceilings and a wide balcony. As I climbed to the top and looked anxiously around, I finally saw Leila at the side of the pool that separated the hall and the balcony. I made my way slowly and finally got closer to her. She was wearing a shirt made of white satin trimmed with silver and a light blue shalwar. Her beautifully shaped, thin feet were bare. Her right ankle was encircled with a silver, chain-like bangle. The colors she had chosen highlighted her dark complexion.

Eventually she noticed me walking towards her, smiled and waved. Her thick, black hair hung loosely around her face, making the perfect backdrop for her silver, circular earrings. She seemed to have dressed differently tonight. I couldn't help but think it was all for me. Her beauty, mixed with my emotions made things even more complicated for me. I was pained by the way she underscored her uniqueness, both from jealousy and too much delight.

As we got close enough to speak, she said, "How are you, Adem!" showing her delicate white teeth once again. "Look, I'm laughing! Don't be upset! But you have to laugh too!"

Once I heard her words, my mind tripped upon itself, falling a few steps back. My body though, was struck numb as if bewitched. She seemed to know everything about me. However, her eyes, falling towards her nose like two blades, were sparkling with curiosity. Maybe it was because she had highlighted her eyes with eyeliner now, that their shapes had aroused my interest.

"Can you..." I grumbled, "read thoughts?"

"Did I guess correctly?" she mumbled modestly. "How nice! That makes me happy. But I still don't see you smiling?"

I laughed.

"All right! Now you're set!" she said.

Her voice had a strange effect on me. The tone was soft and mellow, her words a warm caress. Maybe this was exactly what I needed. Perhaps because we hear before we begin to see. She had spoken my name; my name had passed her mind, lungs, trachea, mouth and out of her scarlet-colored lips.

"You guessed right, yes!" I complained, "But I'm doomed if you're able to guess everything that goes on in my head."

Laughingly she asked, "Why doomed?" Then taking a more serious air, "There's no reason to feel doomed," she said. "Maybe I enjoy it too. Can you fathom that?"

"I hope so," I mumbled. "I'm not used to having my thoughts read. Back in my day, people didn't speak their mind. In fact, at times, even I may not have been aware of what I was thinking." I laughed. "So make sure you warn me if you sense anything odd!"

She laughed in response. Most of the places at the dinner table had been taken so we weren't able to sit together. The same group from last night were again present. It seemed I was slowly mixing with this entourage. I was pushing my way into their circle, but no one seemed to object.

We began a pleasant conversation anew, joking with each other as we ate. As I got to know the people, as their roles became clearer to me, it became easier to speak with them, to start new topics and simply to be with them. Although the food was as delicious as before, this time I did not feel very hungry. I barely touched any of it. I didn't drink any of the soporific sherbet this time either. I ate a little bit of the *mezes* on the table, along with some rakı and wine. Discreetly and as the opportunity arose, I tried to watch Leila. She tried to assist the robots serving us, where they had difficulties, as if they were alive, which pleased me. Once she placed a slice of bread on my plate after taking it from one of the waiters. When the desserts arrived, she cried out to me, "An extra portion is on its way! Want to share it with me?"

"Sure," I said. "Sounds good. I'm not really hungry anyway."

She began to slice the cake on her plate in half. I leaned over and took the smaller part onto my plate.

Music was this evening's after-dinner entertainment. Every one chose an instrument: lutes, reed flutes, zithers, darbukas... Someone thrust a tambourine into my hands. Thus we began to sing and play all together:

Bloody waters flow from my eyes looking at your rosy cheeks

O beloved, 'tis the season for roses, spring is nigh, rivers are misty

Before the song could come to a finish, Kasım broke in: "Stop! You're out of tune!"

Cheshminaz retorted: "I bet you've got the perfect ear, eh? No one's aware of it and we're having fun. Why don't you leave us alone?!"

"Can we not at least play something a bit happier, with more joy?"

"How about *Suddenly I may appear near you?*"

"Sure you may, Cheshminaz!"

"Oh, shush! I'm talking about the song."

"I meant jovial, not frightening, Cheshminaz!"

We laughed.

"Let's sing my song now!" interjected Leila.

They began to play again. This time the rhythm was faster. I tried to keep up with my tambourine. My eyes met Kasım's, who was playing the lute. With utmost seriousness I tilted my head sideways and both approvingly and with a greeting, nodded my head once. Kasım silently replied in the same vein.

I thought you were the light of my life.
Everyday without you turns dark, Leila.
Our parting has made me love-crazed,
My heart aches, I'm in dismay Leila.
Love is truly pure torment.

The afflicted become the talk of the town
Separation is worse than death
Those that leave do not return Leila.
My rose, and my leaf have dried up
My heart's mood is in the autumn
My whole life, destitute
Though she doesn't know it, o Leila!

As I sang along, I did everything I could not to meet Leila's eyes. As the rhythm picked up speed, she dropped the zither in her hand and stood up after tying her hair up on top of her head, revealing her elegant, bare neck. She moved to the stage next to the pool and began to belly dance. Like a voyeur, I mingled in with the crowd and watched her body sway to the rhythm. Although she moved under her loose shalwar and long-sleeve shirt, the curves of her gorgeous body still were revealed every now and then.

Eventually, the others also dropped their instruments and one by one, went to accompany Leila on the dance floor. I followed them as well, of course. As everything was somewhat easier with my new body, I was quite the dancer on the floor. We swayed together in harmony, to the same rhythm. Nobody was playing the instruments, but as they could play themselves, the music continued while everyone danced.

Once the song was over we returned to our seats. The rhythm had somewhat calmed down as well. In unison we sang, *'There's only you, there's your hair,'* and then went on to *'Your lips are like scarlet rosebuds.'*

When I thought of Leila with reference to the lyrics, which I hadn't done up to now, my heart almost skipped a beat. The alcohol I had drunk on an empty stomach must've also helped with the effect. I knew these feelings would be too much for me; I could sense the slow rise of a gigantic wave, but there was nothing I could do to stop it and it crashed onto my heart and left me breathless. I felt the ground beneath my feet being pulled away and I was left suspended in mid-air, after which I began to plunge but hadn't fully reached ground zero yet. In deep melancholy and heroic enthusiasm, my heart played hopscotch instead of beating. It seemed like only one day in paradise was enough to engender such emotions. Although I knew that falling in love took place in a split-second, I had never thought the feeling would be this intense. Perhaps all this was simply my soul in frenzy after going through solitude and death.

Hold still please,
Let's watch you once again
The departing may return
Or may not ever again
...
When you're not there, I have neither time nor space
Don't leave me stranded, alone amidst those storms
You're the only port of refuge I know

Then my thoughts drifted to those whom I had left behind. Just as fast I felt happy, now I felt like I was suddenly split into two, as though my insides were being torn to tatters. Like someone who had murdered their offspring, I felt as if I had betrayed pieces of me. Those whom I loved had used their right to live in a very distant, strange past and had disappeared, and I had totally forgotten them with the joy that paradise had kindled in me. How had I forgotten them so quickly? Once I couldn't live without them; I was concerned for them so... How had I become so indifferent? This was a cold feeling, like ice, like a silent or howling desert; as it indicated that we would all be eventually forgotten, or had been already.

However, realization wasn't always an easy load to carry. We had to forget and at long last, the fact that we had forgot, or had been forgotten, had to also be forgot.

How I loved thee, do you recall?
If I called from Aşiyan, would you hear me?
...
Don't trust your eyes, that's not me
Oh when you love me, that's when I'm me.

Tears welled up; I had to wipe them off with the back of my hand.

Suddenly all the songs stopped. With prudent but compassionate smiles, Leila held one of my hands and Kasım the other as they pulled me to my feet and walked me to the large marble balcony in the hall. We went out into the cool, dark air. Smiling faces adorned the balcony, while we were served amber-scented, silky coffee in ornamented porcelain cups. All the balconies of the palaces, the windows, promenades at the top of the high castle walls, the treetops were all full of denizens of paradise. Everyone watched the Bosporus. I too, imitated them. I rested my hands on the cool, marble railings designed as vines, and waited.

After some time, the ink-colored waters were illuminated with orange lights. Ships passing through the Bosporus lit their lanterns and became visible. The calm surface of the water reflected their lights like a giant mirror. Lanterns were hung suspended between the minarets of the mosques across the water where Arabic inscriptions were formed with oil lamps. Colorful paper lanterns were strung down the sides of the minarets, oil lamps were cast out to the sea from the castle walls and fireworks shot out from the ships... The crescent moon already looked like a lantern hung up in the air. Suddenly a noisy explosion from the castle walls on to my right made me jump. As I turned my gaze, I saw that a person was shot into the air with the speed of a bullet, all ablaze, then plunged deep down into the Bosporus. I shivered. As I tried to comprehend what was happening, Leila turned to me in joy, saying, "Look at that!" and pointing where the cannon had exploded. The she chuckled, "Do you see them? Ahhahaha!" There was indeed a queue of young people gathered at the cannon. They were waiting for their turn to climb into the barrel and be shot out into the open air.

"No way!" I grumbled.

"Oh, come on!" said Leila with a mischievous grin, knowing that she was forcing me to try something new again.

With a tilt of my head, I pointed at the Arabic script on the other side of the Bosporus and asked, "What's written there?" I had taken up a serious tone, emphasizing that I was trying to change the subject. Then I smiled.

"You mean the suspended writing?" she said.

"Yes, those words over there!"

"You mean the old ones!"

"What do they mean?"

She looked at the one far left and translated it for me.

"One says, *What they call true love, is that which doesn't exist!*"

Hearing the sentence plunged me deep in thoughts as I continued to watch the fireworks.

"What about the others?"

She read the rest one by one, probably because the words were written in large letters.

"*The...best...person...is the one...who knows that...true goodness is unattainable!* What does all this mean? A bit contradictory, right?"

"Don't know... There can't be anything worse than believing that a dream, no matter how beautiful, has actually been realized."

"But what if you can't accept that it's not real?" She looked at me with glazed eyes. Was she implying something? "What if you're hooked onto your dream?"

"If we think that the dream has already come true," I replied, "then we cannot realize that dream any longer."

"What if the realization of the dream is impossible, what if we don't know how to do it?"

"There could be a way!" I grumbled. "Since the dream is conceivable, perhaps we can invent a way, out of nothing."

"Things can get unbearable sometimes," she said.

"Yes!" I replied. With this we both fell into silence. She forced a smile, squeezing out the last drop of brightness from her melancholic eyes. Maybe it was just me, but seeing her force a smile like that pained me. I wondered what troubled her.

"Are you okay?" she asked.

"Yes, I'm fine!" I replied, "How about you?"

"I am too!" she gazed at me with her dimples spread out wide. In the cutest fashion, she tilted her head to the right. Then she turned towards the Bosporus and as if she tried to give an impression of joy, began to read the remaining sentences loudly.

"Those who do not want to know, may forget; those that don't want to see, should just close their own eyes!" *"We didn't become isolated; we just realized that we are alone."*

The people on the balcony had begun to go back inside. I looked at Leila and Kasım. As they joined the others, I followed suit. The only light inside the hall was the provided by the dancing flames of the fireplace. Once everyone had gone in and had sat down, one of the young girls began to recite the first chapter of the *1001 Nights*. As I had forgotten most of it, listening to it again sparked my interest. The sultan who had been cuckolded by his wife had had her and her lover decapitated, after which he asked his vizier to bring him a virgin girl every night. Once he had "deflowered" the girl, he would have her killed in the morning. "Do not heed the words of women, my friend. Laugh away all their promises, because their moods are determined by the desires of their genitals. They speak of love, but treachery embraces them and takes its form from the undulations of their garments. Remember respectfully, the words of Joseph. Do not forget that the devil used the woman to have Adam cast out of paradise!"

Once the country had been depleted of virgin girls, the vizier realized that he wouldn't be able to fulfill the sultan's wishes, and was terrified. The man had two daughters; the older one, Scheherazade, had seen her father's troubles and asked him to tell her. The girl had read thousands of books, was wise and spoke well. Once her father told her the problem, the girl hatched a plan and told her father that he should present her to the sultan. Although the vizier was adamantly against her plan, faced with her determination and the fact that he had no other choice, he complied with his daughter's wish.

The sultan was pleased and asked the vizier 'Is everything ready?' The vizier, bowing in respect, replied, "Yes!"

However, just as the sultan was about to possess the girl, she began to weep. When the sultan asked her what was wrong, the girl replied: "My eminence! I have a sister. I would've liked to say farewell to her!" Once the sister was summoned to the sultan's chambers, she embraced Scheherazade and then went to the corner of the bed and sat down. Then the sultan got up and took possession of Scheherazade, deflowering her virginity. Then they began to talk. The sister said to Scheherazade: "May Allah be with you! Dear sister, will you tell us a story so we pass the night in joy?" Scheherazade replied: "I will, with all my heart and the loyalty to my duty. Of course, with the permission of our benevolent and great sultan!" Upon hearing these words, the sultan, whose sleep had already left him, did not see any harm in listening to her tale.

Thus Scheherazade was able to put her plan into motion and chose a tale that triggered much curiosity, leaving the ending untold right as the sultan fell asleep. The sultan was so engrossed with the end of the tale that he did not have Scheherazade killed that morning and, having taken her again that night, wanted to hear the rest of the story. As desired, the girl finished her tale but straight away began to tell another, even more interesting tale. Her hope was that she could survive by playing this game each night.

The girl who recited the tale also stopped her narration at the most interesting part, like Scheherazade. Then with a smile, began to undress. As her buttons came undone and her silky gown dropped to the ground, her naked, smooth, dark body appeared from underneath. Her body was so youthful that as she let her clothes slide off, the sweet curvature of her limbs and her perfect legs and arms were fully motionless. Only her large breasts swayed slightly, as her shirt slid off her nipples. I was excited and aroused.

I looked around; others were also focussed on the naked storyteller but did not look surprised in the least. Once she was stark naked, they also began to undress. I did not know what to do. I was left there standing, frozen and staring at them all.

Laughing, the people all began to enter the pool separating the hall from the balcony. In joy, they began to bathe. Due to the alcohol, they all were happy and were fooling around in the water.

I was completely taken aback. On the one hand I was excited from what I was witnessing, but on the other, I was unable to accept that Leila was among them naked, though I knew this thought was egotistical. I felt my heart being scorched by flames of jealousy. My cheeks burned bright red. Instead of standing there and watching them, I decided the best thing to do was to avoid the whole scene. I turned around and, like an army that deserts the battlefield out of fear of total annihilation, left the hall without looking back.

***

For some time I wandered among the dark corridors, the mysterious chambers of the palace without an inkling as to where I was headed. There was no light save for the flickering candles placed in sooty lamps. I could barely see the next step. This journey into the unknown would've scared me, if I hadn't felt the fatal wound in my heart. But now, as I passed by all these dark places, I was comforted by the dangers I felt, sort of like when contemplating suicide. Unafraid, I pushed open giant doors ornamented with precious stones that held unfathomable dangers behind them, pushed down brass handles and turned huge, rusty keys. I opened all the silent chests I could find and rummaged inside, with the hope of uncovering some clue.

My mind was aflame; my thoughts jumping uncontrollably. I felt waves of emotions surging forth from the jealousy and love burning in my heart. I was nauseated and my chest felt too tight for my beating heart. I was away but who knows in whose arms Leila lay? It was as if I was trying to further distance myself from a desperately difficult problem, or a an incurable wound I tried to ignore.

Could I have invented it all? Or had I been carried away by a mistaken thought that Leila was also interested in me solely because I desired it to be so? I had imagined that our feelings were mutual and I had surmised that all her actions were an indication of this desire. It was truly painful to see that the line separating reciprocal love and madness could be so thin.

After half an hour of wandering aimlessly in the labyrinth made of corridors and rooms until lost, I felt some movement around me. There seemed to be something slithering in the dark corners. As I focused to figure out what this was, I noticed that ghostly garments and the dirty pots and pans were fluttering about the corridor. While wool shirts of all colors, vests, furs and robes were flitting in one direction in one side of the room, on the other slid plates, cups, pots and pans. Perhaps they were carried by the miniature, flying robots to their places like ants moving towards their lair. Then I began to smell food. The kitchen must've been somewhere close by and that was where the dirty pots and pans were headed. Curiously, I began to follow this bizarre current. Eventually, at the end of the corridor I arrived at a giant, ebony door. I hid behind the closed wing of the door and peered inside.

I saw a line of seven or eight giant stoves topped with copper chimney hoods. A jovial group of cooks were grilling meat on skewers over flames of coal. They wore bizarre hats made of a felt-like material. Underneath, probably in recognition of the intense temperatures, they wore loose shorts. Their hairy legs were exposed for all to see.

The cooked food was placed onto serving trays or large parcels and was placed onto the robots that were sent away to another door at the far end of the kitchen. Meanwhile, clay pots full of drink, bundles of vegetables and meat were carried up from a place below –most likely a cellar– that had stone stairs. The dirty dishes were carried to a corner of the kitchen that was out of my range of sight, where I imagined there were giant dishwashers.

As I watched this frantic work going on, I guess I had made myself rather conspicuous, because my eyes met those of a chef. He was a stocky young man, about my age. Instead of surprise, bizarrely he began to wave his hand to me. I could read from his lips that he was beckoning me to come. I wandered inside as if I had no other choice and approached the chef.

"Welcome brother," he said, "Are you hungry?"

"No! I said. "I'm not in the mood for food."

He picked up the lid of one of the ornamented pots and threw a dash of salt into the tomato-sauced mixture. Then with a smoke-stained metal pair of tongs he began to churn the hot coals.

"What troubles you?" he asked.

The flames on the stove heated my face. After I waited a while pondering what to say, "Am I being deceived?" I answered with a question. "Am I being had? Like a madman among a crowd who is disdained by others and is unaware of this fact?"

"Are you in love?" he asked.

"Yes!" I replied.

He went over to one of the wooden shelves nailed to the wall. The shelf was full of metal and wooden pots and pans, all ornamented with precious stones. He fetched two large tankards among the clutter and poured a thick, red liquid from one of the pots near the stove. He held the two tankards in each hand and banging them together, handed the one on the left to me.

"Let's drink!" he said, "Come on, tell me!"

Without asking what the liquid was, I took a large gulp. It was a sherbet that tasted of strawberries. As I spoke with sadness and excitement, I felt like I was going to vomit after each word I uttered.

"It's as if I have a fever!" I said, "I'm burning."

The cook nodded in understanding while he put some cracked wheat into a sieve and poured water onto it.

"Things change so quickly in one's mind!" I continued, "I feel like I'm falling off a cliff. As it was built on nothing, the whole building comes crumbling down in a heartbeat, with no one to blame but myself! I'm so ashamed! What kind of paradise is this anyway?"

"You're being dramatic!" he muttered as he brought out large, red onions from a straw basket. "Calm down! You're mistaken if you think she's not interested in you. Go calm down a bit, take a nap, tomorrow will be another day!"

The food in the cauldron had come to a boil. As I spoke with the cook, I had begun to regain a sense of joy and curiosity, perhaps due to the sweet sherbet.

"Are you preparing for the journey tomorrow?" I asked.

The young chef had peeled the skins off the onions and had begun to dice them on a cutting board.

"That too!" he replied, "dinner continues and then there is the breakfast tomorrow."

"Are you one of them too? One of the new people I mean..."

"Yes, of course."

"But you look different. Besides, the others are having fun upstairs..."

"It's my choice to stay down here. People have their own destiny to fulfill. This kitchen here is my paradise. I find happiness working here. Preparing things that others enjoy, seeing their happiness and accepting their compliments make me feel better."

"I think I understand. What's your name?

"Abdullah!"

He dumped the diced onions onto a small pan sitting on the bed of coals. They began to sizzle.

Suddenly I was swept with the urgent need to sleep. "Good Lord!" I mumbled. "What have you given me to drink?" Involuntarily I gave in and slumped forward though I didn't feel the fall. Soft hands had held onto me yet again.

"Will you be coming tomorrow too, Abdullah?" I barely mumbled.

"No!" he said. "My place is here."

"You should!" I said. "Come along! Please!"

"Maybe... In fact... I'd also like it... Let's talk it over... They will need someone to cook food anyway, right?"

"Exactly!... Now I have to sleep though. I have to get my strength back. I can't be weak! See you tomorrow."

I was carried to a room and laid onto a bed where I was covered with a soft blanket up to my nose. Then the doors were locked.

"He'll be safe!" I heard one say.

"He drank the sherbet anyway!" replied Abdullah.

3

I woke to a soft breeze lapping my face. The light was so bright that it felt like it pierced my eyelids. When I took in the scent of fresh air, I opened my eyes in surprise. I was lying on a bed with colorful linen set on grass in the middle of the palace garden. The garden was crowded with people all round, jovially preparing for the journey. The stone-paved concourse was full of camels mounted with gear and tall horse carriages that resembled walking castles. The carts had round lines, like those in fairy tales. In fact, they looked like huge eggs, placed vertically on top of large, wooden wheels. Some were pulled by stocky bulls, while some by Arabian horses with markings on their noses.

I felt extremely vigorous, perhaps because I had slept in the open air. Still it felt strange to be lying there asleep in all of this activity. I covered my face with my hands, rubbing my eyes as if I were trying to sober up.

"You awake?" asked somebody from behind me. I turned around and looked. It was the storyteller from yesterday, which took me by surprise. She was at my bedside, packing some clothes into leather bags. She began to fold a fur coat.

"You think we'll need this in summer?"

"It can get cold over there!" she replied. "It may even snow. We packed some fur caps too, see?"

"What is your name?"

"Gülşah."

"Nice to meet you."

"Likewise."

"Anything I can do to help, Gülşah?"

"No, we're almost done."

Kasım and Abdullah were dressed in warrior garb. Upon seeing that I had awoken, they approached me in a way that suited their attire, in single file and marching formation. They wore leather quivers and old fashioned, decorated rifles slung crisscrossed on their back. On their waists they carried blades and pistols, slung over sashes decorated with gold. On their feet, they wore hunter's boots.

"We donned our heroic armor!" they said and chuckled.

"Looks good," I replied. I guess they were well aware of the fact; they looked like they had come to show off their appearance.

"Do you guys know each other?" I asked.

"At least for a thousand years!" said Kasım. "Abdullah would never come to our promenades. It's not among his duties. But you seem to have convinced him to do so."

"We are to hunt monsters!" Abdullah jumped in. Then he pointed towards the garments and weaponry resting on the chair at the side of the bed and said, "You've got to dress up too!"

I rubbed my eyes and asked: "Don't you guys ever sleep?"

"This is how we are!" replied Kasım. "We party hard but recover quickly afterwards."

"I guess that's what you get for being a super-man!" I grumbled.

"What else would one want?" said Kasım.

I nodded in approval for a few times. Suddenly I heard Leila's delicate voice and inadvertently went all ears. She was talking to someone, somewhere behind me. So as to not show my feelings, I tried hard to not turn around. I fiddled with the clothes that were left for me: armor in a silver-like color, a black cape, a cutlass with a decorated sheathe...

"Heyyy, how are you?" said Leila. "Hellooo!"

I enjoyed the way she addressed me in elongated syllables as if she were talking to a close friend, a brother or a child. I turned around. Two sets of sad eyes met. She came to stand in front of me as I continued to sit. I wanted to grab her thin waist. It was as if she was trying to apologize for something, as if nothing had ever happened. Her gaze disclosed a curiosity as to what I was thinking. I tried to put a bold face on, though with a tinge of hurt that I felt, and smiled. It took only a few cute gestures from her to lower my colors. I had missed her. All the girls here were gorgeous but she shone bright like a star. It was extremely difficult not to show how much of an effect she had on me. However, I thought, there would always be a thin glaze over my eyes when I look at her from now on. Like neighboring countries' having an invasion plan at hand for when necessary, I was secretly getting ready to pull back if need be.

"You left yesterday?" she asked in reproach. Maybe she was disturbed about what I had been thinking. "Don't worry, ok?"

As if she hadn't gone stark naked in front of everyone, and hadn't fooled around with the whole crowd in a giant orgy...

"Listen, I'm obviously an old-fashioned man," I said. "I wasn't curious to see Kasım's wiener."

They chuckled. Then, as if they had decided before, they left me to my own devices for some time. I looked around for a place to change my clothes. Leila had gone into the crowd and joined the preparations. I watched her from afar as if I were watching myself. She was poking fun at others, saying things that didn't sound like they came from her mouth. Her sweet joie-de-vivre hurt me a little for some reason, perhaps because I thought her to be fragile. Like a bodyguard, I was ready to swear on my honor to preserve her happiness.

It took about an hour to complete all the preparations. Suddenly an announcement to set out was given. I mounted one of the chariots using the ladder on the side and settled onto comfortable cushions that lay in one corner. Then I peered through the curtains to look outside. I was perched quite high. This caused in me both a sense of security and a pleasant shiver. Looking down I could see our escorts mounting their horses. An excitement not unlike that which I felt as we set on vacation with my family enveloped me. Then my buddies joined me. I was keeping a slight distance from them out of pride but they didn't leave me alone.

"Off we go!" said Abdullah as he clapped in excitement.

"My, he's happy!" said Leila and leaned over to pinch Abdullah's cheek.

As our chariot began to move with a jerk, I looked outside. We were now being followed by hound dogs whose job was to guard the convoy. Flocks of predatory birds descended from above and perched on the chariots, camels, and the arms of the cavalry troops. The Janissary members began to beat out and sing a war song as if we were setting out on a siege:

The head of the column's white horse o,
Is rearing up yet again
Oh dear, again I'm spent,
Our path will lead us to the border
(---)
Rosy-faced beloveds too,

We love them by cajoling
Oh dear sons of soldiers,
Can't go without campaigns.

"Look what I'm going to show you!" said Leila. Then digging into her bag, she took out an old book whose pages were falling apart.

"What is this?" I asked.

"Your book!" she said.

I was shocked and excited.

"Really? Has it been printed then?"

"Yes."

I took the book and began to inspect its cover, the pages, and the words printed on its back cover.

"How did this survive until today?" I asked, panting in excitement. "Where did you find this?"

"At the library," she said. "They preserve old books there."

I think she was happy to have cheered me up. For this, I felt even more drawn to her, even more in love and grateful... I smiled; I didn't know what else to do. I didn't have the courage to turn the pages. "Thank you," I said and drawing her closer, planted a kiss on her cheeks and wrapped one arm around her waist. Then, pulling back, I asked: "Have you read it?"

"Yes," she said. "In fact..."

"In fact what?"

"I had read it before."

"How much before?"

"Before I met you..."

I was taken aback.

"Before we met?... Did you like it then?"

"Yes, it is really good. I do like it."

Our strange convoy set its course towards the rising sun.

After being so far away from paradise, the return was too beautiful for words. Again I thought that everything was actually really wonderful and that I would never again encounter anything bad. The clouds on the horizon had enveloped the sun in a way that made the rays peer out from below, with a curtain that was smoky black above and that gave us the sensation of moving towards a magnificent burning pyre.

* * *

Our shadows chased us from behind as we moved by Istanbul's steeped roofs, spired gates and stone fortresses, the last buildings of the city. We eventually found ourselves in a colorful rural area that seemed to have jumped from a painter's canvas. Farmers handling strange machinery were tilling farms and orchards; healthy livestock grazed in open fields.

This was the first time that Leila and I were so physically close to one another. My left and her right sides touched the lengths of our bodies. I felt the outline of her curvaceous body on my legs and shoulders. Her softness and warmth tore through our clothing, inspiring in me a serene excitement, and draining me of life's distresses, comforting me. It was as if two corresponding pieces of nature had finally found each other and had re-connected.

"Your eyes disclose sadness at times," I said suddenly.

She blushed a little.

"This place is a paradise..." I continued, "but you look troubled from time to time. Or maybe it's me. What do you think?"

"When have I looked troubled for instance?" she asked, seemingly trying to gain some time.

"Well, when I first saw you on the road... Then the other night..."

179

I suddenly noticed that my questions might be sounding a bit bizarre and perhaps a bit intrusive even, so I blushed back.

"No, what I meant is..." I said, changing the tone of my voice and letting out a small chuckle, "Is there something that should be troubling? I'm just afraid!"

She bowed her head down as if she wanted to hide it and quietly let out an spurt of joyful laughter. This cheered me up.

Meanwhile someone's guard dog had noticed the convoy and, barking loudly, had begun to follow us. From this safe spot he looked more amusing and cute than hostile. Upon hearing his barking, the farmers on the fields noticed us and turned towards the convoy, waving their hands. Then, resting on their sickles and rakes, they watched us as we moved on.

Abdullah asked, "So are there giants in these areas?" he asked. His tone revealed joy mixed with anxiety.

"Of course there are," said Cheshminaz, "These are fairy tale lands!"

"How about thumblings?" I asked.

"Homunculi! Yes, little people; they exist too. We might even see some."

As I watched the flower gardens that we were passing through, from the window of the cart, I grumbled, "Homunculi eh?"

Some peasant girls ran towards our chariot, their arms laden with baskets full of daisies and violets. They caught up with us and gifted us the flowers, as if we had entered a country that we had just liberated. We thanked them and took as many as we could fit in the chariot and began to place them wherever space permitted. I felt a warm halo of affection surrounding us though I didn't know the reason; I tried to enjoy the sensation rather than questioning it. We barely had room to sit amongst all the flowers.

Kasım was examining my book. He pulled himself out of the pages, looked around in discomfort and grumbled, "It's as if we're stowaways in a flower wagon." I laughed.

In the meantime, Abdullah had begun to play she loves me she-loves-me-not with one of the daisies.

"She loves me, she loves me not, she loves me, she loves me not..." Eventually he threw out the now leafless stem of the daisy. "This'll drive a man mad!" he groaned.

Smiling in mischief, Leila asked: "Whom are you playing the game for now?"

Abdullah pondered the question then said, "For Kasım of course!" We all chuckled.

While I was with them, I noticed how much I actually enjoyed spending time with others and joking around. The natural surroundings also assuaged a certain sense of homesickness I had been feeling. The valley we were passing through was covered in carpet-like green grass and beautifully shaped trees. As I looked around, I began to slowly feel tipsy from the scenery.

"I think, I was just excited," whispered Leila, suddenly. I was taken aback at first because I had forgotten I was awaiting a response, perhaps due to the fact that at that moment, asking questions felt more important than actually receiving answers. "I was trying to make it to the games that day, remember?" she completed. Now I had recalled what we had spoken of.

A silence ensued for some time. I concluded that she felt a bit upset for trying to avoid my question. She bent towards me lightly, bowing her head a little and said, as if confiding in me a secret, "Sometimes... I do not know what the truth is! The truth switches places with the lies in my head."

I had no idea as to how I should respond to this disclosure. When it came to "reality" I felt at such a loss...

"But you kind of enjoy this as well, no?" she mumbled with a

181

smile. "I mean, seeing a pessimistic side in me, just like you have... For thinking alike..."

I laughed as I recalled what I had thought about just a few minutes ago. "Could be," I responded. I liked how she read my thoughts too... "But it upsets me too..."

"You egoist!"

"It's hard to find anything that isn't egotistical though, don't you think?"

"It is. You're right."

As she spoke, she slowly turned towards me. "You were saying the other day..." she said, "'The worst is to think that your dream has come true...' That is so true."

As she spoke, I fell under her spell, watching her shapely eyebrows, her noble nose ridge, and her succulent, glossy lips. I was basking in the pleasure her sight offered me.

"How is it you came about?" I asked.

"What do you mean?"

"The way you are!"

From where I sat, the color of her eyes had a different hue. As she sat facing the sun, her eyes had taken on a sparkling purple. Her skin seemed to have adopted a hue that matched her eyes as well. Leila was in constant metamorphosis, though her essence remained intact. Therefore I was not surprised as much as I should have been. It was like when, in a dream, you regard a face as being the face of another, or how in a TV drama one –somehow– gets used to a character changing actors.

Kasım had finished examining my book. He bent forward and with strength, squeezed my right shoulder with his left hand. "It looks great!" he said, though I just perused through it, reading a few sentences only, out of curiosity. I do want to read it from front to back one day though." At the same time, he dropped the volume into Leila's lap.

"Thanks," I mumbled. I felt proud and smiled. "Now I'm really curious as to what I have written." Leila handed the book over to me. "Do you want it?" she asked in the sweetest voice. "Will you read it?" I made a move forward and held her hands holding the volume. We sat there together, perusing the pages. The pages looked extremely antiquated. Hundreds of thousands of years had passed of course. If it weren't for the warmth issuing from the small, dainty hands I was holding, I could've succumbed to melancholy. Instead, I felt the utmost joy.

"I wonder how many read it so far?" I grumbled.

"Not just a few!" she said.

I was taken aback. "How do you know?

She laughed.

"I did my research," she answered. She had her legs crossed and was almost squeezing me into a corner. As I tried to sit upright, my foot touched hers. "Sorry," I said. She said nothing; neither did she pull her foot back. This, I really liked.

Suddenly I imagined us two, together in bed, naked. My heartbeat picked up such speed that I swooned; I had to gulp.

Cheshminaz proposed we play a game to pass time. She insisted we all join in. So we split into two teams and began playing a word game. As Leila and I were sitting side by side, we ended up in the same team. Since we were able to think similarly, we made a good duo. We were able to decipher right away what each of us was thinking through our jests and movements. Our rivals couldn't stand in our way. As I whispered words into her ear, I felt the warmth emanating from her hair. At one point, she touched my lips with two fingers motioning me to shush and the touch remained there as if suspended.

Then Abdullah impersonated a drag queen and amused us a little. Although I felt that we were being silly, because the others were so cheerful and childlike I was also able to chime in and derive pleasure from these games. Perhaps they all thought similarly but I guess the point was to be together after all. What really made us happy and gave way to laughter was feeling a part of something. Once many people unanimously agreed on the same game and fantasy, albeit a lie, the fantasy could very well be taken as reality.

We continued in this vein until late afternoon when the convoy stopped for a rest. We ate at a hearty, rich table set in the middle of the forest and also drank a little before again setting off on our way. As the others slowly fell into a slumber in the chariot, I was finally able to concentrate on my book. Reading my own words, some of the sentences gave me pleasure, while the others gave me a sense of deep shame. Suddenly, without knowing exactly why, I turned towards Leila. Maybe I had felt her eyes on me by instinct. I had caught her; she had opened her eyes and was staring at me. Before she blushed and dropped back into her sleep, I was able to catch the admiration in her soft, sparkling eyes. It was as if she worshipped me, although it should've been me worshipping her. Her strange behavior, an anxiety that I caught a glimpse of every now and then, maybe an inkling of passion... Could she really be in love with me? Could it really be true? It was hard for me believe it because if I did, and it turned out to be untrue, I feared this would lead me to a bottomless, unendurable disappointment, after which a man could find himself stuck amidst a load of lies.

When I heard some yelling and tremors, I stuck my head out from the window to see what was going on. We were passing over a cobblestoned old bridge. Below flowed a river whose waters were as scarlet as blood. The yelling I had heard previously came from a heavily built, dark warrior who guarded the bridge.

"Who are you people?" he asked in utmost seriousness as he saw me.

I looked back inside the cart but everyone was asleep.

"I'm not really sure myself!" I replied. "Who are you?"

"Dumrul!" he said.

"Dumrul the Mad?" I said in wonder.

"Whoa there! You're the one who's mad!"

"Pardon me! It's just because we know of you in that manner... May we pass, Dumrul? We're on our way to Cappadocia."

"For what reason?"

"None."

"What do you mean none? Who travels for no reason?"

"I guess you're right... Let's just say for recreational purposes... A promenade, like."

"You're entering dangerous territory!"

"Apparently so."

"I haven't even allowed the Grim Reaper to pass by this bridge!"

"That's what they tell me! Very brave of you! How's your wife?"

"Good."

"You're lucky to have a spouse like she!"

"I know."

"Was she angry at you?"

"What for?"

"For asking for her life so you could save yourself?"

Dumrul was infuriated. He obviously didn't like to be reminded of this affair.

"I apologize!" I said. "I had a wife like her as well once! She would've died for me! I don't think anybody else would die for me like she would!"

"What happened to her?" he asked. I think now he had calmed down a little.

"She decided to stop loving me," I said. "Or maybe I was

fooling myself into thinking she actually ever loved me. So either her love, or the mirage of her love... Whatever it was, I lost it."

"You probably deserved it," he said.

"That may be so, but you deserved even worse! Why does your wife still love you anyway? Is she obligated to do so? Tell her to stop!"

"Is that what one should tell a lady?" he rebuked.

"Then..." I said, "let us pass."

After a while of thinking, "You..." he said. "You're cursed aren't you?" Then he stepped aside, letting us pass.

I had begun to weep but as the chariot began to move, the others woke up and I hurriedly brushed my tears away.

"Who were you talking to?" asked Leila, still sleepy.

"Dumrul the Mad!" I said. "He was guarding the bridge!"

"Oh! Are you upset? Don't be!"

She touched my cheek with her hand then pulled it back. Her touch was healing. I took her by the wrist, squeezed it, and then let it go.

As the convoy passed the bridge, I saw a number of fallow deer grazing on the side of the road scurry into the pine forest. As I tried to hold my gaze on them as they tramped into the forest, I suddenly recoiled seeing a troop of cavalry waiting in hiding.

"There are cavalry out there!" I whispered.

"Where?" asked Leila bending towards me.

I showed her the troops in the woods.

"Köroğlu!" she said.

The evening had begun to fall. Rocks, leaves all glittered like they had been varnished.

"They're not thieves, are they?" asked Kasım.

"No!" said Leila.

The others had woken up and were also now peering out of the window.

The troops in hiding were a band of light cavalry, dressed in white shirts and red sashes, carrying rifles. Accompanied by the wind that shook the leaves and weeds, the hundreds of warriors suddenly took off in a gallop towards the mountains, like a migrant flock.

Cheshminaz began to sing a folksong:

Meandering in the orchards of Gesi
Lost my beloved, been looking all over
Placed my trust on a hello she might've given
Come sit a while. Let me tell you of myself.
What sort of lover is this, ignorant of my troubles!

I have three roses in the orchards of Gesi
You with no fear of God, know that death awaits us both
If death does exist, then a tyrant is this world
Oh mother, don't cast me beyond mountains!
I only want my mother to weep for me, no one else.

May all pass by the orchards of Gesi
May tables be spread, rakı, cognac be drunk
May everyone take their beloved and embrace in a corner.
Come sit a while. Let me tell you of myself.
What sort of lover is this, ignorant of my troubles?

We all applauded when she finished singing this haunting song. We still wanted more songs however, so we sang a few more in unison, until we dropped silent with fatigue.

The sun had gone down and the shadows had grown lean. Leila sat next to me but I couldn't find words to say to her anymore. All I felt like telling her was my declaration of my love.

We had to find a way to be alone again, someway or another. Not only so I could open up, but also so I could talk to her to my heart's pleasure. I did not know if I had to plan or arrange things. Was there really a destiny that we could submit ourselves to?

In fact, so far I was content with the imaginary world that I lived in which made me feel good even if for a short while and I feared it would topple down. Whatever the case may be, what I had been seeing was still just a dream; nothing about a person could be considered proven with such little data at hand. Implications always harbored a sliver of indeterminacy, a route for escape. In effect, this was a part of my generations' flirting game; we couldn't imagine it otherwise, to the point we found it displeasing when lacking. I thought, *what you sometimes tell me with your eyes is enough, even if it may be an illusion I myself created.*

Eventually, albeit half-heartedly, I began to peruse the pages of my book again... I was kind of curious to tell the truth; curious to see its pages, print, what was written on the writer's biography, the introduction and the epilogue, though I didn't want stories to steal from life's reality anymore. Words were mere images and could only signify as much as they reflected reality. They were only valuable insofar as they were read, understood, talked about and augmented the facts. This is why they shouldn't be separated from their homeland, the concrete world and people. They should never cast a shadow on truth and others by way of an illusion.

"It's rather late!" said Leila suddenly.

"Yes!" I mumbled back.

"Do you like the darkness?"

"I do, how about you?"

"I do too! We must both be vampires! Tee-hee-hee!"

I smiled. Her interest, a few words from her mouth, her sweetness could rejuvenate me immediately. I felt like my life was saved.

"It's very quiet!" I said. "I guess there are no bugs here, are there?"

"None!"

I nodded.

"Actually..." she began as she pointed to my book, "I wanted to discuss your book with you but the opportunity never arrived!"

"Oh we'll get to talk about it," I said, allusively.

Then we heard steel rattling. Those who sat by the windows of the carts were sticking their hands out and pulling down the steel blinds.

"Is this protection from the monsters?" I asked.

"Yes," said Leila, "Time for bed!"

"There are also humans who were turned into animals by witches of course!" added Kasım, "Half-animals, or half-humans... Bandits."

I was rather taken aback. "Can they attack us? Cause us harm?"

"A small possibility!" said Leila, "But yes, they may."

"Excellent!" grumbled Abdullah with an infantile joy.

"Let's go to sleep!" said Kasım, "Tomorrow will be a tiring day!"

"Really?" I grumbled back. "How come?"

"No, man! Just kidding!" he responded in laughter.

I laughed back. Then they each curled up in their corner and went to sleep, one by one. As night fell completely, I was the only one left awake. In the meantime, our chariot continued its path on its own. Staring at the dark lands as we passed by, I was more excited than afraid. These giants and wild monsters, coupled with love, were making me enthusiastic. *Let the bandits attack the caravan*, I thought insanely, *I could die protecting Leila, oh what bliss!*

She was sleeping next to me. I hoped that her head would fall on my shoulder. Maybe she'd like that too. The pleasure I felt from being in the situation I was in made me stave off sleep, just like a child refusing to go to sleep. A full moon was on the rise and the stars were plentiful in the sky. Like ancient peoples, I tried to make out meaningful shapes and patterns while watching them. As my eyelids slowly drooped, a large, white bird was circling us up high. *The phoenix,* I though dreamily as I fell into slumber, so much so that I might've just mumbled it as if asleep.

* * *

Before dawn, I woke up this time before everyone. I always went insomniac when in love, but this time it was an odd nightmare that had awoken me. I dreamed that all contrasts and colors had disappeared and the whole world resembled a giant, grey heap of debris. It had turned into a void; a solitary, empty, insignificant desert. I had gone blind and couldn't find my way around any longer. It took me a while to shake off its effects once I had awoken.

Even though the day had begun to rise, the hills we passed through were still pitch dark and their ridges were so round and proper that they could've easily been mistaken for giant, sleeping beasts. As the navy blue light of day rose in the horizon, I began to make out the faded bushes that covered the ridges not unlike a sparse beard. Among the greenery I could see the marble-like stone that had a skin-like hue of pink and white. The full moon had almost descended out of view but kept on shining like a weak oil lamp.

We must've made it into the inner regions of Anatolia. We were heading faster than I thought. It's as if we were on a theatre stage and had gone for hundreds of miles in a few steps. Nobody questioned it either; just took it for granted. *We've arrived,* we'd say and we'd be there.

The sun shattered the darkness, breaking it into pieces here and there, before swallowing it up completely. I felt a sense of affinity with the nature around me. Surrounded by these rocky ridges, it was as if I had come close to something that I had once loved dearly, then forgotten. I wanted to re-unite, get enmeshed in it, melt and become one again.

Leila slept next to me. I felt a sense of excitement, as if my heart was touched on the inside. Her innocent, blond head was tilted a bit to the right, and had fallen onto her sweet bosom. Her warmth made me realize how cold I had felt. I sighed and looked away at the rocky ridges. We were passing through a valley whose ridge ascended in steps.

Then came the birdsongs; the birds had also awoken. I wanted to wake everyone up. I was feeling as if among siblings after a very long time.

Eventually I couldn't bear it any longer and started grumbling: "Come on, wake up! You used to be so perky, what's happened now?"

Like beasts of the fields, they uttered discontented grunts. As they were still asleep, one could posit they hadn't turned human yet anyway.

"Oh, geez!" mumbled Abdullah.

Leila awoke smiling and said "Good morning!" Right away she started to gather together her disheveled hair.

They dove into their bags and brought out some food, which we all shared as one. I, though, wasn't really feeling hungry. It was if I didn't need food any longer; my feelings seemed to have fulfilled all my requirements. As I chatted with my companions, I also continued to look out at the landscape through which we were passing. I saw that they took the pieces of food I had taken bites from, and ate them without hesitation; I sort of found this pleasant, but didn't let them know.

The horizon was covered in clouds and we were surrounded

by bizarre stone monuments that rose up in the air. It was as if we were in an abandoned sculptor's workshop. I took a sudden pause, though, when I saw a large, malformed head bobbing up and down among these monuments. A gigantic creature was walking besides us as if accompanying the convoy.

I turned to Cheshminaz and trembling, said: "Did you see that?"

"There's a giant, yes!" she replied calmly.

I had turned around in the chariot to see the others reaction when I heard Leila say, "Watch it!" with a nervous expression.

As I turned my head towards the window I shuddered as I noticed that the creature had drawn closer to us. Its face was at the level of our window and it was so big that it covered our whole sight. I would've screamed if I hadn't been able to restrain myself.

The giant mumbled incomprehensibly out of his distorted mouth as if ruminating. I think he was trying to tell me something.

"He's saying he's got a house beyond the hill," said Kasım. "He's inviting you for a dinner of lamb. Says he has three daughters, one of whom he will present to you."

"Don't believe him!" said Cheshminaz, "He's trying to lure you into a trap! The lamb he'll eat is you!"

"Begone ye demon!" yelled Abdullah, "You go and devour yourself why don't you!"

The creature replied in grunts.

"What's he saying?" I said.

"'And I'll show you a hell of a time!' he says," replied Leila. "Just ignore the beast!"

"I'm not doing anything!"

The giant could've easily tipped the chariot over by leaning on it just a little, but decided to stop following the convoy. Thus we left him behind as the convoy progressed. I stuck my head out of the window a little and looked behind. He was watching me with fearful and hungry eyes.

"Don't be upset for him!" said Kasım. "Why are yo sad?"

I sat in my seat and leaned backwards, staying put for a while. I was shaking. I tried to calm myself down. From where I sat, I could only see the clouds behind the hills. They too were formless like the ridges and triggered the imagination.

In a few minutes my pulse went back to normal. In fact the tremors of the chariot on the road had begun to make me drowsy. As I thought a nap would do me good, I did not struggle against my drooping eyelids.

I had probably slept around two hours when I felt the chariot stop and I opened my eyes.

"We're here!" they said. "This is the place!"

I watched them pack up their bags and joyfully descend from the carts one after the other.

"Come on!" said Leila, "we're off!"

I tried to smile and nodded my sleepy head. Then I glanced outside and, taking a deep breath, rose from where I had been sitting. We were on a flat stretch of land with a giant tree rising in its middle. The top of the tree looked like a hemisphere and was dense in foliage and red fruits. This gigantic mass cast a cool shadow that extended a few acres. Large tents made of red baize with brocaded fringes had been pitched in the shadows afforded by the tree and the entire tented area had been enclosed by tall fences draped with hand-woven rugs embellished with geometrical shapes. Thus was a strange, small fort; a barracks as it were, just for us.

Potato and wheat fields surrounded the arid plain on three sides. On the last side lay a canyon, a cleft that formed a natural border, from which I could make out the tips of poplar and willow trees.

Those in the convoy had immediately spread out over the plains, like kids difficult to control. Some drank from the fountains at the base of the tree, while others wandered among the tents, or chose to recline lazily on the rugs spread out on the ground. I too, took refuge under the ancient tree's shadows and began to wander around the camp. Wooden tables and grills were being set up in front of the tents. I strode the area for some time with my head down. Then I quickened my pace and joined my friends in the tent in which they had all congregated.

Inside, Abdullah lay on one of the beds placed in the corners. The others were gathering up strength, sitting on the rug-covered ground and sipping wine. In one of the farthest corners of tent were baskets full of fresh fruits and vegetables. Leila had let her hair down. She looked simply beautiful.

"Are we a herd?" I grumbled. "Are they fattening us? Will they butcher us?"

They laughed but did not persist for long, as I maintained my seriousness. I think I might've been having a small nervous breakdown.

"What are we supposed to do here?" I asked.

"First we rest a little!" said Kasım sympathetically. "Then we prepare and go out to hunt altogether! We'll draw nets between the valley walls and chase the creatures towards them."

"What sort of creatures are we talking about?"

"Evil ones!"

What they were saying was frightening and vague. Besides, I hadn't killed any creatures, except perhaps plants and bugs up to then and didn't plan on doing so, unless I had to.

"I don't think I want to go hunting!" I complained.

"Don't worry. You can remain in the background for now, then!"

"I'll go to the other side of the valley!" I said, "Who planned this trip anyway? Let's do something spontaneous. Come on, let's discover the area on foot!"

"Yaaay!" lunged Leila.

"There's nothing to discover!" said Kasım, "It ends after a while!"

"What ends?"

"The world!"

I was aghast.

"What is this?" I asked laughing nervously. "Has the world gone back to being flat?"

Abdullah laughed.

"The new world ends!" said Kasım, with a stress on the second word.

I was getting excited.

"Great!" I exclaimed. "Let's go see the old world then!"

"There's nothing there to see! Besides it's not really safe."

"How do you know?"

"That's what they say!"

"You've never been?"

"No, we have never gone there. Nor have we the need to..."

"We'll be back before dusk!"

"I wouldn't advise on going Adem!" said Cheshminaz, "Please! It's dangerous!"

"I'm curious. And you don't know much either. Who knows for how many years you've trod on the same path. A thousand? A hundred-thousand?"

Nobody, save Leila, looked interested. In fact they looked a little scared. This was the first time they were resisting such a proposal. Considering their calm when we had encountered the giant, this felt even more bizarre. However, I wasn't going to stop insisting. Besides, here was a chance to be alone with Leila once again. Gulping, I awaited their reaction.

"Fine, we can't stop you anyway!" grumbled Kasım. "You're a free man. It's up to you! But don't drag us down with you!"

"Never mind them!" said Leila. "Let's go, just the two of us!" she said and sprang up on her feet.

Everything was moving according to plan. I tried hard not to put on a wide grin and mumbled, "Come on then!" I didn't want to speak so much lest my beating heart's noise would escape my lips. Besides I did not know if I could utter anything else apart from what I had just said. I nodded over to the door, Leila responded likewise and we moved towards it together. I let her pass before me as I lifted the tent's flap.

"Are you guys insane?" yelled Abdullah from where he lay.

"I guess we are!" said Leila, laughing.

"Take something warm with you! It gets cold at night!"

"This vest is quite enough!"

"Right, fine, do whatever the hell you want! Just come back in one piece!"

"Take some water with you!" said Kasım.

Laughingly I dropped the tent's flap. I held my smile in place and looked over at Leila. She smiled back. Together, we walked towards the fences, passed them and headed towards the deep canyon. Someone was singing a song behind us, like voicing a requiem.

Haven't laughed since we departed, friend
Without you, possessions mean nothing friend.

The voice became indistinct, as we got further away from camp.

"All right then!" I said to Leila, "We're off!"

I was almost tongue-tied. Nothing else had come to mind anyway. Maybe because the last thing I wanted to do was talk then but to make love, oh to make dear love, right then and there.

"Let's go then!" She replied.

The rift on the eastern part of the plain was deeper than I had thought. The poplar trees whose tips one could barely see from camp must've been at least 100 yards tall. Thin trees, they leaned against the ridge, and rose straight up into the air. Below them were lines of yellow reeds that grew among a slowly moving shallow brook. The trees' thin leaves swayed in the wind and, thanks to the various tones of each leaf, they looked as if they were covered with sparkling lights.

The valley was deep but since we were determined, we easily descended by helping each other. We were thus able to climb to the other side in about half an hour. When we reached the high point, I pulled Leila up, catching her by her right wrist. In front of us lay a vast bed of multi-colored, multi-formed rock that stretched all the way to the horizon. Far off into the distance we could see the outlines of a magnificent mountain, just barely visible due to the distance. "Is that Mount Argaeus?" I asked pointing towards the mountain.

"No!" she replied, "It's Mount Kaf!"

"Shall we go?" I said, smiling.

"Let's," she replied.

Fire and gunpowder together, we marched jovially towards uncertainty.

4

The deserted plain was covered in thorns. I felt as if the sun's rays were looking over us. My instincts told me that the light was safe.

The rocks' outlines appeared mostly soft, like kneaded dough or ice cream, and their surface were smooth as marble. Some of the rock formations looked like someone or something had stretched and elongated them by pulling on them from opposite sides. It was as if these thick strains had been stacked and cooked into a solid mass. Only by touch was I able to ascertain how hard they were, despite their smooth and soft appearance. At some point in prehistory they must have actually melted and then had suddenly all hardened. Maybe it was a volcano eruption that did this, or the remains of a horrible battle, who knows?

After a while, we found ourselves in the midst of a spooky fairy tale forest full of fairy chimneys that were 30-40 yards tall.

"Some say they are soldiers turned into stone," said Leila. "See their helmets? The heads?"

"Well why were they turned into stone?" I asked full of curiosity.

"Because they came here to invade this place!"

We passed newly forming pillars that jutted out on the side of a flesh-colored hill. Pieces that had broken off from the main rock forming new monuments had lined up, spanning from the complete columns to the newly forming ones.

"Look!" I said. "See how they are formed..."

She lifted her head and shielding her eyes with her right hand, started investigating the spot I had pointed out to her. She had let her long, fair hair, dripping with sweat, down and was straightening out the ends with her free hand, as if she was trying to flatten the waves on her head. Her silken, white blouse revealed her midriff. I looked at the smooth, dark skin of her thin waist. Her beauty was too much, too perfect.

Although being alone meant I could take this chance to open up to her, I didn't like the fact that we were so far away from the others; and I didn't want to scare her while trying to get more intimate. If she saw me as a brother or a friend, my coming on to her could destroy any trust she had in me. I suddenly became nauseous and covering my mouth discreetly with my right hand, I tried not to gag.

"They're soldiers!" insisted Leila, laughing. "Soldiers turned to stone!"

I laughed. "You're right!" I said. "But this fact is so upsetting that I can't accept it and have to create other excuses!"

We kept on walking. I was able to wade through the thorn-covered plains easily, without bruising my legs or feeling any pain. I didn't feel tired one little bit either.

"Look!" I showed Leila, "Hyacinths!"

"They're gorgeous!"

"Do you know their story?"

"I don't!" she replied eyes agape.

"There was once this king who had a beautiful son called Hyakinthos. Apollo was in love with the boy; they used to throw discs together on grassy plains... Now I'm not really sure what the disc-throwing really implies..."

She laughed.

"Anyway, let me not lose the thread of the story. One day when they're playing again..."

Leila started laughing again.

"Ok well, here they are again, throwing discs... However, a wind called Zephyrus also was in love with Hyakinthos and was very jealous of the two. So, Zephyrus can't stand it anymore and makes one of Apollo's discs strike the boy's head."

"My goodness! Does he die?"

I nodded.

"So there's blood pouring out of his nose and out of the wound on his head. Upon seeing him Apollo says..."

"What?"

"Oh you beautiful boy, he says, I murdered your youth with my own hands. Since I can't join you in the grave, I will make you immortal like myself. You will turn into a flower and thus live on! Whenever I draw closer to the earth, in spring, you will point your head out of the ground. I will caress you with my rays..." So it was that Hyakinthos became the hyacinth and has been so ever since that day."

As I approached the stories' end I became a bit sad myself. When I finished, Leila said nothing. As we were walking I was looking carefully at the path we were on, but I suddenly became curious and turned around. She was crying.

I touched her shoulder, "Look!" I said to cheer her up, "at least since the disc is able to kill the boy, it can't be a metaphor eh?"

She laughed, or feigned laughing so as not to upset me.

Then we gossiped about the others we had left behind. "Abdullah's a funny chap!" we said. "So glad he came along too!" she said.

"I wonder what they're up to?" I grumbled. "What is this business with the hunt?"

She told me that what they actually hunted were all robots. "It's really fun!" she said. "Like a war game... You see... Remember the giant?"

"Yes?"

"That was also a robot!" she laughed. "A toy! We just didn't tell you so we could scare you a little!"

"Well, I would've been afraid even if you had told me it was a robot!"

"But it's benign, see! I'm telling you they're all toys."

"I get it," I replied.

We were moving our arms a bit too much while talking, as if we wanted to embrace each other with them. After some minutes of silent trekking, I began to feel a cool breeze. The flora around us had become denser as well.

"Remind me," she said, "to take you somewhere really nice once we're back in the city. I'm sure you'll love it!"

"Now I'm curious!" I grumbled.

"Surprise surprise!" she said flirtatiously.

"All right!" I said.

"Remind me though! Don't forget!"

I laughed. "I can't!" I replied and turned towards Mount Kaf. It still was quite afar. We hadn't even gone halfway yet.

"How about..." I said, "How about after it? Does the playground end there?"

"I guess," she murmured. "I don't know what lies beyond, so..."

I wanted to reach the mountain as soon as possible. Like an obsession, I had somehow tied it all to this goal. I even thought of declaring my love of Leila, screaming down its cliffs. Maybe I was just looking for reasons for my silence.

"Remember," I said, "the time we flew with you... In Istanbul... Can't we fly over there again?"

"We never flew!" she replied.

I was agape.

"It was a metaphorical scene!" she explained, laughing as if she had told a joke.

I laughed along and did not insist on soliciting a more serious answer. It was already beautiful to be walking alongside her. Our progress was heroic, in unity. A veil covered all problems; the darkness dissipated. Again, I felt like the protagonist of a story.

"Isn't it nice?" asked Leila looking around.

"The surroundings right?" I asked. "Yes, it is."

"No!" she said, "The fact that we're walking together like this!"

At times like these, I couldn't be sure if it was she or I talking. I wanted to embrace her. I didn't think she'd object. I was going to do it. I felt the thrill of being on the verge of diving into lucid, deep waters at the tip of a cliff.

We arrived at the top of an area that resembled a pyramid made of stone. A clump of weeds and a solitary mulberry tree had pushed their ways out of the stony ground. The tree was wet.

Suddenly a brisk wind picked up speed, throwing up dirt and dust to the point that a small tornado appeared in front of us, eventually culminating into a hologram image of a young man.

"I!" said the hologram, "served my country for 25 years battling on the earth, air and sea. In the end, I was martyred here. I do not have a grave but I am buried under these rocks over there!" As he said this last sentence he disappeared as quickly as he had appeared.

We were both taken aback. We looked at each other, with one eyebrow raised. For a while, neither of us knew what to do.

"I guess he wants us to pay him a visit!" said Leila excitedly tugging at my left arm. "Come on!"

"Poor guy!" I said and after yanking my arm away, started walking back in the direction from which we had come.

"Where are you going?" asked Leila.

"I'm getting out of here!" I said, "I'm scared. I'm terrified of ghosts!"

"Come on Adem, don't be silly!"

I went towards the place we had seen the hyacinths and after uprooting two bunches, returned back.

"We should put flowers on the grave, right?" I said. Then I handed her one of the bouquets of hyacinth. "And this one is for you... So you don't get jealous."

She blushed a little upon receiving the flowers and gently thanked me. "The Hykakinthos flower!" she mumbled.

"The discus flower!" I said.

We laughed. Then, upon remembering our duty we became serious again and respectfully placed the other bouquet on the soldier's grave.

"Let's pray!" said Leila. She opened her arms and turned her palms upwards to the heavens. As a non-believer, I was reluctant to do so. "Come on!" she said, "For him!"

I also opened my arms and tried to mumble a few prayers in Arabic as much as I could recall but I think unknowingly I had muttered something incomprehensible. Then to myself, I entertained some thoughts about my sadness for the soldier in Turkish. I shut my eyes.

"Are you done?" asked Leila after a while. I believe she had gotten bored. She laughed. "Have you fallen asleep?"

"I couldn't contain my laughter anymore. "All right!" I said, "Let's go! Chop-chop!"

Then I worried that we may not make it to the mountain

before dusk. But we couldn't turn back now either. We had already set on the path, and changing our mind now might disappoint Leila. Moreover, if we returned, I might never again get the chance to be alone with her.

If she's able to read my mind, I thought upon a moment of fury, *why isn't she helping me? I can't read her thoughts and be sure of what she's thinking!* I wondered if she expected me to open up first. I wondered if she thought I'd want to be the first to speak, as an old fashioned man–quite literally. If this were the case, she was indeed correct. I felt an indiscriminate smile pass along her face.

We came to a grove of fruit orchards. As we walked, the thin layer of dust now covering my body had made me a part of the surroundings. We passed apple trees with pink branches and apricot trees whose leaves looked scorched by the sun and drought. Leila couldn't restrain herself from picking a few and eating them. She handed me some, which I tasted.

As I looked around the surroundings, I suddenly noticed another rupture in the ground ahead of us. We hadn't noticed it until we had come closer, but it extended horizontally all over the path we were walking. Another natural obstacle to our path to the mountain I thought, disconcertingly.

"Look here Leila!" I said, pointing at the rift. She turned towards me and smiled. She came to me with the fruits she had just picked. "Look!" I repeated.

"What is it?" she asked.

"Looks like a deep gorge!"

"Want to check it out?"

We began to slowly make our way to the edge of the cliff. An ebullient river flowed along the floor of the gorge, whose waters sparkling like molten gold. Both sides of the gorge were lined with scores of little burrow-like caves. The fertile plain that we stood on extended throughout this strange sheltering area, reaching the other end of the gorge. In the middle stood a thin, stone bridge that joined the two sides. Covered as it was with moss, the stone bridge had taken on a greenish hue.

"How pretty!" said Leila, "Dovecotes!"

"Yes!" I said, "I wonder who lives here? Or did. We can use this bridge to cross over.

"We'll have to go through the caves."

"Yes, come on!"

We descended carefully down a narrow, rocky strait, entering the first cove we came across. Although it was hot outside, the interior of the cave was quite cool. The rocks seemed to have absorbed all of my tension as well, leaving me relaxed.

The aperture through which we passed also functioned as a window, letting light flow into the space. With curiosity mixed with fear, we investigated our surroundings. This was a basilica carved in tuff rocks. It must be extremely ancient, or was constructed with the intention of making it seem so. Columns in relief had been carved into the stonewalls. I presumed that the residents must have wanted to preserve the kind of church construction to which they were accustomed. The red rectangles they had drawn on the tuff resembled a brick wall.

"It's so silent!" said Leila.

"Yes!" I replied, "As if it was abandoned!"

"A playground for djinns and faeries!" she said, laughing.

"Where?" I asked.

"Over here!" she pointed haphazardly, "In fact, one of the balls they're playing with just struck you in the head!"

"Dear me!" I said, "What bad luck! How do I look?"

"Fine! You're in tip-top shape!"

"Thank you!"

We chuckled.

The walls of the church cave were covered with dark colored frescoes depicting religious imagery. One wall offered a scene of Jesus and his mother Mary, with their golden haloed heads turned opposite to each other. Angels watched them from above in sadness. In another fresco, knights on white steeds threw spears at giant monsters that looked like snakes. There were also scenes of heaven and hell. Some of the frescoes had been rubbed off and the grey tuff below was visible. I looked at the face of Jesus. His expression was calm and made me feel at peace.

Suddenly I felt the room light up in the direction of the pulpit. Leila must've also felt it because she turned to the same direction at the same time as I did. The candles inside were burning and behind the pulpit appeared a tall, black-robed man.

"Welcome to the land of the happy clerics!" he said in a soothing tone.

Leila and I exchanged surprised glances.

"If you're hungry you will be fed. If you are thirsty, you will be given water."

As soon as he uttered those words, a robo-platter appeared on four legs serving us dark bread and grape juice. I remembered my hunger as I saw the food on the platter. I took the offerings gratefully and slowly walked towards the pulpit as if hypnotized. There were benches in rows in front, all carved in stone. I hopped over a few, careful not to drop the food in my hands and sat at the third row from the front. In the meantime I continued to watch the dark robed figure.

"Thank you," I said. "And who might you be?"

He did not reply. He kept staring for a while with a cool expression that either signaled he was analyzing my question or was formulating the answer. In the meantime, Leila had sat to my left, and had huddled up to me as if the church was too crowded.

"Is this place taken?" she whispered.

I smiled. "No!" I said. I opened my arm as if I was to embrace her and said, "Come!"

"Thank you!" she laughed, "It seems I have the best spot!"

"I'm an assistant!" said the man suddenly. "I am not a cleric!'"

"Doesn't matter! Not to worry!" I whispered with my head down so as to not be heard. Leila snorted as if concealing a chuckle.

"Unfortunately, I must advise you not to stay too long!"

I tilted my head down in shame as if I had been chastised. "And why's that?" I asked.

"Because this is the home of the happy clerics!"

This time Leila barged in, finally showing some interest in the matter: "Are the happy clerics dangerous?" she asked.

"No!" said the assistant. "The residents have stopped seeing other people for a long time now!"

Every response brought another question to mind but instead of cutting him short, I restrained myself so he could go on speaking. I continued to listen, all the while sipping at my grape juice. It tasted a bit bitter. It was in the process of turning into wine.

"My master, Simeon, told me that he would not come to visit you!"

"Oh now that won't do!" I said. "We came here solely to see Master Simeon." Leila pinched my arm.

"I'm sorry! He doesn't wish to see anyone."

"Fair enough!" I said bowing my head. "Actually, we were just passing by. All we want to do is go on to the other side. How do we make it to the bridge?"

"Of course!" said the man in the same soothing voice. Then he moved and grumbled: "Follow me!" As he exited the church, he took the burning torch affixed onto the wall.

Together we wandered from one cave to the next, towards the

rocky depths of the valley. The walls, doors and windows weren't smoothened completely. Especially the ceiling, probably deemed unnecessary do to otherwise, was left in its original state, with the axe marks still visible. The hollow parts were covered with iron grills. It was as if we were in a 3D labyrinth and I couldn't remember the path we had taken anymore.

I shuddered at the thought that if we were to lose our guide, we would never make it to the light of day again.

Finally –and fortunately– we came to a large grotto that the chambers led to. Some light seeped from above. This must be a kind of ventilation system or a chimney, I thought. It might've also been used as a sort of meeting place down here. Humidity had changed some of the colors of the walls of the grotto and some had gone black from soot, as if a fire had broken out some time ago.

The man waved the torch in his hand to and fro, as if he was in a danger zone, or did not want to miss some fearful thing hiding in the corners. I swallowed hard. The chamber and the path seemed to get narrower and the ceiling lower than before. I became worried that we would get stuck in the cave as we moved forward.

Leila followed from behind, huddled close to me. I held her hand, to which she didn't object. Then I pulled her over to me and placed her in between the two of us, in the middle. This way she'd be safer. I cursed myself for not having thought of this before. She was completely defenseless in the back. Something bad happening to her would've meant something far worse for me.

"How much longer do we have?" I asked the man.

"Have patience!" he said calmly, "Very little left!"

And lo and behold, in about ten minutes our path began to light up again. I also caught a whiff of clean air, which relieved me. Eventually we arrived at another church that was poised at one end of the stone bridge.

"Here we are!" said the assistant. "After you cross the bridge you won't need a guide any longer. You have to follow that path over there!"

By looking in the direction to which he had pointed, I could make out a clear path that ascended the ridge. I thought it must've been steps carved out of stone. After thanking the man, Leila and I began to walk towards the bridge.

I took a few steps, then turned back and complained, "It's not really nice what your master did!"

"Go now, please!" he replied, "When there's no one present, neither is there a judgment to be made!"

For a few seconds I tried to ascertain what he meant then asked: "No one? How about you? You count as somebody, right?"

"That is a very rude question!"

"Adem, let's go!" said Leila tugging at my arm.

"Is Simeon even alive?" I asked.

"If you don't leave right now, I'm going to have to involuntarily harm you."

"Adem, come on!"

I lifted my arms up high and said "Fine, fine!" turning back towards the bridge and thus we continued to walk together, without looking back.

As I we were crossing the bridge, I found that I couldn't gather up the courage to look down towards the river flowing far below us. Even though I didn't see it, I could still feel its coolness and hear its rumbling roar.

Once we arrived on the other side we began to climb the steps the man had pointed out to us. We had almost reached the summit when we were caught under a shower of pebbles raining down on us. A glance to a spot higher up the slope revealed a fleeting view of deer antlers among the bushes.

"Look!" said Leila in excitement, "Deer!"

We continued our climb in a quicker pace and eventually arrived at a flat, arid plateau that seemed to go on forever. The only things to enliven the view were some rocky ridges and caverns to our right. The deer must've hidden there. For a while we stood there and caught our breath. Then Leila asked, pointing to one of the larger caves, "Shall we go inside?"

"Let's not lose time!" I replied, "The sun is about to set."

Suddenly two noses, then the whole bodies of two animals, emerged from the cave. These were two gigantic horses, one red, one white.

"Great Lord!" she murmured as she ran towards the beasts and began to pet them. "Come over here! Look at her! What a beauty!"

I didn't know what to do. Unsure of what to do next, I looked around. The beasts were truly beautiful. Of course I enjoyed watching Leila engrossed by them as well but I was still a bit nervous, thinking we might be in danger. Suddenly an idea came to me: "Come on!" I said, "Let's mount them!"

"Yes!" exclaimed Leila enthusiastically.

We petted the animals for some more time before slowly climbing onto their backs. We started off at a slow walk before we broke into a canter as we headed towards Mount Kaf, which lay directly ahead of us. We had regained our high spirits. Even though this was the first time I had ever mounted a horse, I found I was able to keep up with Leila; in fact I was able to do fancy tricks on the horse like a Mongolian cavalryman.

* * *

Darkness had fallen by the time we arrived at the mountain. We climbed slowly through the deep blue darkness, not really know-

ing what we were about to encounter. We had left our two horses at the base of the mountain, at the end of the great plain, right
where the mountain began its ascent like a giant wall. We had
told them to wait for us there, as if they could understand.

We climbed through rocks and stones. The place seemed to be
devoid of any living creature. The rocks jutted out like gnarly,
sharp teeth or broken bones. The air had definitely cooled down,
but not so much as to cause discomfort.

"It's very dark!" said Leila.

I smiled. "Let's see!" I said, "Let's see what's going to happen now. Thanks for coming all the way here with me. I don't
know why I insisted so on coming to this mountain. I'm really
sorry that I put you in danger. We probably should've gone back
when we had the chance."

"You were curious!" she said. "And bored. So it's all-good!
Come on, we don't have very far left to go."

This time I followed her in silence. She was wearing white
pants with deep slits in them showing her elegant, dark legs as she
walked. I watched longingly.

We were a bit worried when we realized that we were moving
past some dried-up water-beds.

"There's no water, Leila!" I said. "How long can we go on
like this? Come now, let's return! There's nothing here! I
should've guessed!"

Don't worry!" said Leila. To my amazement, water spurted
out of the dry earth when she whammed her fist on the ground.
The ground grew darker from the water seeping under it and
soon a muddy pool began to form. The water pooled and then
began to flow, directly towards me. The small stream became
wider, larger, and clearer. I leaned forward and drank heartily.
Then I dried my mouth with the back of my hand and looked at
Leila.

"What was that?" I grumbled.

"A miracle!" she replied smiling.

"How are you able to do such things?"

"What you saw wasn't real!"

"But my thirst is gone!"

"Because that wasn't real either! We don't feel thirsty unless we want to. We only feel thirst so as to savor the pleasure of drinking. This is true for your body as well."

All I could do was sigh. I stopped asking my questions. "All right then!" I said. "Then let's make it up that hill! And if we don't need to rest, let's not go to sleep please!"

She laughed. "Can't we take refuge when it gets dark, Adem dearest?"

"No, come on!"

I moved to her front, grabbed her by her right wrist, and began to climb with determined steps. I was practically dragging her behind me. Night had not yet fallen completely and there was still enough light to make out our direction. Luckily enough, we had a full moon and that moon reflected onto the yellow stones, which seemed to have been prepped for a photo shoot. The climb was too steep to allow us to move straight forward, so had to jig and jag our way, walking in circles in order to climb. This round-about climb took us to the farther side of the mountain. I thought that we should probably stop for the night. In the morning we could get a better look at what lay in the direction beyond the mountain which at this point seemend like nothing more than a dark ocean.

"That night!" said Leila suddenly, "when we undressed, did you get aroused?"

The way she said this led me to believe that she wasn't really sure whether she should have allowed these words to spill from her mouth.. It was a pretty shameless thing to say, even though she said it shyly. Timidity went well with a goddess such as she, I thought.

"Look how subjects change once the night sets in!" she said almost in a whisper and laughed a little.

"As if you don't know the answer!" I grumbled, partly because I was at a loss for words. I also felt a bit angry, though for what I did not know. I guess I didn't like to be reminded of that night. Maybe the anger I felt was actually towards myself, but she –probably– couldn't know this. I realized that she was becoming sad and upset.

"That day..." she said, "You were cross with me right?"

"Let's say jealous!" I replied tensely.

She fell silent. I was upset. I moved towards her. Then I caught her arm and pulled her towards me. We came face to face. I looked deep down into her sad, beautiful eyes.

"I couldn't care less about Mount Kaf!" I grumbled. "All I wanted, all I want, is to walk with you. You are the only aim I have, can't you see that? Spending time with you is my ultimate destination. If it weren't for you, this whole place would be a sad amusement park, nothing else!"

As I talked, I straightened the hair that had spilled onto her brow. She looked at me unwaveringly with her dampened, slanted eyes. Her cheeks were like burning coal. It was as if we were in ecstasy together, in an initiation ceremony of some religious ritual.

"There's nothing else really!" I said. "The only time I feel that there is something worth to hold onto in this world is when I look at your eyes looking at me!"

In front of my eyes lay a perfectly sweet expression on her face that was so close to me now that I couldn't hold back any longer and started to kiss her to my heart's content. She wasn't irresponsive. A threshold was thus crossed and our cares disappeared as if we were trying to satisfy a hunger, a thirst that we had been repressing for a long time. Our caresses took the form of a revolt, a reproach for the time that had passed. It wasn't enough for our lips, our hands to touch; more flesh on flesh was required. I started to move my hand on the contours of her body, over her dress. The more we became aware of what we were doing, that we were doing it to each other increased our thrill by tenfold.

I sat on the rock behind me and moving towards her, pulled her over me.

"Do I feel like a stranger to you?"

"Not at all!" I replied. She was a part of me. It's as if we had been in an embrace for years. She was giving herself to me completely, with no holds barred.

I found her exquisitely beautiful and felt so undeserving of this beauty. She was a willing partner and time seemed to condense and grow extremely slow as it revealed all its colors. I wished time could stop, I tried to hold on to each meaningful second. My personal story could end here. I could make love to her for eternity; we'd be like two heroes of an epic legend.

***

In my dream, Cappadocia was a huge, disheveled bed. Leila and I slept on it side by side, like two giants. I opened my eyes, overjoyed to see that she was right next to me. I felt a mix of pride and excitement; this filled me with the exuberance that starting a new day brings.

"Good morning!" said Leila, waking up and gently stretching her body a little.

I smiled. I pulled her over to me, drawing her on top of my body.

"Good morning."

We began to kiss again. My eyes were shut, but when I opened them back up, I was startled to see what was lying behind Leila, what lay behind Mount Kaf.

Upon feeling my hesitation she asked, "What's wrong?"

"Leila!" I said, "Look over there!"

She turned her back, and then with surprise asked, "Oh my goodness! What is that?"

In front of us were graves, rows and rows of graves that extended until the horizon. What was even more eerie was the fact that each grave was exactly the replica of the next, as if it was the graveyard of a whole battalion.

"Did all these people die on the same day?" I whispered. For some reason, I suddenly began to feel my energy drain out of me

"I don't know!" replied Leila, in concern.

We were too far away to be able to make out the names and dates on the tombstones. We stood up and walked to the edge of the rock that we were sitting on.

"It must've been a huge massacre!" I said. "In the past I guess... Do you remember?"

"I remember people dying... And war... Then there was an epidemic... If this was the reason for... I did not know so many had died. Horrifying!"

"When did this take place?"

"Thousands of years ago I guess! When people's lives were extended... I was recently born."

She must've recalled bad memories as she went quiet. I moved forwards and hugged her. "So you were just born eh?" I said compassionately. "Good thing you were!" She smiled.

Suddenly I went numb as I heard a shriek from the top of the mountain. It sounded like the voice of a giant beast who was on the verge of madness.

Staring at the cloudy peak of the mountain Leila asked, "Did you hear that?"

"I did!" I said, my voice trembling.

"I think it's best we start back, don't you think?" she asked.

"I couldn't agree more!.. Come on!"

I stood up with difficulty. We began to put our clothes on, gathering them up from where we had cast them so haphazardly the night before. I was finding it difficult to move, which surprised me.

"Are you all right?" asked Leila.

"I feel weak!" I said. Then I added, laughingly, "You must've drained me! I am an old man after all!"

She laughed but her gaze was full of concern.

"I wonder what's wrong?" she said worried.

"I can't believe it!" I said, "so we actually..."

"Yes!" she replied smiling. "It really has happened, it seems!"

We began to descend the arid rocks hand in hand. When we touched like this, it felt like a circle was complete. I felt myself lighter, relaxed and in peace. Something that was bubbling inside found the target it was looking for in Leila.

Our joy had returned. The colors around me were brighter and I was able to make out the beauty of all the details around me. Although I was tired, I was also experiencing a shock of joy. Just as one tries to shake oneself awake when in a dire situation, as if in a nightmare, there often lurks the same kind of uncertainty in a real experience that resembles a beautiful dream. It was dangerous to believe in such a dream anyway.

She squeezed my hands suddenly and caressed my fingers in silence. Did she understand what I was thinking? She approached me and smilingly embraced me. "Are you a dream?" she asked me.

I first did not know what to say. Then, after a bit of thought, "I don't know what to say..." I mumbled caressing her hair. "I can't make you believe that what I am saying is true, that I'm not a dream. To me, you are also a dream."

She escaped my embrace and laughed. "I think I can make do with this response."

"The question was enough for me!" I added.

We were able to hold a conversation together. I wouldn't have minded if there had been silence between us, I was free to be myself and she accepted me for what I am; everything was happening in its own time.

"When I first met you..." I said, completely at ease, "I knew you were the only one for me in this world and I felt extremely lucky that you were here. Meeting you was like finding an oasis in the desert."

She smiled. "Such nice words..."

"When we arrive back at the church," I said laughing, "I will light a candle and say a prayer! You've made a believer out of me!"

"Hurray!" she screamed, running and jumping on my back. I held her strongly by her legs and tried to carry her for some distance. She had forgotten how weak I had gotten and I didn't want to spoil the moment by drawing attention to it. I hoped that I would regain my strength the farther I got away from the mountains and the graves and the closer I got to the city. We jested about our first encounters a bit more.

"You..." she said, "were desperately trying not to look at me while singing! It was quite funny!"

"And you..." I replied, "were obsessed about me being the Sultan for a while..."

"Which I am still suspicious of."

"I'm about to suspect it myself, due to your insistence! What does this Sultan do?"

She thought about this for a while, and then said, "He organizes things! Everything here is actually under his control. The trips, the creatures... He does all the designing. The little deity of the amusement park..." she laughed.

"It sounds like the title of a book!" I said. "Can we meet this... little deity? If it's not us, that is."

"He usually hides himself from others! It is said that this is the way things should be done. So that the artificial nature of this world doesn't stand out so!"

"I see," I replied.

I had gotten really tired. I stopped by a dried tree husk to catch my breath. Though it was too dead to provide us with any shade, it lay in the middle of the road like a milestone, a sign. Below lay a rocky, narrow path. Leila planted a cold, wet kiss on my cheek and got off my back.

"Are you all right?" she asked, her slanted eyes full of worry. "Look at me! You are feeling weak and I had you carry me! How selfish of me!"

"Oh, it was worth it!"

"Stop now, and lie down a bit!"

I did as I was told and lay by the dried-up husk.

I had begun to worry as well. "What is this about?" I wondered aloud.

"All you need is some sleep!"

"Maybe we have to escape from Mount Kaf!"

I tried to get back onto my feet but it was as if the whole weight of the mountain was now on my shoulders. The rocks drew me like magnets. I decided to stay put.

"Rest a little, love!" said Leila, "You'll feel much better, I'm sure!"

I involuntarily nodded and continued lying on my back.

"What has come over you?" she asked. "Hold my hand! Don't you go away now!"

I embraced her narrow waist. "Let's take a nap," I said, "together."

She lay her head on my stomach and lay still. I caressed her hair.

There were bad thoughts brewing in me. While on the one hand I thought I could depart now with no regrets, on the other hand, I didn't want to lose somebody like her whom I had just recently found. After a while I began to understand that my thoughts were becoming muddled. Leila touched my cheek with one hand. How delicate her hand was; how well formed! She gently lifted my head and put something soft under it.

5

I saw Hale. At our old house in Gümüşsuyu, I drew the curtains of the living room just enough to see that the city outside was in ruins. Then the ruins themselves also became indistinct and slowly disappeared, leaving its place to a dark desert. I couldn't find anything to get a grip on, in order to continue my path. In panic I decorated this empty abyss with dreams, re-forging the world anew, and opened my eyes.

Though it was not severe, I had a slight, creeping headache. The familiarity of the pain upset me. I tried to recall what I used to do to make it pass. Leila was there by my side. "Are you all right?" she asked when she saw that I had awoken. She put her hand on my chest, where my heart beat. "I was terrified. You were sweating and mumbling in your sleep!"

"Mumbling? What did I say?"

"Meaningless words!"

"I have a headache Leila, dear." I mumbled as if I were still asleep. "I wonder if I wasn't cured? Maybe the illness is in relapse! I knew it actually..."

She scowled as if she too, felt the same pain as I did. I had forgotten how much I had missed such compassion. She moved closer and placed my head on her lap. Thus my head had finally found a warm, soft lap of a woman. Leila started caressing my hair. "The mountain didn't do you well!" she said, trying to console me. "My love, don't get sick! I need you here! I'll take care of you from now on!"

Trying to smile, "I put you in danger too, dragging you here with me!" I said, apologetically.

"Don't say that! All that matters for me now is that you don't suffer!"

I had become quite emotional from the pain and I felt teardrops welling in my eyes. I held her hand and squeezed it tight. "What sort of a wonderful creature are you?" I grumbled. "How did I find you? How did you come to me? Is it destiny?"

She took my two hands into her palms. "I think we must be soul mates!" she mumbled as if she recited a lullaby. "Your hands are coooold!"

Her curls fell on my head like the branches of a tree, under whose shadow one takes refuge. I was just about to say how more could not be asked for, that it is unnecessary, that more would be meaningless.

"I know!" she shushed me. She took my head between her two hands. "I know everything you wish to say. You embroider your thoughts actually, perhaps exaggerating a bit even. I am no sacred creature though I can't say I mind being called one." She laughed. She had a sense of humor. I was amazed that we were actually lovers and blushed like a teenager.

"I'm not saying enough!" I said, "You're more than that!"

"Oh my love! I don't deserve your words."

Suddenly the pain became excruciating. I shut my eyes. I clenched my teeth to not make a sound, but I couldn't stop a quiet moan from escaping from my lips. Leila cradled my head in her two hands. Then she took one and placed it on my brow, after which I felt a cool dampness. I slowly opened my eyes a little. She was drying her eyes. She had been crying because of my pain.

"What is there to do?" she moaned. "I'm leaving!" she said. "I'll bring back help! We have to get you to a doctor! I'll get a vehicle too... If we get out of here soon, we can..."

"Don't go!" I said. "If there were anything to be done, they would've done it by now! Just stay by me! If I am to die, I want it to be by your side!"

"Don't," she said pleading, "Don't talk like that! I don't want to leave you alone here either, but I can't let you suffer like this forever!"

"It's too far!" I grumbled. "You'll be traveling alone!"

"The horses are down there!"

"Can't you fly?"

"I can't dear!"

Both of us were engulfed with fear and melancholy.

After some silence, I unwillingly agreed, "Ok, fine! But you take care of yourself, you hear? Be careful, ok?"

"Ok! And you be careful! And don't worry about me!"

We held each other in our arms tightly, trying to meld into one another. The sheer possibility that this may be our last embrace was beyond endurance. She rose to her feet and started to quickly descend the mountain, using the path we had trodden on our way up. I watched her leave from where I lay. She couldn't seem to move correctly; her confusion and concern seemed to be reflected in her steps. She got smaller and smaller amidst the rocks; eventually turning into a white spot and disappearing out of sight. She was putting her lengthy life in danger for me. I was terrified that something bad would happen to her. There was no other Leila! *Why did I let her leave* I thought to myself; I was filled with an unbearable sense of guilt.

***

A day had elapsed since Leila had departed and darkness fell on the earth for the second time. Although I was a bit worried the night I spent here alone, a very silent but burning sense of concern extinguished all my fear. At every beat of my heart I felt Leila's absence, which even during the times my pain subsided, would leave me shaking to and fro from where I sat. Once you start loving somebody, you also presume to bear the pain of losing him or her, I thought. In fact, losing someone is much worse than getting lost, worse than perishing. Perhaps it was pure selfishness to do away with oneself in the name of the beloved.

I tried to push away these thoughts. The reality perceived by one solitary person is only that of a deep, bottomless abyss in which we –and we alone– are free to roam. However, I thought, when two people reflect each other like a mirror the abyss can be bridged.

As the hours passed I found that I could barely remember kissing Leila. What we had experienced seemed more and more like a distant dream. There were no traces left save for moments that became more and more blurry in our minds, indistinct from dreams. It wasn't only Leila but myself as well that slowly felt like a dream.

As I dwelled on these thoughts and time passed, being aware of the fact that Leila hadn't returned yet felt like rubbing salt on an open wound. I was filled with terror at the thought that her special light might've been harmed in some way. I felt I was falling down a bottomless pit. Both my brain and my heart swelled and tensed. Though my mind failed as if pain engulfed my thinking, the torture just did not cease.

I lay on the ground and rested my head against the cold rocks in order to alleviate my anxiety. My hopes would be stirred by each and every noise I heard, then would be dashed with bitter disappointment. The monotony of one's heartbeats could drive one mad in this silence. I wanted to yell and scream but the idea that my scream would receive no echo, or would turn into an echo that slowly dissipates only made me feel worse.

I shut my eyes. Just like when in pain, every detail bothered me. I did not want to fall asleep though, as I couldn't bear the thought of waking up and finding that she hadn't –or couldn't– arrive yet. I felt my teeth go numb. None of these worries were unfamiliar though. I had felt the same worry when Hale hadn't come home and hadn't called to tell me where she was. She had later told me she had done this purposely to hurt me.

From where I lay, I watched the sky with sullen eyes. The stars were not as I remembered them. An unfathomable stellar migration had happened. The map of the universe must've changed drastically. Maybe I was on another planet.

Suddenly a dark shadow bore over me and began to grow. The only thing I could see were the stars going dark one after the other. After a while I noticed that this was due to an illusion caused by a transparent object that was drawing closer. In a few minutes the object had become large enough to fill the sky above me. The wind that ruffled my hair signaled the advent of a huge mass, but my eyes couldn't perceive anything more than the stars going dark. Although the view had become blurry, I was still able to watch the sky.

The object, whatever it may be, closed onto me like a predator bird. I saw light seeping out from a slit in the object. Suddenly I found myself in the bottom of a spherical room. Leila was there as well and was next to me. I was filled with relief and felt that I was able to finally breathe again after a long time. She smiled at me in joy and opened her arms. We embraced.

"Where have you been?" I asked. "I was worried sick about

you!" She tried to explain. "It's okay!" I said, "Hearing your voice is enough!" I had come back from the dead and the fear and pain of losing her had begun to dissipate.

"How have you been?" she asked with a tremor in her voice, "I was also worried out of my mind! And now, to hear such words from you..." She held back her tears, trying to force out a smile.

Hearing the concern in her voice a feeling of peace and calm spread through my being. We truly had a strong bond between us; stronger than I could ever imagine or believe. I didn't know the reason for this, I didn't understand nor did I want to. I was very happy with what had been handed to me and I didn't want it to disappear.

"I'm sorry!" I said, "The thought of losing you was horrible. I understand your concerns better now. I won't lose hope; I'll try to live for you."

"Oh, love!" she whispered.

Her being near made me stronger. I was in better spirits and felt my health getting better too. If I had been left alone for longer I probably would've died, but just one touch from her was enough to restore me.

"I could..." I said, "I could probably live on just hearing you say that again and again!"

We remained locked in the embrace for several minutes. I could've remained there forever, in fact, I could've died there in her arms, if I knew it wouldn't make her upset. I believe we were gliding through air, though for a brief moment I felt like we stopped. Wherever we were meant to go –I hadn't even thought of asking Leila where for some reason– I guess we had arrived.

***

The hospital's wide, high-ceilinged corridors were completely deserted. I thought how the idea of illness might've become something of the past. So I must've been lucky to find someone to treat me. To the left from the large, square windows I could see a campus made of single story buildings amidst a forest, whereas on the right I could see a well-kept inner garden. Apart from the sound of flowing water, there was nothing to be heard. This way, we were able to hear the sound of the nurse's high heels approaching. We obliged her request to follow her to the doctor's office. A bizarre contraption was cleaning the corridors. I felt like a victim on death row, marching to imminent doom. The task of walking left me drained and fatigued and I was out of breath... Leila's face was really pale as well. She held my left hand and I replied by squeezing hers.

It took us only a few minutes to arrive at the examination room. The nurse indicated that I could go in. Wooden benches stood in rows in front of the door. I thought how they might've not been used for maybe thousands of years. The wood would rot, new benches would be brought in and this probably went on for god knows how long.

I turned to Leila and said, "Darling, you wait here! All right?" For some reason, I felt like I had to confront the awful truth on my own.

"No way!" she interjected, her voice trembling. "I want to come in with you!"

"The doctor might only want to see me for now!" I replied, "Besides, let me tell you what my condition is, once I grasp it, ok? Your waiting here for me is already huge support."

Though unwilling, she complied with my request. She must've understood that her mere presence was enough to relax me. Moving towards the door, I walked in with trembling steps.

The walls of the office were whitewashed. A row of monitors

about 1.5 meters tall, lined the walls of the office. On the screens were high-resolution, 3D images not unlike those taken from an MRI test.

The doctor was a lean, tall fellow; he wore a nicely ironed white gown and had on thick-rimmed glasses. Upon seeing me enter, he rose and moved towards me saying, "Welcome Adem Bey!" His voice carried a soft but troubled tone that gave the impression that he could sense his patients' troubles, which was in fact simultaneously comforting. He signaled me to sit. As I settled into a leather chair, he pointed at the images on the screens and said, "Let me not waste time and come directly to the subject at hand. To be frank, unfortunately the situation is not very positive."

I felt as if my whole life force was being sucked out of me by a syringe, only to be replaced by a dark, brooding melancholy. "When did you get these results? I asked with one last valiant effort. "I don't recall going into an MRI machine."

"The MRI? Oh yes! They were taken while you were in the ambulance."

"I see."

After a few seconds of silence, "For you..." the doctor began, "I investigated every treatment option possible. The whole hospital has been working on it believe you me. In fact, I even consulted other colleagues from around the world to find a solution... However, so far to no avail. Medically speaking, there isn't much we can do... We will try until the last minute though! We are ready to mobilize all our resources for you!"

"Thank you!" I mumbled. "You do mean the cancer, right?"

"Yes, yes! I didn't mention it as you hibernated for this purpose. We've investigated every minute detail of your medical history. To be brief, we have a serious onset of metastasis on our hands. The tumor has spread."

"I don't understand why I was woken then!" I grumbled. "Why was I woken up before a proper treatment was discovered? Do you know why?" An uncontrollable fury had begun to seep into my voice as I talked. I was almost chastising the doctor, as if it were all his fault.

"I have no idea!" he said, troubled. He had taken his eyeglasses off and was holding them like a defensive weapon. After waiting a while he said, "But if you like, I can check your records and see why…"

"Please!" I said sharpy as if issuing an order.

Pictures of documents replaced the 3D anatomic visuals on the screen. The data seemed to be stored digitally, though the reports seemed to have been drafted on a typewriter. Some sentences were crossed out; some were underlined or highlighted for emphasis.

"It's an old law…" said the doctor, thoughtfully, "But I presume it is still valid. It says here that you have a right to know the truth! The high court has issued a ruling based on this law and similar ones."

The patient has the right to decide what to do with their condition, was written on one of the documents.

"What decision?" I asked.

Hundreds of pages flashed on the screens, one after the other. "Though I couldn't catch what was written on them, the doctor seemed to have full grasp of the content. "It says here that you have two options," he said. "Either you can wait and live on until your illness kills you, or you can continue to sleep forever."

"Forever?" I lunged forward. I was really confused and my fury was at a boiling point. "Why am I to sleep forever? I thought I was to be hibernate until a treatment was developed."

The doctor gestured with his head and hands indicating he understood my point of confusion. "But progress has stopped

Adem Bey!" he replied. "There is no such thing as medical progress anymore. That is why the court had to come to a decision regarding your case! And look, it wasn't an easy one either. It seems your case dragged on for quite some time."

I shook my head disconcertedly. "How in God's name can progress stop? Don't people generate ideas anymore? No new combinations? Can there be a limit to all that?"

"Believe me, I am at a loss of words Adem Bey! I'm only a doctor. My expertise is in medicine. The application of it, I mean. I don't do research. Nobody does it anymore. They can't."

"Why?"

"Unfortunately, I do not have an answer to your question! I've never really thought about it!"

"How can you not?"

"It isn't my duty!"

"Whose duty is it then?"

"Once upon a time, scientists published articles. New drugs, new treatment methods were discovered and we would apply them, providing the researchers with feedback. Then suddenly it all stopped. Thus we had to administer what we had at hand."

"This is unbelievable! And you've never wondered why? Why medical research stopped I mean?"

Sadly he shook his hand meaning *no*. "Like I said," he continued, "This has never been my duty."

"Then where can I learn the truth from?"

After some thought, "History!" he replied. "You can very well obtain information from historians, I think."

I nodded and grumbled, "Fine! Let's go back to the hibernation process then. I am here because the technology for re-animation has matured, right?"

"Correct!"

"But the treatment hasn't been developed yet..."

"Unfortunately not."

"How is this possible? I mean, you're able to bring back to life someone who hibernated but can't treat a measly cancerous disease? I'm sorry, but this is all very troubling..."

"Not to worry at all, I understand!"

A silence ensued. The doctor was probably thinking on the reply. "Since you were woken, there has to be an explanation!" he mumbled. Then, as if he had discovered something important he said, "Predictive maintenance! That must be it! We haven't had a patient for a long time because predictive maintenance has been carried out regularly. Precautions are taken before the patients fall ill. In this sense, it hasn't been necessary to develop new treatments. Research must've stopped because it was no longer a lucrative business."

What he said was logical. "You may be right!" I grumbled.

"These possibilities probably didn't come to mind during your hibernation!" added the doctor, as if trying to emphasize the effect of his response.

"But isn't it a bit late?" I asked. "I mean, why is this situation explained to me now?"

"A placebo treatment was administered as a last resort. They made you think your illness had been cured. In this way, you might've spontaneously healed yourself on your own."

Suddenly the MRI images re-appeared on the screen.

"So what happens now?" I asked the doctor, "What do we do? What can we do? I mean...about the illness."

"We don't give up!" he said quickly, "We continue to fight until the very end! We'll try all known methods! But you have to stay here as an inpatient! We've arranged the prettiest room in the hospital. This way we can at least keep your pain at bay. I promise you we'll make sure you're not suffering."

Grasping tightly to the handles of the chair, I barely was able to push myself up. My head was spinning. I moved towards the man and shook his hand.

"Thanks again, Doctor!"

"There is no need for that! This is my duty! I wish I could do more. But I will continue to try as I said... Your room is ready. The nurse will direct you there. See you soon, Adem Bey."

I nodded a few times. Then, just as I was about to leave, something bizarre on the screen caught my eye. All of the images seemed to show a formless, ghost-like mass around my body. It was as if I had been possessed by a kind of ghost while the photos were being taken. I felt my spine tingle.

"What is this?" I asked, my voice trembling.

The doctor slowly turned around.

"What's that again?"

"Do you see this dark silhouette on the pictures?"

He put on his eyeglasses and began to inspect the images more closely.

"A dark silhouette?"

I moved towards the screen and pointed at what I saw. The doctor came by my side. I guess he eventually understood what I meant.

"Oh!" he said, calmer now. "You mean these shadows?"

"Yes, exactly!"

"That's your toy! You probably had an android with you while the visuals were recorded, right?"

* * *

Upon seeing me exit the doctor's office, Leila stood up excitedly and came to me. "What happened?" she asked, "Are you all right, dear? What is the situation? Please Lord; let it be good news. Please!"

She opened her arms to hug me but I didn't know what to do. I was afraid of her and pulled back. She was taken aback.

"What's going on Adem?" she asked, "What's the problem? What does the doctor say?"

I cut her short: "I'm dying!" There was humming in my ears and my tears welled up in my throat, crying to be released.

"Oh dear God!" she screamed. She covered her mouth with her right palm. Her eyes were wide open in surprise and sadness, but soon began to brim with a shower of tears. These were reactions I expected. Anyone, upon learning that their lover had caught a fatal illness would've displayed the same. I leaned forward and touched her tears.

She looked at me with hope, feigning this as an act of compassion, meaning that her artificial intelligence had mimicked such behavior, to tear my insides up even more. I, on the other hand, was like a disinterested scientist towards her. I squeezed her tears between my thumb and index finger, in order to understand what they were made of.

Unwillingly I was being nasty towards Leila, as if she had lied to me, as if she was the sole source of my suffering.

Faced with the abyss, I had become dark and evil, almost abysmal.

"Don't scare me!" she mumbled. "Is the tumor eating your mind? Your personality is changing! Damn it! It's me; me! Darling... What is wrong? What have they done to you? What have they said?"

Her concern was so genuine that for a minute I did not know what to believe in. I cringed in pain and held her by the hand.

"Are you real?" I asked.

"What does that mean?" she replied with a question, surprised. "I don't know? Are you?"

"I meant to ask whether you are an android or not. You aren't human, are you?"

"What are you talking about Adem? An android? A robot, you mean? That's ridiculous! Where did this come from?"

She was truly perplexed. She could've been acting of course and maybe I was wrong; perhaps she didn't know the truth either.

"Ok!" I said, "Fine!" I tried to force a smile. Without reason, I hugged her compassionately, out of habit. "Remember you had mentioned universities? I would like to meet a professor or someone similar from the history department. Can you take me there, Leila?" I had addressed her with her first name, no darling or love, this time, thinking there was no life in that body. I felt like I wanted to rip her bosom open and look in; I wanted to feel the warmth of her blood, her essence; but of course then, if she were indeed alive, by the time I discovered this, she would already be dead.

She got out of my embrace as if angry and moved away.

"Fine!" she said, "I get it! You're not in a good mood now! You're saying strange things! I won't press any longer, until you come back to your senses! Fine! I'll take you where you want to go... I'll do whatever I can! And won't ask for the reason either!"

I was at a loss for words. I was hurting her. She looked consumed. Both her eyes and her lips dropped in sadness. I tried not to be affected by it. Her words echoed in the empty corridors, slowly disappearing into the silence.

"Why isn't there anyone here? Why aren't there any other patients?" I asked.

"Because no one gets ill anymore, that's why!"

Nausea crept up. I tried not to vomit. Suddenly the pain began with a strange itching sensation in my ears. I tried holding my breath, as if a predator beast was approaching but to no avail. The pain increased exponentially, I understood that I wouldn't be able to push it back any longer. Then suddenly, I felt as if my brain exploded. I didn't know what to do save for closing my ears with my hand, sitting on the floor and screaming.

"Baby, what is wrong?!" said Leila. She hugged me as if to drain the pain, kissed my hair and called, "Doctor! Doctor, help us! OK! Don't worry; nothing can come between us! We won't let it! The channel between our hearts is open and will remain so. We understand each other... As long as you love me... I will love you even more and this will go on forever..."

I could no longer hear her words.

First the nurse, then the doctor rushed in... They put me on a stretcher. They gave me some drug by a needle, which dampened my pain a little, making me recall the paradise that was so far away now. Leila held me by the hand and continued to stroke my hair, all the while weeping.

"You have to stay here with us!" said the doctor.

"Why aren't there any other patients?" I asked him again. "You mentioned predictive maintenance... Don't they come for regular checks then? If not, why is this hospital still standing?"

"Calm down!" said the doctor, "You have to rest; you're exerting yourself too much! Please, don't waste your strength! There are answers to all your questions! Don't worry! There is nothing to be afraid of!"

"Then take me to someone who can answer them!" I retorted.

They looked at each other as if they didn't have a clue as to what to do.

"Ok!" said the doctor, "Now let's take you to your room! You don't have to go anywhere! I will arrange the meeting that you requested. We can arrange a conference call."

"Can you look at the records for me as well? When was the last client admitted? Can you learn this? You'll do this for me, right?"

"Of course I will, now to the room..."

"Can you run and check right away?"

He nodded and left us, like a soldier that received his orders, and I squeezed Leila's hand. She smiled at me with genuine concern and I tried to smile back.

I felt foolish with the Ottoman garb I was wearing. I must've looked like a tragic clown, or a woman whose mascara had come off while weeping.

"Change my clothes..." I mumbled.

"Ok!" said Leila with an understanding that one would have, speaking to a child.

The stretcher began to move.

"The doctor!" I said, "The doctor was to come back!"

"He has, baby!" said Leila, trying to console me.

She was right. Upon turning my head, I saw that the man had caught up with us.

"I checked the records Adem Bey," he said in a concerned tone.

"And?"

"It's been quite a while actually..."

"How long?"

"About 972,000 years! The last record is from the year 3280!"

6

The elderly man's 3D image appeared in my room like a ghost. The professor, with his outfit and glasses had –as I expected– the appearance of a classic academic. As I lay on the bed, connected to a myriad of medical equipment, he appeared to be sitting across from me, as if he were on patient call. Sitting in front of him was a small, light green desk holding books of various sizes. I couldn't quite make out if this piece of furniture belonged to my room or his. On the wall behind was the projected image of a wide and well-lit library. I guess it had been quite some time since morning or the professor was on the other side of the world.

"It is extremely thrilling to be talking to a real human being," he began. Obviously I didn't fall for this fake sincerity. However, I didn't have the strength to pinch myself constantly in order not to be fooled. Both because of the mastery of the human-replica manufacturers and because I preferred not to believe that the professor was somehow artificial, I was tempted to disregard and forget the truth.

The old man –meaning, his simulation– continued, "History

had stopped from happening for some time now. There was only the past. Now, however, there is a *present* again, things are happening again! Imagine, you're a live fossil, almost a million years old!"

"One that will be a dead one soon, though!"

The professor changed his tone of voice. "Yes..." he said pensive, "I know about this and am very sorry... What can I do for you?"

"Am I the last human being?" I asked.

"If the rest haven't been hiding somewhere for the last million years, yes you must be!"

"What about others that hibernated or were frozen?"

"As far as I know, you are the last! Hibernation was banned before it became pervasive, thus there already weren't very many people in a similar case such as yours. Moreover, your case seems to have dragged on for a long time."

I was at a loss as to believe in him or not, and I couldn't utter a reply. I felt my face droop, my expression becoming more and more indistinct. "What happened then?" I asked, "What happened to all the people?"

The old man took some seconds to ponder on the question. Perhaps he was trying to retrieve the information I needed from the dusty archives of his mind, collating and summarizing them, making connections, if there were any unmade connections left, that is.

Finally he began: "Evolutionary-wise, it is not surprising that the human race became extinct, like all other species. The free competition system, or the lack of a system that is, fanned the flames of unruly wars waged over resources that were nearly depleted. All sides employed WMDs."

"Didn't anyone predict the extinction of the species?" I retorted. "How can this be? Can such a struggle go on until there is no one left standing? Did the androids have a role in this extinction? Perhaps it was you who replaced the human species!"

"I'm a historian Adem Bey! I'm telling you the facts. Once under a certain critical number, a species is more vulnerable to external effects and in danger. The biological weapons used created mass epidemics, which in the end, killed every last human being unfortunately. We did not replace you. We continue to live on exactly for the purposes for which humans had designed us."

"Which is?" I asked automatically.

"The first robots were assistants," said the professor. "They were designed for heavy and dangerous labor, as you well know. Once technological progress enabled the manufacturing of androids, we began to be employed as practitioners, in jobs that humans did not want to work in, but wanted to preserve the ability to have contact with creatures in their own appearance. In this sense I do acknowledge that as there was no need for a labor force, we might've been the cause of the decrease of the human population to a certain extent."

The professor straightened his spectacles and crossed his arms. He would not take his eyes off me, which looked larger than they are behind the light-colored, optical lenses he wore. Maybe he was trying to impress or hypnotize me. Perhaps even revenge was on his agenda. Maybe he too suffered, and wanted to give a dismal lesson to a representative of the human race, the race that was responsible for his being there in the first place. Or it was I that imagined, or even desired that he had such an intention.

"However, the needs of your race were complex!" the old man continued. "In fact, ever since the dawn of history, you've been dependent upon ways to pass time. Everyone was born with the need for unconditional love, respect and the desire to communicate with others. Perhaps this was a trait that surfaced in time, necessary for the continuation of your species. The lucky ones among you were able to satisfy these urge and desires in childhood via parents, other relatives and friends, but the same urges re-surfaced in adulthood, imprisoning you to a certain hunger that was temporarily satisfied – if you were lucky again-with love, the relationship with your own offspring or groups that united under a common cause. Once you were on your own though, you had to find other ways to keep yourselves busy. Apart from *rented* others such as prostitutes or psychologists, other creatures, other peoples' dreams, memories, books, recorded songs, films, games, beliefs, chemical substances and objects affixed with an identity were ways to alleviate your hunger to a certain extent. In fact, any human endeavor was simultaneously a pastime. The business world, politics and science even, all completed the amusement park that is human life. Moreover, even though the senses of reality they engendered were relatively weak, these ways of substitution were usually much more reliable and sustainable than relationships with other humans, which were full of inconsistencies and vagueness, to say the least."

"Instead of half-baked systems of order, capitalism, with its disorderliness, turned each human being into an explicit rival towards each other, thereby unearthing your loneliness. In fact, what destroyed the old world were its own inconsistencies, meaningless beliefs and implicit inequities. Humanity was not able to construct a more consistent order that learned from its shortcomings, thereby being stuck in a semi-savage lifestyle among the ruins of the past. Artificial methods of substitution emerged. Technological innovations also enabled a sense of reality that was more and more tangible. Eventually a race devoid of love could've emerged, but instead, perfected human replicas, androids, the last techno-wonder of the free economy, replaced the others who were lost. We are the world's most advanced toys. We are made in your appearance, but we are also loyal and reliable to an unbelievable degree. Actually, even your first designs had been in your own appearance and finally your golem fantasy was realized. Before the human race went completely extinct, each remaining human was already living in isolation, surrounded by their androids. This future was already apparent way back to your time, the signs were there: In fact, it had already begun to emerge in several ways."

I took a deep breath with a final effort from my lungs. That's when I noticed that I hadn't been breathing for some time. My heart began to beat in dismay. This terrifying *paradise* I encountered, was a dream that had become an object, before its realization!" Leila came to my mind and I felt utterly depressed. This pain was familiar though, it was the creeping sense of nothingness and loss, a shiver that could only be recalled once re-experienced.

"How can they have accepted all this?" I asked, mumbling, "How could they go on living, knee-deep in such lies? Did they never suspect? Weren't they ever concerned?"

"Once you have your mind set on it," continued the professor in a calm and confident tone, "or when you think all other options are exhausted, the most simplest dreams can replace reality. The new-borns, in particular, had even more difficulty questioning this paradise, which was handed down by their predecessors. Besides, why should've they? There wasn't another reality they could compare this one with. *You* too, Adem Bey, lived in such a theater house. And you didn't feel the need to question it either, until you ran up against problems. Don't take this as me blaming you! My duty as a scientist and an historian is to lay the facts on the table."

"I know!" I replied, as if I were trying to console him. I couldn't fully accept that he was artificial too. "Thank you!"

Tears ran down my cheeks uncontrollably, though I wasn't aware I was weeping. "When all the people were gone..." I said, "How did everything else remain and continue to exist then?"

The professor smiled. "The least that the system required to exist..." he said, proud that he had touched upon an absolute truth, "were people! Everything was built to live on without any human labor required. Therefore to your question *how did they continue to exist,* I would answer with another question such as *why shouldn't they?* As humans did not foresee their own extinction, they never felt the need to add a feature that would pull the plug of the mechanism once they were gone. Besides, what good would it've done?"

"972,000!" I grumbled. "Almost a million years!"

Everything had remained as it was. This artificial paradise, this last and most horrifying human endeavor, had kept surviving for an unimaginable duration.

"I feel admiration towards them for this creation!" said the Professor. "But isn't it also terribly tragic that they focussed on building this pyramid, before they satisfied their most basic needs? Perhaps while they tried to heal themselves, they distanced themselves more and more from each other, remaining forever wounded "

It had become difficult for me to focus on what the man was saying. I wanted to stop thinking. My pain had come back as well. I took my head between my hands and moaned as I clenched my teeth. Then something was injected into my left arm, probably a painkiller. I relaxed a bit and felt sleep slowly taking over. I wanted to let myself go and disappear. Then, just like it happens, had happened with all people every day, without being aware of when it happened, I slowly drifted into sleep and the world of dreams.

***

The next morning, I was able to flee the hospital before sunrise, unseen. When I exited the building, I found I was in the middle of a desert that seemed to go on forever. Nonetheless, I continued to wander, like a lost ghost, in a direction I chose haphazardly. It was as if I was changing locations to desperately get rid of my anxiety.

"Very bad! Very bad!" I began to mumble to myself.

As I withdrew as if from a terrible defeat, I looked at what I had left, but couldn't find anything that would make me hold onto life, that would make me continue to live.

Then suddenly a little spider crept out of the sand and began to rush in one direction. First with disinterest, then with a curiosity that slowly increased, I followed the creature, which fled faster the more I followed it. When I was a child, I was told that the dead's spirits came back in the form of spiders to visit us, that's why nobody would bother them. Suddenly the insect turned into a dove, but still, it continued to escape from me with hesitant steps. Every now and then it would turn its head and look at me. Just as I was about to catch it, it took to flying. After a few feet in the air, this time it turned into a girl-child with soft and disheveled hair, dropped from the sky landing on its crooked legs and without knowing where to go, took a few steps, looked around with surprise, pulled a sour face and began to cry.

"Hey! Come on!" I said. "Don't cry! What are you doing here?"

She stopped as if consoled, began to run, her hair trailing wildly, and as she ran, this time she began to grow and turn into a young girl. I felt my heart skip a beat because the young woman I saw in front of me was Hale. She stopped and bent down to pick up something on the ground. I looked to see that it was the sapling of a tree she was interested in. She caressed its newly sprouting branches and smiled in sincerity, then rubbed her nose on the buds as if she was pouring light over them from her face, as if her face was more radiant than the sun itself. The sapling looked very happy and seemed as if it hadn't tasted such love before. It seemed to me that the sapling was at a loss of what to do next. It grew, turning into a huge apple tree. Hale reached out and took an apple from its branches. The fruit was too big for her hands, but she was exuberant for having it in her possession.

I had not liked the sound of her voice when we spoke on the telephone one day, "*You sound troubled,*" I had said. Her voice had begun to tremble and she couldn't keep herself from crying. I guess she thought crying stained her honor, thus she cried even more, eventually hanging up as she couldn't bear talking any longer, leaving me dumbfounded for a while. I didn't call her back, I didn't go to her and try to hug and comfort her. I thought it would not have been the right thing to do. These had all come to pass, done and over with, with no possibility to return! I had no other solution than trying to forget, trying to justify my actions, to continue living.

I walked towards the mirage of Hale.

"I'm sorry!" I said, "I took the wrong paths. I focussed on sharing everything so much that I forgot that there is virtue in possessing and being possessed, that we actually are dependent on it. If love is spread to all, there isn't much left for anyone... This didn't need to happen... Some strange twist of fate... There were many things I had and wanted to do. It was unfair of me to think that you should've been more supportive. I guess I was trying to use you."

She looked at me and smiled as if she just now had become aware of my existence.

"This is who you are!" she said, "Writing, trying to change the way things are is part of your character. You shouldn't let anybody, not even me, make you feel guilty for this!"

I did not know what to say.

"I..." I stuttered, "See how even I forget? I thought something bad could've happened to you, that day. I had gone to your place and checked to see if your lights were on. As your bedtime drew closer, the lights had gone out one by one. I cried out of joy. Even if you weren't mine, at least you were alive. I wonder if I came close to truly loving you that day?"

Tears welled up in her eyes. She reached out with her right hand and touched my face.

"I don't know!" she mumbled.

I bent down on the ground, on my knees. I dipped my hands in the sand and tossed handfuls of it into the air. Everything had turned into dust; all had gotten mixed in the earth and disappeared. Was it all worth it? In the end, words aren't alive and the readers are strangers. Are you all worth it?

I felt a shiver under my skull. The pain had returned and begun to increase again. My heart beat faster with fear and I held my breath. For a moment the pain was so intense that I thought my eyes would burst out of their sockets. It felt as if my mind was about to explode. The pain briefly subsided before again becoming stronger. It was like torture... I was dead tired. My heart and lungs had had enough. Unable to bear it any longer, I dropped to the ground.

***

As I slowly opened my eyes, I saw that they were all around me: Leila, Abdullah, Kasım, Cheshminaz and the others. They looked as if they were experienced the same pain I was.

"When you think about it..." said Cheshminaz, "How can one endure such a thing?"

I wasn't feeling any pain. In that hospital room, even if reality and dreams were intertwined, I could feel that at least the pain was real and that a drug relieved it now. The end of physical pain made one temporarily intoxicated. Of course this could be the drug's working as well.

I tried to sit up. Upon seeing me awake they all got excited and nervous. They didn't know what to do at first, like slaves afraid of their master. They were joyous when they saw that I did not chase them away but smiled at them.

Kasım was in front, "We've missed you, bro!" he said.

"I too," I said in difficulty, "I too have missed you."

"One shouldn't lose hope! Let's keep our minds sharp and open! I think you're going to get better. We will exit this place together!"

I nodded, trying to thank him for his kind words.

Cheshminaz approached the bed holding a box in her hand. "We brought you your things, look?" she said.

I reached out and touched her beautiful cheek with my left hand, then started perusing the box of things she had set somewhere where I could reach it. I pulled out a water glass; it was an old gift that made me sentimental. Even a simple glass was so valuable! But one had to forget, yes... However, if we were to never forget the pain we felt in our heart when thinking about an ex-lover, if we could constantly recall the way those tears that we stop from flowing, flowed back done into our stomach, if we could only remember these, this world would've been a truly different place.

Upon seeing the tears running down my cheeks, "Don't be sad!" said Cheshminaz, "Oh dear! It's entirely my fault. Please don't be sad, you're making us upset as well!"

Abdullah was wearing all black. I wondered if he was in mourning, in his own way.

Hesitant, Leila approached me and touched my face with her right hand. It was soft, delicate and 37 degrees warm. "Please!" she said, her voice trembling, "Please stay with us a little longer!

You know how long it has been since I asked this from someone? If you go... I'll feel terribly lonely."

"I'm sorry!" I uttered, "I know I suddenly got distanced from you. It is not your fault. You are a magnificent being!"

Like a mother, she cradled me, as if trying to envelop me back inside her, the way I had hugged her in Cappadocia.

She was only a character out of a novel, yes, but wasn't I the same as well? If she was made of plastic and steel, wasn't I made of earth?

"I believe you!" I said, "I know your smile, your embrace, your love are all real!"

I shut my eyes; even if I were mistaken, there was nothing I had to lose. I only wanted to die right there and then. I wasn't worried about what death really was anymore. I didn't believe in its existence even and I was determined to not to do so until it came to me.

"Please don't go!" they screamed. I heard cannons being fired. Women and children chanted beautiful, peaceful songs and lullabies. Bells rang out, the call to prayer sounded.

Suddenly, at the most unexpected moment, I felt an unbearable pain again and couldn't breathe; it was as if my chest was being torn in half. I tried to open my eyes, but this time I couldn't but the pain suddenly had stopped as quickly as it had begun.

Then I saw a light. A hand touched me and I felt the disease disappear. I felt a joyous sense of peace that emanated from my mind to my spine, and from there, all the way down to my toes. My heart beat calmly, with happiness. My feet left the ground and I began to hover in air. The light was breath-taking. The colors were extremely clear. The fresh spring weather consoled all, making me feel that all this was just a joke. Everything I had ever worried about, the pain and the sadness all seemed insignificant like a child's game. What we lived through was nothing but a story!

Then I thought how sad this fact was! Then again, sadness didn't really exist anymore either!

I flew over valleys that were covered in trees and where rain clouds hovered over towards a coastline and travelled into the open sea. A heavy wind was blowing. It wasn't an easy trip, but it felt real. The light became brighter and brighter, until I too, became a part of it.